TAKE THE KEY AND LOCK HER UP

ALLY CARTER

TAKE THE KEY AND LOCK HER UP

BOOK THREE OF EMBASSY ROW

Scholastic Inc.

This book was originally published in hardcover by Scholastic Press in 2017.

This book is a work of fiction. Names, characters, places, and incidents are either the product of the author's imagination or are used fictitiously, and any resemblance to actual persons, living or dead, business establishments, events, or locales is entirely coincidental.

ISBN 978-0-545-65501-9

10 9 8 7 6 5 4 3 2 1   18 19 20 21 22

Printed in the U.S.A.   40
First printing 2018

Book design by Yaffa Jaskoll

FOR THE ALLY AMBASSADORS.
THANK YOU FOR COMING TO ADRIA!

CHAPTER ONE

When the screams come, I can't be sure that I'm not dreaming.

I bolt upright in bed. The walls are thin, and I can hear the shouting, the force of something being thrown against the outside wall of the cabin, shattering in the place just above my head.

The wall shakes.

The ceiling creaks.

And I roll off the narrow cot, shaking.

I know better than to be afraid, but it's instinct now as I wrap my arms around my knees, pulling my legs close to my chest. In the age-old war between fight and flight, I'm Team Flight. Even in my thin T-shirt and bare feet I want to run faster and faster, farther and farther until I reach the end of the earth.

1

But instead I creep toward the window and look out the dirty glass, and a stark truth hits me: I'm already there.

"Is that all you've got?" Alexei's voice slices through the morning air. The sun is up, but the rays have yet to burn through the heavy fog that covers the ground like a blanket fort we can't help but hide inside.

"I'm gaining on you, buddy," my brother yells.

"Yeah." Alexei circles around him. "Let's see you do it again."

How many times have I seen them fight like this? Too many for me to count, I'm sure. This is the part where my brother is supposed to launch himself at his best friend, where they are supposed to tumble to the ground, Jamie a little heavier, Alexei a little taller, the two of them a whirl of limbs and strength. But that doesn't happen.

Instead, my brother takes a step, unsteady and uneven. Then another. And another. It's like he's being sucked into quicksand.

Despite the dew on the ground and the chill in the air, sweat gathers on my brother's brow and his body shakes as he takes an unsteady swing at Alexei, who ducks, then swings back.

Gently.

Alexei is being gentle with Jamie. That's how I know that things really are as wrong as I remembered.

Jamie lashes back, but Alexei just pushes Jamie's fist away.

"Again," Alexei says, and they resume their positions.

It's like Alexei's training a child, a little boy who is a long, long way from being his equal. And the thought makes me want to cry.

The pair of them dance around, maneuvering slowly, until I come into view.

Alexei stops. "Well, I guess the princess decided to join us."

It's a joke. A taunt. A tease. The fact that he's technically correct is what's supposed to make it funny, but I don't feel like laughing.

I can barely remember what laughter sounds like.

"Some of us need our beauty sleep," I taunt back.

"I'll say," Jamie comments, and Alexei smacks him on the shoulder in a way that has nothing to do with Jamie's recovery or his training. Instantly, my brother's countenance changes.

He looks at Alexei. "Don't make me hurt you."

Alexei smiles. "My friend, there is absolutely nothing I would welcome more."

He means it, and so the next punch is slow but steady. It's like watching two fighters wearing training wheels. I'm supposed to think that Jamie's getting stronger, faster. I'm supposed to be pleased with his progress.

But I'm too busy being happy he's alive.

The slap of skin against skin echoes through the stillness. In the distance, a bird calls. As the fog lifts, a pair of bald eagles swoop across the sky. I've seen their big nest on the other side of the island, near the steep stone cliff and rocky ledge. They've spent their morning pulling big, fat salmon from the cold water and are now returning to the nest. Safe. Sound. Free.

Not for the first time, I find myself officially envious of birds.

My brother stumbles, catches himself, and doesn't fall. But he's slow to regain his balance. He's still too thin and far too weak.

3

"Jamie, why don't you rest for a little bit?" I suggest.

"I just woke up," he tells me as he slaps at Alexei's broad shoulders one more time.

"Good," Alexei says as if he hasn't heard me. "Again."

"Jamie," I say, "you don't want to push it."

"No, Gracie." My brother stops and whirls on me. "That's exactly what I *have* to do."

He sounds like Dad, which means there's no use in arguing, so I ease away from the cabin and the boys. "We're running low on kindling, so I'm going to go . . ." I trail off but gesture toward the tall pine trees that surround us.

"Don't go far, Gracie!" Alexei yells as I move toward the shelter of the trees.

There is no place far enough.

It's not a forest—that isn't the right word. But that's how I've grown to think of the tall trees that grow straight into the air from the rocky soil beneath my feet. The ground is covered in moss, and it cushions my footsteps. I feel like the hunter for once. Not the hunted. I only wish this feeling could last.

Finally, the trees stop, and I step out from beneath their sheltering branches to look across the huge rocks that are covered by receding waves. The air is too cold. The sky is too overcast. And, most of all, the water is the wrong color. You wouldn't think it possible. Water is water, after all. But instead of the cool blue of the Mediterranean I'm looking out at an ocean that's as gray

4

as the sky, and that's how I know for sure how far we've come. It's the one thing that gives me hope that maybe—just maybe—we've come far enough.

I'm careful on the rocks. They're big and smooth, wet with the dew and the breaking waves. I leapfrog from one to another as I move down the shore. I close my eyes and think of fire, of sticky nights and the burning sun, and, most of all, another island and another time—another place on the other side of the world.

I can feel the fire as I plunge my hands into the icy water. Instantly, the cold burns and my skin goes numb. I wish I could submerge my whole body in the frigid depths. I wish I could turn off my mind, so I lean down and duck my head, feel the cold swallow me, jolting me awake. I stay under as long as I can, until my lungs burn and my eyes feel frozen shut. Then, with a cry, I hurl myself back, clawing against the rocks, pushing my wet hair from my face and drawing in deep, burning breaths.

There's no one to hear me. There's no one to see me—nothing but water stretching out to the horizon. There's no dock. No boat. No witness to my crazy as I throw back my head and scream. Cold water drips from my hair onto my T-shirt, freezing me more with every drop, but I'm not numb yet, so it's not enough. I want to wade out until I'm too cold to feel.

But then who would gather the kindling? I remember. I turn around and start up the rocks again, toward the trees.

Down the beach I can see the tall tree where the eagles have built their nest. They'll mate for life, returning here day after day. This is our home now. And a part of me wants to stay here, cold and isolated forever.

That's why I think it must be in my mind, the sound of the motor that carries on the wind. I stand on the rocks and look out through the fog. I can barely make out a shadow in the sky. I have a hard time breathing as I watch and listen to the sound of an engine getting closer and closer.

Then I bolt toward the tree line, hiding like the coward that I am. It's a water plane, but it doesn't get any lower. It doesn't land in the water off our shore, and so I breathe deep and start back through the trees.

As I go along, I pick up wood and check the traps that Jamie's set, looking for any small game that might stretch the supplies we brought from the mainland. I'm getting sick of fish.

My route takes me the long way around. The island is about the same size as the one off the shore of Valancia. I can walk the perimeter in less than two hours, and when I reach the far side, I climb steadily until I reach the highest ridge. The stone is solid beneath me, nothing but a steep cliff that has stood for ages against the battering ram of the sea.

I stand there for a long time, waiting.

And then I see it, bobbing on the waves: the plane.

It didn't fly on, I realize now. It circled. And then it landed.

I don't even realize I've dropped the wood that fills my arms until I hear it hit the rocks. I'm spinning, my feet slipping as I rush down the rocky ridge. I've got to tell Alexei. I have to help Jamie.

I have to run—I know it like I know I need to breathe. But then I freeze.

The woman wears a white suit, a fur stole around her neck. The breeze pushes her white hair back from her face, and she looks almost like an angel—like a ghost.

I'd give anything for this island to be haunted, but the woman on the rocks is flesh and blood. I'm certain of this as soon as the prime minister of Adria says, "Hello, Grace. You've been a very hard girl to find."

CHAPTER TWO

This isn't a dream, and I'm not sleeping. If anything, it's a nightmare, the waking kind.

"What are you doing here?" I say. One piece of wood is still in my hands, I realize. I grip it like a bat, ready to swing, to fight, to get dirt all over the prime minister of Adria and her pretty white suit.

My pulse is pounding, and the roar of the waves has been drowned out by the pounding of my blood.

I want to scream for the boys, but maybe she doesn't know they're here. Maybe I can delay her—delay this. Maybe, just maybe, my brother might live to fight another day.

"How did you find me?" I ask.

Alexandra Petrovic studies me, then shakes her head, as if I'm so sweet and naïve.

Just goes to show what she knows.

"Grace, we've been looking for you for weeks. We've all been very worried."

"How did you find me?" I shout this time, but the PM merely smirks.

"We have our ways."

I don't ask who she means by *we*. If there's one thing I've learned, it's that the secret society that my mother and grandmother were a part of doesn't take kindly to answering questions.

I grip and regrip the piece of wood. Splinters bite into my hands, and I welcome the pain.

"Leave," I say.

"Grace, we need to talk."

"Leave!" I repeat. As if I'm in a position to give orders.

"I came alone," she says. I glance down at the plane that bobs on the water near the rocks. "There's a pilot, but, don't worry—he will remain with the plane. I came alone. For you."

I start toward the woods, skirting the tree line and walking along the rocky shore. I have to lead her away from the boys. I have to—

"Gracie!"

I skid to a stop just as my name echoes through the air. Someone bursts from the trees.

"Grace!" Alexei is out of breath, and I know it's not because he's been running. It's because he's terrified. "A plane is circling. We've got to—"

I turn, and he follows my gaze to the woman in white.

"Alexei," she says, and something in the word stops me. He's supposed to be the most wanted man in Adria—a murderer. A fugitive. But the prime minister isn't shocked to see him. She is anything but afraid.

Alexei couldn't care less. He never takes his gaze off her as he tells me, "Gracie, come over here and get behind me. Now."

"Don't be silly, young man. I've come a long way to see Grace. Now, who is going to take me to Jamie?"

On our way through the woods, we climb down steep ravines and over muddy trails, but the prime minister doesn't complain. Neither does she try to talk to Alexei. He keeps his head down, leading the way, almost like he's trying to outrun something that he can neither see nor name. But I know better. There are some ghosts that live inside us, and we can never lose them, no matter how far we run.

When we come around the edge of the cabin, I hear the cocking of a gun. I don't bother to turn, but I can see Jamie out of the corner of my eye. The shotgun is heavy, I know, but he's found an untapped reservoir of strength somewhere and both barrels are steady as they stay trained on the prime minister.

"What are you doing here?" Jamie practically growls.

"Hello, James," the PM says, then slides her gaze to me. "My, what a family resemblance."

"Stop!" Alexei yells, spinning on her. "Stop your lying. Stop . . . Go away. Go back."

"Alexei," she starts, but then seems to realize he's not her ally here. She has no allies. No friends. But she still has a mission, and when the woman speaks again, she very much resembles the most powerful woman in Adria. "Gentlemen, I need a word with Grace. Alone."

"I don't know how you found us, but we're not—"

"It's okay," I say, cutting Jamie off. It's not that I trust her. It's that, so far, there are no black helicopters on the horizon, no SWAT teams bursting through the trees. If the prime minister wanted us dead, we would be, and all of us know it. She certainly wouldn't have come herself and risked getting blood all over her pretty white suit.

"I'm fine," I tell the boys. They don't try to stop me as I lead the PM into the cabin.

It's dusty and dim inside. Three rooms with a roof and a generator and a well for running water. It's not much else, but it's home. For now. I try to put on my best *Ms. Chancellor* smile. I ask myself, *What would Noah do?*

"Would you care for some tea?" I ask, and the PM smiles.

"That would be lovely."

I can hear Jamie and Alexei pacing across the porch while I boil the water and steep the leaves.

They might be outside, but the door is open, so the PM doesn't say a word. I learned a long time ago not to ask questions that no one is going to answer, so I don't ask again why she's here. I don't demand details about who's been trying to kill us. Or why.

"It's not that good, but it's hot," I say as I hand the prime minister one of the mismatched cups.

"Lovely. Perhaps we can enjoy it outside?"

When we step onto the porch, my brother and Alexei glare at us, but neither says a thing as the prime minister of Adria and I wrap our hands around our steaming mugs and walk toward the trees.

The sun is higher now, but it still doesn't burn through the fog or lighten the gray. Inside the cover of the trees it might be dawn or dusk or the middle of the day. It doesn't matter. The clock is the same in any case, and it simply reads, *Time's up.*

We walk in silence. Whatever brought the most powerful woman in Adria to the other side of the world, she isn't in a hurry to share.

Overhead, birds squawk. If the fog would clear, we might see whales breaching in the rough waters in the distance. But we stay shrouded in our cloud cocoon.

"I've not seen this part of America before." The prime minister brings the hot tea to her lips and takes a sip, careful to avoid the chipped section of the old cup.

"Few people have," I say. "That's kind of why we chose it. You didn't tell me how you found us."

12

"You're right—I didn't." She takes another sip of tea. "You can't run forever, Grace."

I stop. I grin. "Watch me." The words are like a dare.

"Your brother doesn't look well. Is he receiving medical care?"

It's my soft spot, and she knows it, so I snap back defensively, "Jamie is fine."

She raises an eyebrow but doesn't say a thing.

"Do they . . ." I start but falter. "Does the royal family know where we are?"

"I am not certain." Her words are clipped, measured. There's something she's being very careful not to say.

"It *is* the royal family, isn't it?" I ask. "I mean, my brother is supposed to be king. He is Adria's *rightful* king. Why else would someone want to kill him? So it has to be them. *Is it them?*"

The words are desperate, but I can't help it. I need a face for the threat in the dark. I need her to tell me that I'm right. Because I don't know how many more times I can survive being wrong.

"There is much we do not know. Yet."

"Yes or no?" I snap. "Is the royal family of Adria trying to kill me?"

The PM carefully considers her answer. "Probably."

It's all the verification I need. The truth hurts, when I let myself remember. Better to keep it like a thorn pressing against my skin, never quite piercing through.

"I met the king once," I tell her. "He was nice. But that was before he needed my brother dead."

13

Sometimes I hate my mother for what she found, what she learned. She was about my age when she first started this hunt, and now she's gone. I think about my mom's best friends. One now lives in the palace with the people who want me dead. One hasn't been seen in a decade.

"Where's Karina Volkov?"

The PM studies me. "Where is who?"

"Alexei's mother. Where is she? What happened to her?"

I expect a lecture on understanding my place or respecting my elders. I'm not at all prepared for the look in the PM's eye as she turns back to the gray waters of the sea and says, "Why should I know?"

"Because she was part of the Society. And the Society knows everything."

"Karina went away several years ago, but that was no surprise to anyone. She was always . . . flighty."

"Why does everyone think she could just run off and leave Alexei?"

"Are you saying *you* could never leave Mr. Volkov, Ms. Blakely?"

I don't know if it's her smirk or her question that knocks me back a step, but I move anyway, carefully across the slick rocks.

"I'm saying moms don't do that."

"Your mother didn't do that."

"No. She didn't. She just kept picking at a wound that was two hundred years old until some powerful people needed her dead. And now they want to kill me. They've already gotten way too close to killing my brother."

14

I take a step closer. She might be powerful in Adria, but I know every inch of this rocky shore. This is my turf. I'm not going to be intimidated by anyone here. Even her.

"Why are you here?" I demand, but the PM only smirks again.

"You've been a very bad girl, Ms. Blakely."

I ease closer. "You're under the impression that I care, Ms. Petrovic."

The wind blows her white hair around her face, and it's almost like she's risen from the sea, an omen or a curse.

"The Society has operated in secret for a thousand years. Four times longer than *this*"—she gestures to the land and water that surround us— "has been a country. Regimes rise. Dictators fall. Wars rage the world over and still we stand. Do you know why, Ms. Blakely?"

"Because I wasn't around to ruin everything?"

She raises an eyebrow as if to indicate I have a point, but she doesn't say so.

"We survive because *we take care of our own*. I'm here because you need a friend. I'm here because you need *us*."

"Am I supposed to believe that you care about me? Or do you just care about the lost princess of Adria?"

That I can even ask that with a straight face shows how surreal my life has become. But, then again, maybe it's *not* real?

Maybe I'm still in a psych ward, strapped to a bed. Maybe that would be better than this, because then, at least, Jamie would still be at West Point—Jamie would still be safe.

"The Society needs you, Grace. And you need the Society."

"The Society needs me for what?"

Sometimes the scariest answer is silence. I stand in the wind, listening to the waves crash and the birds cry. It sounds almost like Adria. Perhaps I could close my eyes and pretend that I am back on the beach, looking up at the wall. But I don't want to. I'm on the other side of the world for a reason.

"You are significant. And for that reason you've been summoned."

"I'm doing just fine on my own, thank you."

I'm starting to turn. I'm desperate to leave. I'm going to run, swim . . . fly. But then the PM calls, *If I found you, then others will, too!*

And that's the point, isn't it? That I wasn't safe in Adria. And, in time, I won't be safe here.

Someone managed to blow up a car belonging to the Russian government. Someone managed to kill a West Point cadet and frame an ambassador's son. Someone wants my brother dead.

The wind blows the PM's chic white hair across her face, but I can see her eyes. I just can't read them.

For a second, I am tempted. I really, truly am. But then the PM says, "Come with me, Grace. Come home," and something inside of me snaps.

"I'm not going back to Adria. I am *never* going back to Adria. I made that decision while I watched my brother lie on a dining room table with his blood all over my hands. I am never going back there. Ever."

I turn and start down the beach. As I round the bend, I can see the little water plane that brought her here, bobbing on the waves, waiting to fly far, far away.

"We can help," the PM offers, as if it is a last resort.

But it just makes me want to laugh.

I face her. "Like you helped my mother? Like you helped my brother? He's learning to walk again, by the way. He doesn't even need the canes anymore if he goes slowly. We're just lucky that he never lost blood flow to his brain, because then . . . Excuse me if I think your help might be a little too late."

I spin and start back toward the cabin; the conversation is over. It's not really up for debate.

But Alexandra Petrovic did not become the most powerful politician in Adria by taking no for an answer.

"You seem to think that I'm asking, Ms. Blakely. Which I'm not."

I stop and turn. "And you seem to think that you scare me, Ms. Petrovic. Which you don't."

The conversation is over, but the PM is smiling. "Aren't you going to ask me why I'm here?"

"I think we've already established that. Thanks."

"I mean why I am here and *not* Eleanor Chancellor."

At the sound of the name of my grandfather's chief of staff, I go still. The PM's right. Ms. Chancellor should be here. She's the one who took me deep into the tunnels beneath Valancia and told me the Society's tale. She's the one who introduced me to this world and started guiding me on this journey.

She should be here.

But she isn't.

"What have you done to her?"

"This problem is larger than you, Ms. Blakely. It is larger than me. It is hundreds of years old and lives in the shadows of the darkest halls of power in the world. So once again I'll say: *You need to come home.*"

"No." I shake my head again, like my consciousness is trying to drag me from a very bad dream. "No. I'm not going back to Adria." It's a mantra now. "I'm never going back to Adria."

The smile on the PM's face doesn't belong there. She looks like someone who has almost won.

"Well, that works out nicely, then, because that isn't where we're going. I will be in Washington, DC, for a few days, and I'd like you to come with . . ."

She doesn't finish. She just looks at me, a confused expression upon her face as her steps falter. It's like all her strength is fading, her mission clearing from her mind like the fog.

I look down at the cup in my hands. My tea has gone cold, so I toss it to the moss-covered ground. The prime minister has almost finished hers.

"No, *you* misunderstand, Madame Prime Minister. I'm not just good at staying alive. I'm also really, really good at drugging people."

She slumps slowly to the ground, getting mud and grass stains all over her pretty white suit. Well, that ought to show her, I think. It's time she learns that I mess up everything I touch.

There's a shout in the distance. I can hear my name being carried on the wind.

"Gracie!" Alexei is standing on the rocky shore of the beach. Behind him, the water plane is coming to life, and I know it's time to go.

I don't look back at the woman on the ground; I just run along the rocks to where my brother waits inside the tiny plane.

Alexei moves to help me inside as Dominic punches at the plane's controls. The pilot lies on the rocks, unconscious, and the Scarred Man looks at me.

I knew he'd see the plane, subdue the pilot, collect my brother, and take him to safety. I'm only a little disappointed that they bothered waiting for me. The smart move would have been to leave me here on this island, but I'm not the only one who acts stupid sometimes, and I'm my mother's daughter, so the Scarred Man will never, ever let me go.

"Grace Olivia, hurry!" he tells me as I climb inside. Alexei follows and slams the door.

The water is rough, and the plane bounces, fighting gravity and the current. Soon we're in the air and rising through the fog. This must be how Jack felt when he went up the beanstalk. I wonder if we might find treasure, up here in the air. More likely there are just bigger, meaner people who want to see us dead.

Jamie's in the seat beside Dominic, a headset over his ears, and the two of them talk like soldiers. Like grown-ups. Alexei and I are in the back, and with the roar of the air around us—the whirling of the small plane's engines—it's almost like we're alone.

He puts his arm around me and pulls me tightly against him, warm. Solid. Beneath us is a massive mound of stone, but Alexei is the rock I lean on. He is the only thing that can still make me feel safe.

"What are we going to do?" Alexei asks.

"I don't know."

If my brother and Dominic hear, they don't reply. The four of us just stare out at the clouds and the horizon, looking for a safe place to land.

CHAPTER THREE

It takes three days for them to break me.

Three days of flying and then driving, of fast food and sleeping in the old car that Dominic may or may not have stolen. But I'm too tired. I'm too sore. And, frankly, I smell too bad. We all do. You'd think running for your life would involve a lot more exercise, but so far it is just a long strip of asphalt and an endless stretch of sameness that lies before us, day after day.

So it's no wonder that, eventually, I snap.

"Where are we going?" I say while Dominic pumps gas.

Jamie's in the backseat of the car, covered with blankets but sweating, shaking. He's been like this for hours, but I'm the only one who seems to care.

"Dominic!" I shout, and slowly, he turns to me.

It's dusk—that time of day when you may or may not need headlights. It's neither day nor night, bright nor black. We are in the gray area of life, I know. And I don't like it.

"Where are we going?" I ask him.

"Mexico," he says. It's not a question, not a debate. "There is a woman there who owes me a favor. She will help us."

"Mexico?" I ask.

"Yes. Don't worry about the language. I am fluent. It will be—"

"I'm not worried about speaking Spanish, Dominic. I'm worried about my brother."

"It is for your brother that we go."

"He needs to rest." I glance down to where Jamie leans against the window, eyes closed. He looks worse than I've seen him in weeks, since the hospital. Since Germany. "We've got to stop. He's not strong enough for this."

"America is no longer safe."

"America is a big freaking country."

"We must get you both someplace safe," he says again, and for the first time, I hear it. Dominic isn't just worried. Dominic is scared.

As a boy, he loved our mother. As a man, he watched her die. It is far too late to save her, but it's not too late for us, and so he is going to keep driving—keep moving. He will never, ever stop.

"How did they find us?" I ask, thinking back to the sight of the prime minister in her white suit, appearing out of nowhere like a ghost.

22

When Dominic turns back, he looks me squarely in the eye. I'm not just the pesky kid sister anymore, the brat, the burden. Dominic and I have been through too much together, and now he knows me well enough not to lie. I almost wish he would, instead of saying, "I don't know."

If there was a leak we could plug it, a trail we could clear it. There are few things in the world scarier than the unknown. I've learned that the hard way. And now the only thing Dominic knows is to run and keep running until there is no room left to take another step.

"Jamie's fever is back," I say.

"We will give him fluids in the car, hang a bag. He'll be—"

"He will not be fine!" The gas station parking lot is empty, but I don't care. I'd yell even if a crowd were watching. I have to make him see. No. I have to make him *stop*.

"He needs a bed, Dominic. And a shower. And a meal that doesn't come out of a bag. We all do. When was the last time you slept? I mean really slept?"

"I'll sleep when you're safe."

"Oh, Dominic." I shake my head slowly. "I will never be safe. And that goes double if you collapse or give out on us. We need you. I know you know that. But I'm saying it anyway. We need you at your best. And you're not now. You can't be. It's just not possible. So . . ."

I don't realize Alexei's behind me until Dominic glances over my shoulder, but even before I turn I can hear it: the conversation they are having without me. It consists of glances and shrugs.

23

Neither one of them wants to admit that I'm right. But they probably don't want to spend another night sleeping in a twenty-five-year-old Buick, either, so Alexei shrugs.

"I will see about getting us some rooms."

The little motel on the far side of the parking lot probably has only twenty units, and it doesn't seem busy. The opposite, in fact. Which is worse.

"Stop," I call out, and Alexei turns. "You're still front-page news," I tell him. With all that's going on with me and Jamie, the fact that Alexei is a wanted fugitive is easy to forget sometimes. But the headlines are real. The manhunt is months old but on-going. "Even if no one in their right mind would expect you to run to the US, we probably shouldn't take the chance."

Then I look at Dominic, the scar that will forever mark his face. "And you're . . . memorable," I tell him, then hold out my hand until he passes me his wallet. "You two stay here. I'll go see about the rooms."

There's a smell that comes from being on the run. It's the odor of stale, reheated coffee and dim, abandoned rooms, of seedy motels where a decade's worth of cigarette smoke has seeped into the curtains. Inside the little motel office, the coffeepot has been on all day, and the smell of it hits me as soon as I step inside.

But, otherwise, the place is clean. Tidy. The woman behind the counter is busy with a pair of knitting needles and pink yarn. Then I realize that the entire room is covered in yarn. There is a knit sleeve over a jar of pens, a calendar holder on

24

the wall, and at least a dozen dolls with brightly colored yarn dresses. Whoever this woman is, she really must believe that idle hands are a devil's plaything. I doubt she's been truly idle a day in her life.

"How can I help ya, hon?" she asks me, a big, bright smile on her face. I might be the only real person she's seen for hours. Maybe days.

"Do you have any adjoining rooms?" I ask.

"Well"—she gives a little laugh—"we're not exactly fully booked at the moment. I think we can take care of you."

The sun is almost down now, and a neon light is coming to life. The word *VACANCY* glows green against the glass.

"Can I have two, please?"

The woman eyes me then, a little skeptical. I don't want to know what she's seeing. I'm still too thin, too tired, too haggard and dirty and worn. I probably look like the chased animal that I am, and there's not a doubt in my mind this woman sees it. From her place behind the counter, looking through that perfectly clean window, this woman sees everything.

"You okay, sweetie?" she asks me, tilting her head.

"Yes. Thank you."

Dominic is still by the car. Alexei is looking under the hood.

"Who you got with you out there?" she asks.

"Uh . . ." I glance over my shoulder as if I can't quite remember the answer. "My dad," I lie. "And my brothers. We're . . ."

Running.

Lost.

25

But not quite lost enough.

"Where's your momma?" the woman asks.

I look down at a neat stack of knitted coasters, finger the stiff yarn.

"She died."

You can't fake the way my voice cracks, my fingers tremble. And finally the woman is convinced that I'm not lying.

"Oh, heck, sweetie. I'm sorry. Here. I'll get you those rooms."

She's busy for a moment, typing on a computer that might be older than I am. Then she reaches in a drawer for two heavy metal keys attached to massive plastic tags. Rooms five and seven. Our home for the next twenty-four hours, if we're lucky.

The woman runs one of the many credit cards the Scarred Man gave me. They all have different numbers, different names. I have no idea where they came from. They may be stolen or just attached to one of his many identities. It doesn't matter as long as they're clean and untraceable.

"What brings y'all to Fort Sill?"

For a second, I'm sure that I've misheard her. I hope that I've misheard her. But I haven't. I know it in my gut. I should have seen it before now. I should have felt it like a magnetic pull, a steady, constant tug. There's a flag on the wall that was knitted out of yarn that's red, white, and blue. I see the map now, a pin over where Fort Sill sits in the southwest corner of Oklahoma. I should have noticed the tidy stacks of flyers like tourists always grab, announcing the local sights. Almost all of them have the words *Fort Sill* blazoned across the top.

Maybe this was why, deep down, I was so desperate to stop here.

Maybe this is why the Scarred Man was so desperate to stop *me*.

"Sweetie?" the woman says, bringing me back.

"We . . . we used to live here."

I'd give anything for it to be a lie, but the woman brightens at my words. She glances through the window again. Dominic is still standing by the car, so broad and tall and strong.

"Oh. Was your dad a military man?"

I look out the window at the coming darkness. A cold seeps into my bones as I say, "Yes."

The room is dim. Heavy, old-fashioned curtains cover clean windows, and only a little light creeps into the room from the bathroom. I'm part bat now: I can see in the dark, hear every drip of water from the leaky faucet, every buzz and hum from the bathroom lightbulb that is getting ready to blow. But, most of all, I hear Jamie.

His breath is deep but labored. Just lying in bed is hard work for him. He's no longer the boy who could wake before the sun and run around the great walled city twice before breakfast. He'll probably never be that boy again. But he's alive, and that's enough.

That has to be enough.

I lie atop the covers and watch him. When he shudders and

mumbles something in his sleep, I get up and feel his pulse. Faint but still there. At least his fever seems to have broken. There's no blood coming through his bandages and staining his white T-shirt. My brother is alive. For now. And I know it's up to me to keep him that way.

But that's just the start of the things I have to do.

The connecting door is slightly ajar. There's silence on the other side. Dominic is in one bed, sleeping. But I know that with the slightest noise, even the smallest disturbance, he'll bolt awake, alert and alarmed, so I move slowly to where Alexei sits in an overstuffed chair that's pointed toward the window. The curtains are open just a crack, and the light from the parking lot slashes across his face, an eerie yellow glow. He's supposed to be keeping watch, I know, but I don't wake him. He needs his rest.

And I need the keys.

They're on the tiny table between the two beds. I pick them up gently, close the door behind me when I go.

Outside, I pull on my cardigan, not looking back. I just keep walking to the Buick. Only Jamie's voice can stop me.

"Don't do it, Gracie."

He's not yelling, but the words are too loud in the still night air. Dominic or Alexei will hear him.

"Do what?" I ask, turning back.

Jamie gives a weary laugh. "Do you really think I don't know where we are? We're five miles away, Gracie. I'd know it blindfolded."

He coughs then, doubles over. His color is better, but he is so far from well that I step toward him, half-afraid that I might need to catch him before he hits the ground.

Jamie holds out a hand, stopping me.

"I'm fine."

He is so not fine.

"Go to bed, Jamie."

"Okay." My brother gives me a smile. "When you do."

"I can't sleep," I say.

"Then neither can I."

"Jamie, you're . . ."

"You can say it, you know. I'm lucky to be alive. I'm not ashamed of that."

He's right, but that's not the point.

"You need to rest, Jamie. You need to get better."

"I need to keep my kid sister alive, is what I need to do. Even if she's dead set against it."

I wish he were joking, but he's not. I wish he were wrong, but Jamie is never wrong. Ever.

"I just . . ."

The town is a few miles away, and I glance in that direction, unsure of what I'll see.

"I know, Gracie." Jamie's voice is soft and understanding. He's maybe the only person in the world who has some idea why I'm out here in the dark, what has called me to this place.

"I need to see it," I say.

"Okay," Jamie says, no longer fighting. "Tomorrow we'll tell Dominic we need to make a pit stop. He won't like it, but—"

"Tonight," I say. "Alone. I need to see it alone."

But Jamie's already shaking his head. "Alone isn't an option."

"No." I'm not shouting, but I want to. "You saw it *after*, didn't you? Well, not me. I was . . ."

Tied up. Locked up. Dying.

Jamie doesn't need me to say any more. When my brother walks closer, every step is a struggle. He's going on steam and sheer force of will. He should be in a hospital. At the very least a rehab center or that motel bed. But he's not going back. Not without me. He just drags himself to the Buick and reaches for the door.

"You drive."

It's been almost five years since we moved here, since Dad surprised our mom with a little white house in town. Since they sat Jamie and me down and explained that Fort Sill would be Dad's last post, our last stop. But it wasn't the end, our parents told us. No. It was the beginning.

But of what we had no idea at the time.

"It's up here," Jamie tells me. I turn the Buick off the highway and onto a street that is bathed in the yellow glow of streetlights. They're so different from the gaslights of Adria; their light doesn't flicker. The fire inside them doesn't burn. Everything around me feels too foreign, too new. The town is small, even by US standards, and it feels like we're a world away from Embassy Row.

It's the dead of night, but morning comes early in an Army town, and I know the streets won't stay empty for long. A few lights shine inside the cute little shops on Main Street, but there is one shop that stands in darkness—like a string of Christmas lights with one blown bulb, a solitary dark spot, fading into the night.

That is where I park. And sit. And stare.

"We don't have to get out," Jamie tells me.

I turn off the Buick. "Yes. I do."

I honestly don't know what I expected to see. It's been three years, after all. "It's still . . ." I start, easing closer to the brick walls, a burned-out shell of what used to be one woman's dream.

"Dad never sold it," Jamie says. "He hired a crew to come in and clean it up, remove the debris and make it safe if kids should wander in or something. But yeah. It's still the same. I think he . . . I think he was afraid to change anything without her permission, you know? It's still hers. In his mind, it will always be hers."

I remember the first time our mother ever brought us here. She made us stand across the street with our eyes closed until she yelled, "Ta-da!" Then we opened them to find her standing in front of an old hardware store, her arms thrown out as if she was showing us a palace.

A palace . . .

Suddenly, I'm shaking. My blood is pounding too hard in my veins. *Jamie is no longer beside me, and I'm alone on the street, looking*

31

through the window at the smoke that fills the shop. I'm screaming out my mother's name, watching a man I've never seen lay her body on the wooden floor.

Cases line the walls, full of old clocks and crystal vases, dolls and watches and books—so many books. And when the man sees me, I yell. I scream. A bag lies at my feet. Shiny metal peeks out from the depths, and I reach for the gun. I reach for the gun, and—

"Gracie. Gracie!"

Jamie is squeezing me, holding me tight.

"It's okay. It's okay." His fingers are in my hair, pushing my face toward his broad shoulder, muffling my screams.

The flames are gone and the night is clear, but I swear that I can still smell the smoke. It hasn't been three years. It isn't over. A part of me wants to lunge through the place where the door used to hang, run back through time to that night, to stop the stupid girl I was. But it's too late.

Inside, the wide wooden floorboards are sturdy but covered in dust. The roof is still standing, and the old tin tiles on the ceiling are now charred and stained with soot. Mom loved those tiles. She spent hours sanding and scraping and painting them to shiny white perfection. But nothing about our family will ever be perfect again.

"Every now and then Dad talks about selling it, but . . ."

I get it, even if Jamie can't put it into words. There are some books you can never get rid of, even if you don't like the ending.

It's not a shop anymore; it's a grave. There is nothing alive within it, and it can't hurt me. I know this, but when I close my eyes, I hear the crackling of the fire, the shattering of the glass.

I shake and I want to scream, but most of all I want to wake up in my old bed and find that the past three years were nothing but a very bad dream.

I don't realize I'm shaking again until I feel Jamie's hands on my arms.

"We don't have to do this, Gracie. Whatever test you think you've got to pass, you don't."

I do. But I can't say so. I just pull away from Jamie's grasp and steady my pounding pulse, take a deep breath. And soon *I'm standing where the stairs used to be. The second-story balcony is breaking free, crashing down and taking Dominic's perfect face with it.*

That's one way the Scarred Man and I are different. It takes more than a glance to see the way that this place changed me.

"Grace?" Jamie is beside me, here to stop me from doing something stupid.

He's three years too late.

"Gracie, come—"

But I don't care what Jamie has to say. There's a brick at my feet, and I pick it up and hurl it as hard as I can through one of the remaining pieces of glass. It shatters and falls to the floor, and I just pick up something else and lash out again. And again.

And again.

Jamie doesn't try to stop me. Maybe he knows he's too weak now. Or maybe he was never strong enough to hold back the wave of emotion that is crashing through me.

One of the interior walls is half-collapsed, but I kick at the part that still stands. Over and over I pound and I pummel until the bricks move. The wall shifts, and soon it's crumbling, just like me.

"Gracie, stop!"

His arms are around my waist, pulling me away from the bricks that are crashing to the floor like an avalanche that's been held back for too long. Dust swarms around us. The old wooden floor creaks. And, suddenly, I wonder how long and how hard I'd have to kick to make the wall around Valancia come tumbling down. I'm half-tempted to try it.

"Are you okay?" Jamie holds me at arm's length and looks me up and down. Poor Jamie. When will he learn that I only get hurt on the inside?

When he sees that I'm as whole as I was when I started, he tips up my chin and makes me look him in the eye. "Feel better?" he tries to tease.

But Jamie wouldn't smile at my answer, so I don't give it.

I just try to ease away, but in a flash Jamie's arms are around me, jerking me back, and he's screaming "Look out!" as I realize that the heavy bricks have crashed through the weather-beaten boards, disappearing into some unknown below.

For a moment, my brother and I just stare at the massive black hole that has opened up before us.

"I didn't know it had a basement," I say.

Jamie shakes his head, a hint of fear in his eyes. "It didn't."

•   •   •

I shouldn't be surprised. My life has become a never-ending spiral of dusty, secret rooms and even darker secrets. We're thousands of miles from Adria, but this shadowy space is connected, I can feel it, like maybe I might drop into that dark hole and start walking and, in a year or so, emerge somewhere behind the wall.

"Do you have your flashlight?" Jamie asks, proving he's one of the few people on earth who really know me, because of course I have it. I hand it to him, and he kneels slowly to the dusty floor.

He's nowhere near recovered, but adrenaline is the most powerful medicine there is, and right now he's not feeling any pain. He has more energy than he's had in weeks as he leans over the broken boards and shines my small, bright flashlight into the space below.

"I'm going down," I say.

"Gracie—"

Jamie wants to tell me to stop, to slow down, to be careful, but as soon as he looks up he realizes he really should just save his breath.

"I'll lower you down."

"No," I say, but I can't tell him he's too weak. "There's a desk. I can just . . ."

In a flash, I'm on the ground next to Jamie and dropping into the darkness below.

The desk I land on is solid; it doesn't even shimmy when I touch down.

"Light?" I hold out my hands, and Jamie lets the flashlight drop.

He doesn't try to join me, and I'm glad. I don't have the strength to tell him just how fleeting his own strength is. At least Jamie is smart enough to know it.

So I stand alone in the darkness once again. The beam of light is small but startlingly bright as I shine it upon walls covered in maps of Europe and Asia and the Middle East. There's a globe on the end of the desk, piles of notebooks; Post-it notes cover the walls. And on every piece of paper there's a handwriting that I haven't seen in years.

My mother's lipstick stains the rim of the cup by my feet, but the coffee has long since grown cold and evaporated away.

If not for a thick layer of dust, the room would look like she just popped out to take a call or help a customer. Maybe she's gone to pick me up from school and will return at any minute. Maybe she's been down here this whole time, just waiting for me to come back.

"Gracie." Jamie's voice breaks through my mind. "What's that?"

I turn and follow his finger, directing the light at the wall farthest from the desk. I have to hop down off the old metal desk, push aside a dusty chair, but soon I'm standing in front of something like I've only seen in movies.

From a distance, it looked almost like wallpaper—maybe a mural of some kind. But the closer I get, the clearer the images become, and I can tell it's really more of a collage.

Newspaper articles are pasted over magazine pictures that cover maps and photocopies of what must be ancient books.

There are more Post-its and calendars. The dates go back hundreds of years.

Ms. Chancellor told me that my mom was responsible for antiquities, lost artifacts that were relevant to Adria and the Society. But one glance at this wall, and I know it was so much more than that. She wasn't looking for *something*. She was looking for *someone*. And now she's dead because, in a way, she found her.

"Gracie, what is all that?"

"It's the inside of Mom's head," I say without even having to think about the answer. Really, the most amazing thing is that I haven't already made a dozen walls just like it.

"What?" Jamie calls.

"Amelia." I turn and glance up at my brother. "It's how she figured out what became of Amelia."

Jamie doesn't believe the story. Not really, I can tell. And I can't blame him. I spent my summer sneaking through the tunnels beneath Valancia— I've seen the inside of the Society and heard their tales, witnessed their power. And even I can't really believe what is, by all accounts, unbelievable.

But you don't send assassins after things that are make-believe.

Two hundred years ago, there was a palace coup and, in the chaos, a baby was smuggled free. The Society hid her among their own. She was raised in secret. Protected. Safe. And, eventually, she grew up, and her bloodline survived.

Until someone started trying to kill us.

I ease even closer, shine the light up and down, sweeping across my mother's old obsession.

Maps. Articles. Notes. And in the center of it all, a picture.

My mother looks so young. Her hair is long and her skin is tanned, and she's smiling as if the future would hold nothing but more good days. Two dark-haired girls flank her on either side. One is famous now, the mother of Adria's future king. And one is a stranger.

"Who is it?" Jamie asks.

"It's mom and Princess Ann and . . . is that Alexei's mother?" I ask. Carefully, I pull the picture off the wall. Then I climb back onto the desk, reach up, and hand the photo to my brother.

"Yeah, that's her," he says. "I remember her. Barely. She and Mom used to get together and tell me and Alexei to go play."

I've always known that Alexei had a mother, of course, but for years she was never mentioned, never seen.

"What was she like?" I ask, as if that is the great mystery here.

"I don't know," Jamie says, pondering. "She was—"

"Gone," a hard voice says from behind him. Soon, Alexei is down on the dusty desk beside me. "She was gone," he says, as if that's all that matters. And I guess, to him, it is.

I'm not surprised when Dominic appears over Jamie's shoulder.

The sun must be rising, because a gentle golden glow has begun to fill the room. It's easy to see the hurt on the Scarred Man's face.

"I never knew this was down here," he says. "I came and . . .
She didn't tell me. I never knew."

I turn and let the light sweep into the corners, and that's
when I see a box sitting on a high shelf. About the size of a shoe
box, it's covered with dust and cobwebs, but I can tell the wood
is gorgeous. There seem to be a bunch of different kinds all
melded together in an intricate pattern. When I reach for it, I
hear my mother's voice.

*"See this, Gracie? It was Grandma's. And before her, it was Great-
Grandma's, and so on and so on for a very long time. And someday,
sweetheart, it's going to be yours."*

My finger traces through the dust and through the years.

"How do you open it?"

My mother laughs. Smiles. "You'll open it when you're ready."

"Are you ready?" Alexei's voice cuts through the fog and pulls
me from the dream.

"What?" I ask.

"Are you ready?" he asks again.

"Alexei, if our moms were working together . . . if your
mom was part of this, then maybe—"

"Maybe Karina's dead? Or maybe she just left me? Which one
of those is supposed to make me feel better?"

There are some questions that even I know better than to try
to answer.

The light that fills the shop overhead is brighter, and I can
hear Dominic return to himself as he says, "We can't stay here.
It's someplace they might expect to find you. We can't stay."

39

"But—"

"Take it down," Dominic orders. "Take it all down. We'll bring it with us. We cannot let it be found."

Obsession.

That's the word Ms. Chancellor and Prime Minister Petrovic used when Alexei and I overheard them in the tunnels. I never really understood what they meant until now, as I stand surrounded by my mother's work.

Her obsession.

Three years have passed, but this room is like a wound, and Alexei and I peel away the layers of it piece by piece, shoving them into boxes and bags, preparing to carry my mother's obsession away.

When the last wall is empty, Dominic reaches down and Alexei boosts me up. The last thing he gives me is the ornate box. I don't care about the dust and the cobwebs—I hold it close to my chest and I walk, almost crying, to the car.

CHAPTER
FOUR

I'm not hungry, but I force myself to eat—to keep my body fed, to be a good influence on Jamie, who is still far too thin and too weak.

Besides, the way Dominic is acting, we may not stop for lunch, for supper. We may never stop again, and so I take slow, steady bites of my pancakes. I eat my scrambled eggs. Because if there's one thing I've learned, it's that I have absolutely no idea what any day might bring.

The diner is cold but far from empty. The only noise is the scrape of forks against plates, the distant, sizzling hum of frying bacon. And, beneath it all, there are whispers.

I can see the girls out of the corner of my eye. They've piled purses and backpacks into the corner of a booth, and the three of them lean across the Formica-topped table. They've pushed aside plates of barely eaten food and filled their cups with more sugar than coffee. But, most of all, they watch us.

No. That's not true. They watch Alexei.

Eventually, Dominic gets up to pay the bill. The girls slide out of their booth and collect their things, shooting glances our way.

"You have admirers," I say.

"Excuse me?" Alexei looks at me as if maybe I am speaking Japanese.

"You didn't notice your fan club?" I jerk my head in the direction of the three girls. They're all wearing cheerleading uniforms. It must be Friday, I realize. Game night. They're probably getting ready to go to a pep rally, maybe take some tests. They are getting ready to be normal for one more day.

They're the queens of their school; I can tell it by the way they sit and talk and toss their hair.

I'm a real-life princess, but I'll never be as royal as the three of them.

"You notice everything," I tell him. "Do you really expect me to believe that you didn't see three girls in cheerleading uniforms checking you out?"

Alexei glances up, blue eyes through dark black lashes. "I do not notice girls," he says. "I notice *girl*."

And with those words, my brother coughs. "Well, I think that's my cue to excuse myself." He slides out of the booth and heads toward the bathroom, slowly. He actually holds on to one of the leather-covered barstools to steady himself as he goes.

42

The cheerleaders watch him. Just a few weeks ago they would have been eyeing both Alexei and Jamie, but my brother isn't well, and it's obvious even to them. Whatever swagger he used to have flowed out of him weeks ago. We left it puddled on the embassy's dining room floor.

It's coming back, I know it. Slowly. Surely. But it's not coming fast enough.

"He's not getting better, is he?" I ask, terrified of the answer, but needing to ask it anyway.

Alexei pushes his empty plate away and pulls mine in front of him, shoves a fork full of my pancakes into his mouth, then considers.

"He has the strongest heart of anyone I have ever known. He will recover."

The frustration that's been building inside of me for days is starting to boil now. It's all I can do not to yell when I say, "Not if we keep dragging him all over creation. Not if we keep giving him fluids in the back of a car and not taking him to a doctor when his fever spikes, and . . . he won't get better like this."

"Yes." Alexei pierces me with a stare. "He will. He has to."

"He needs to rest," I say like a petulant child, complaining about not getting her way. "He needs to stay in one place and rest."

"We can't stop running, Gracie." Alexei pushes away my plate as well, his appetite suddenly gone. "You know that. We can never stop running."

I want to yell and scream about how wrong he and Dominic are to doubt me—that I know Jamie better than anyone and I know what is best. I wish I could tell them that they're wrong.

But they're not.

And I hate that most of all.

"Jamie could stop running, you know . . ."

"Gracie, we—"

"He could." I cut him off, make him look into my eyes. "He could stop if they had something—if they had *someone*—else to chase."

In the silence that follows I can actually feel Alexei shifting, changing. He sits up straighter, leans closer. He does everything but grab me by the hands, force me to stay in this booth and within his grasp. I can actually feel Alexei's fear.

"Gracie, if you think you can—"

"Hey!"

When I see a fuzzy blue figure out of the corner of my eye it takes me a moment to remember the cheerleaders. They stand at the end of our booth, pink backpacks over blue uniforms, all three of them looking down at Alexei, who doesn't even seem to notice that they're there, wearing uniforms that are the exact color of his eyes.

I look up at the middle girl, the one who spoke. "Hi," I say, but the girl acts like I haven't said a thing.

"So my friends and I were wondering . . . do we know you?" She runs her hands along her backpack straps, pushing her chest a little closer to Alexei.

44

"Sorry," I say. "We're not from around here."

"It's just that . . ." the girl says as if she's still under the impression that she's having this conversation with the cute boy and not the annoying girl he's eating with for some unknown reason. "You look super familiar, and we thought we'd come say hi. So . . . hi."

For a second, she's content with the silence that follows, but Alexei's gaze is still glued to me; the worry is still etched on his face.

"He says hi back," I say, and for once the cheerleaders seem to acknowledge my existence.

"I'm Lura," the girl says. "Lura McCraw." She's still studying Alexei. "You really do look familiar, you know."

"He knows," I say because the last thing we need is for these girls to hear Alexei's Russian accent, for them to realize the cute boy in the diner is also the hot fugitive they've no doubt seen on TV.

Alexei didn't murder the West Point cadet, but that's one story no news station is going to carry. He's still a fugitive—a wanted man. And I can't let these girls realize it, especially since they want him for entirely different reasons.

"Lura!" her friend whines. "We're going to be late."

"Okay." Lura turns back to Alexei. "Well, bye, then. I guess I'll see you around. Nice talking to you."

Whether or not Lura realizes that Alexei never said a word is something we'll never know. As the girls head toward the door, Alexei doesn't even glance in their direction. He doesn't wonder

45

what it feels like to spend an entire day sitting in classes, to live in a world where your biggest problems are pop quizzes or whether the person you like might like you back.

I'm a princess, but I'd trade places with the Luras of the world in a heartbeat. I'd trade places and never once look back.

"Ignore them," Alexei says when the door dings and they're finally gone. "They know nothing."

It's true. And, honestly, that's the hard part. They don't know what it feels like to watch your brother lie on a table, life flowing out of him like the blood that stains the floor. They don't know what it means to walk down a dark alley, jumping at shadows, looking for ghosts. They aren't hunted. They aren't marked. They can gather their bags and their friends and rush out into the sunlight while I am cursed to live in the shadows. Not just for now, but for always. I'm thousands of miles away, but I'm still locked in the tunnels beneath Adria. I'm still trying to find a door.

"Grace Olivia." Dominic's voice brings me back. "We must leave."

"Jamie needs to rest," I try one more time, a broken record.

"He can rest in the car," Dominic says, helping me from the booth.

"Jamie isn't well," I tell him, the words automatic now. My body is numb.

"He will be significantly less well if they find him."

The door dings as Dominic pushes it open.

"Dominic . . ."

"Yes."

46

"The Society— can they help?"

Dominic puts on his dark glasses, donning his mask, and I cannot read his gaze. He doesn't want to hurt me further, so he doesn't answer at all.

In total, I have four fake passports. I have almost a thousand US dollars in cash and almost as much in euros. There are two credit cards with fake names and a burner cell phone that has never been used.

Jamie has a packet that's similar. Alexei does, too. Dominic handed nearly identical envelopes to each of us as soon as it was safe to remove Jamie from the army hospital in Germany. For weeks, mine have been in a pouch that I keep hidden, wrapped around my stomach. Always there, itching and rubbing against me, daring me to run.

So for weeks, I guess, a part of me has known this was coming.

It's another night and another motel. But this one is two miles from a bus station, and that's the only distinction that matters.

I'm quiet as I slip on my shoes and pick up my backpack. Jamie's sleeping fitfully, and I ease toward the door. I can't risk him waking as I slip outside.

I don't say good-bye.

There's nothing but darkness and an empty highway and the narrow beam of my favorite flashlight, which, it turns out, is all you really need to disappear.

CHAPTER
FIVE

I've never really liked crowds, but now I truly hate them. I don't see people. I see threats. Who has a gun, a knife? How many people are standing between me and the nearest exit, blocking my very best chance at retreat?

I'm too exposed here, too open. But Washington, DC, has more surveillance cameras than any city in the world, with the exception of London. And as I sit with the Capitol to my right and the Washington Monument to my left, I know there are probably more cameras here than average. So I keep a ball cap pulled low over my eyes. My hair is loose around my shoulders. A few days ago I was cursing how long it was starting to get, but now I'm grateful for that extra layer between me and any facial recognition software that might be scanning the globe at this moment, trying to find the lost princess of Adria.

"Hello, Ms. Blakely."

I might not have recognized the woman who stands before me, but by now I'd know her voice anywhere. Gone is her pristine white suit and fluffy fur stole. She's in a black trench coat today. She wears a black-and-white scarf around her white hair and she holds a small bag of bread crumbs. Without asking for permission she sits beside me on the bench and starts tossing crumbs to pigeons.

No one seems to notice the men in dark suits who stand not far away. Her guards are almost as unobtrusive as she is. None of the joggers or school groups that pass can begin to guess that the old lady feeding pigeons spent her morning with the president. Alexandra Petrovic might be the Prime Minister of Adria, but she's also a chameleon. It's one more reason not to trust her.

But I have to trust someone, and right now she's my only option.

"Some might say you're foolish for coming here," she says.

I have to laugh. "It won't be the first time they've said it. Trust me."

The birds swarm around us, scattering on the ground as she tosses a handful of crumbs onto the grass.

"I was very pleased to hear from you, Grace. Surprised, but pleased."

"I've been thinking about what you said."

"I'm glad."

"I want to stop running."

"That's good, Grace. Let us—"

49

I spin on her. "I want to *end it*."

The PM studies me. We're thousands of miles from Adria, but it feels like we're right back where we started.

"If the royal family is after me, I want to prove it. I want to . . ." But I honestly don't know how that sentence is supposed to end. "I want to *end it*," I say again. "And the Society can help me. Or you can get out of my way."

"I see," the PM says. I know she knows I'm serious—that I'll burn them down. All of them. I won't stop until the wall of Adria is nothing but a pile of smoldering dust.

"Now you can stand with me or you can stand against me, but you should know I have three conditions."

If PM Petrovic is angry with me, she doesn't show it. She just gives a little laugh, as if she'd known this moment was coming all along. Her eyes actually twinkle.

"Of course you do."

"First, you clear Alexei's name. He didn't kill anyone. It's not right that John Spencer's murder has been blamed on him just because he happened to be in the wrong place at the wrong time. I don't care what kind of story you have to spin or how many lies you have to tell. After this, Alexei stops being a wanted man. Okay?"

When the PM looks into my eyes, I can't read the expression that lives there.

"Can you do it?" I ask, and she looks as if I might be joking—like no one could possibly be this naïve.

She tosses another handful of crumbs to the pigeons and says, "Yes. We can do it."

She means it, I can tell. And at last I breathe a little easier, at least for Alexei's sake.

"Second," I say, because it feels like I'm on a roll, "my brother stays out of this."

This time the PM stops laughing.

"Your brother is the rightful king of Adria, Ms. Blakely. He is very much *in this*."

"And that fact almost killed him," I shoot back. "You have me. You have the spare, so you don't need the heir. I am expendable, so you can have me. And if I'm not good enough, then I will get off this bench and disappear and no one will ever see me again. Understood?"

For once, the PM looks at me as if I might be more than a reckless teenager, a liability. A girl. She's looking at me as if I might actually be worth a sliver of her respect. And, grudgingly, she gives it.

"I understand." She nods and tosses the last of the crumbs to the birds before turning back to me. "And your final condition, Grace?"

She smiles like maybe Alexandra Petrovic and I are becoming friends. Or maybe we're just starting to not be enemies.

"My third requirement is the hardest, I'm afraid."

"And that is?"

"Stop lying to me."

I expect her to laugh again, to look at me like I'm playing dress-up inside my mother's world. But the PM simply rises. For a second, I think she's going to say no, to turn her back on me and all my drama.

But instead she raises one eyebrow and says, "Very well, then."

She extends a hand, and I rise and take it. I know we're sealing our deal—that we're partners. Allies. But mostly, she's just the devil I know.

I tell myself it's going to be okay, and maybe I even let myself believe it. But then the PM glances behind me, gives a nod. "Go ahead."

Before I can react, there's a hand on my shoulder, a pinch in my neck. I turn to see a guard behind me holding a syringe.

He's tall and broad, like Dominic. Like Dad. So I don't try to fight. I just spin on Prime Minister Petrovic, staring daggers, feeling betrayed. I want to shout, but my tongue is too thick and the words are too heavy.

"It's not personal, Ms. Blakely. But I can't deny it's fitting."

I want to hit—to run—but my head is starting to swirl. My legs turn to rubber and the men take me by the arms. Eventually, it's too hard to keep my eyes open. I'm just looking for a soft place to fall as they toss me into the backseat of a limousine. Soon, there's nothing left but darkness and laughter.

CHAPTER SIX

When I wake, it feels like I've slept for weeks—years. And maybe I have.

Groggily, I push myself upright on the narrow sofa. My neck hurts. My throat aches. My legs almost refuse to move as I try to swing them to the floor. There's barely any light, but my eyes are so used to the black by now that I can see the smooth walls that surround me, the bare bulb that swings by itself from the ceiling, dusty and dim. The room is small, maybe four by five. If not for the open, empty doorway, it would feel like a cell.

I tell myself that the light is electric—not gas. The floor beneath me is tile. I'm not in the tunnels beneath Adria; I know it in my gut. This room is dim and quiet and damp, but it is not the Society's main headquarters, of that much I am certain. But that's all I know for sure.

I should panic. If I were a normal girl, I'd be terrified and screaming, trying to claw my way out from this dark, dank place and the people who drugged me. But I'm not a normal girl. I haven't been in ages. And when you add the whole "princess factor," normal was always out of my reach.

"Hello there."

I don't know the woman who now stands in the arching doorway. She's young, though. I can't see her well, but I can tell from her voice and the way she moves that she's not much older than I am.

"Where am I?" I ask. I try to stand, but the room spins, and I sink back to the little sofa. The girl comes forward, hands me a bottle of water.

"Here. Drink this."

I eye the bottle skeptically. "Is it going to knock me out again?" I can't exactly blame the PM. Some would say I had it coming.

"No. They want you awake."

"Well, that doesn't sound ominous . . ." I say, then take a sip of the water. It's the best thing I've ever tasted, so I guzzle it all down.

"Easy now," the girl tells me as I start to gag and choke. The water sloshes in my too-empty stomach, and I know I wasn't just out an hour or two. I haven't eaten in a very long time.

"What day is it?" I ask as I rise to my feet.

The girl stands in the doorway, silent.

"Where am I?" I try again.

"Come. They're waiting for you."

"Who?" I snap, but she doesn't answer. She just turns and starts down a long, winding corridor.

Are we underground? I wonder as I follow. *Am I still in DC?* It's possible, I suppose. But I know in my gut that I'm a long, long way from safety.

"Why am I here?" I ask, and the girl glances back, gives me a smile that's too peaceful—too serene. Maybe I'm not the only one who's been drugged, I wonder as I fight the urge to grab the girl by the shoulders and shake her until she's as screwed up and cynical as I am.

I want to tell her that there's no reason to smile, that there is no peace. But, most of all, I want to ask her where I might find a bathroom.

I'm just opening my mouth to speak when I hear the voices. The corridor twists and curves. Brighter lights shine beyond the bend. It's not the flickering gaslight of Adria. No. This light is yellow and blue and red. The girl eases forward, stands in what looks to be the end of a rainbow, but I'm not looking for a pot of gold.

"It is not our place to interfere!" a woman shouts. "It has never been our place. It will never *be* our place."

I might stay in the last shadows, out of the conversation and out of the fight if not for the next voice I hear.

"People are dying."

Eleanor Chancellor is my grandfather's chief of staff, but she's more than that. She is a member of the Society. She is one of the underground leaders of Adria—of the world. She is a woman with secrets. And she is on my side. Or so I've started to think.

Slowly, I inch into the brightly colored light and take in the room before me.

Stained glass. That's the first thing I notice, and I realize that we aren't underground. No. The room before me curves like the corridor outside. Round, with benches and railings atop risers made of heavy wood circling the perimeter. I stand in a narrow gap in the circular bleachers and study what appears to be the room equivalent of Arthur's Round Table. No head. No foot. All the women here are equals, I can tell. Or at least they're supposed to be. And the ceiling above us? It is made of stained glass. I can't help but crane my head up to take in the intricate pictures. I'm reminded of the mural in the secret underground headquarters in Valancia. But this window doesn't tell the story of the king who founded Adria and his knights and their wives and the Society's origin. No. I see pictures of castles and churches and the great landmarks of the world. A thorny rosebush wraps around them all, circling the window. Covering the globe.

"The situation changed as soon as innocent people started paying the price," Ms. Chancellor says. She stands in the center of the great, round room, her back to me, and I know she has no idea I'm here. The women in the risers study her with calm indifference. It's like she's giving a book report and not talking about matters of life and death.

One woman actually shrugs. "People have always died," she says in a British accent.

"You are too attached to the child, Eleanor," another woman adds. She has an East Indian accent and wears a beautiful sari. She sounds almost sympathetic as she says, "You can no longer be objective."

"The child has a name!" I've never heard Ms. Chancellor yell before. Not like this. She's always been so cool that I used to wonder if ice would melt in her hands. Now she is practically radiating fury and heat. "And she did not ask for this. None of us asked for this, but our ancestors made a decision two hundred years ago, and now the responsibility falls to us."

The room sits in silence. It seems to take forever for the British lady to lean closer to where Ms. Chancellor stands. "Are you saying the Society should not have saved the baby Amelia?"

"I'm saying our ancestors knew what they were doing when they hid the princess. They knew the danger she would face. Otherwise, why didn't they reveal the princess was alive once the coup was over? Why didn't they put her on the throne when she was grown?" Ms. Chancellor sounds tired. Desperate.

"Exactly!" the British lady cries. She's leaning over the railing now, practically standing. "Following the coup, Adria was safe! King Alexander's brother was on the throne, and Europe was stable. To bring Amelia back from the grave would have disrupted the peace then. It would shatter it now."

"No." Ms. Chancellor is shaking her head. She looks like a child refusing to eat her vegetables. "I'm not saying that we need to put the Blakely children on the throne. I'm saying we need to keep them alive!"

The words are desperate, and they echo around the room.

Hushed silence descends until the woman in the sari says, "For many, there is no difference."

Nods of agreement and murmurs of ascent follow.

I can see Ms. Chancellor's hands shaking, her body radiating with rage.

"They won't stop until she's dead. Until they're *both* dead."

"The boy is not one of us," says a woman in the back—I can't tell which one.

"The boy will die if we don't help," Ms. Chancellor shoots back.

"Everyone dies eventually," says the British lady with a shrug. "The boy is not our concern."

They're talking about my brother—about me—as if we are characters in a play, pieces in a chess set. Should we live or die? Should they order in Chinese food or pizza? There's really not much difference.

Now I'm shaking. I'm stepping forward. I'm about to do something stupid—which is, of course, what I do best—when the British woman looks Ms. Chancellor up and down again and asks, "The question, Eleanor, is what do we do with the girl? And with *you*?"

For some reason this stops me. I realize what I'm seeing now. Ms. Chancellor doesn't look like a lawyer addressing a jury. Ms. Chancellor looks like the accused.

"You don't deny that you were the one who brought Grace Olivia Blakely into the Society?" the British woman says.

Ms. Chancellor pulls her shoulders back. "I do not."

"And you told her our secrets?"

"I did."

The British woman shakes her head, as if the truth should be so simple, but Ms. Chancellor is just too stupid or too stubborn to see it. "And yet you did not properly explain to her the essence of a *secret* sisterhood?"

The women in the risers sneer. Some actually snicker. It's like the British woman has made an excellent joke, but it's not really funny, and that part is obvious.

"Eleanor?" she says, prompting.

"Circumstances mitigated," Ms. Chancellor says.

At last, the woman grows angry. "There is no excuse for—"

"For murder!" I finish for the British woman. "For arson?" I try again. I can't help it. I've been too silent for too long. It's practically encoded in my DNA. My mother couldn't leave well enough alone either, so I push through the small break in the risers and go on.

"For hunting innocent people across continents? Really, ma'am, please finish. I'm dying to know what you are going to say." I stop, then look at the women who fill that lovely, round room. If it weren't so ironic, I would cry. "Or maybe I'm just dying . . ."

Dust dances in the streams of multicolored light. It's like I've wandered into a kaleidoscope, a fun house. But this isn't fun at all.

That's when I see the prime minister rise. She was seated just out of my sight before, but now it's impossible to miss her. This time, she's dressed all in red. Her suit is stark against her snow-white hair.

"Esteemed elders," the PM says, "it seems our guest is awake. Allow me to introduce Grace Olivia Blakely."

For a moment, they just study me. In the back, someone whispers, "Just like her mother . . ."

I want to think she's talking about my light hair and brown eyes. But more likely she means that I am trouble.

The British lady is no longer scowling at Ms. Chancellor. Her gaze has shifted onto me. "Welcome, Ms. Blakely."

"Yeah . . ." I say, not even trying to hide the cynicism in my voice. "I don't really think you mean that."

Ms. Chancellor cuts me a warning glance.

"Where am I?" I ask.

The British woman looks around, as if gauging the temperature of the room.

"You are before the Council of Elders."

"The what?" I ask, but now that I'm used to the room, I'm able to focus on the faces. Many of them I've seen on the news. There's the prime minister of France in the front row—she dined with my grandfather and Ms. Chancellor not long ago. I recognize the Canadian ambassador to Adria, and another woman who was on the cover of a magazine that was on Ms. Chancellor's desk last month. I think she's some sort of CEO. There's a former candidate for president of the US. A movie star. A talk show host. I'm suddenly all too aware of my jeans and T-shirt—the old cardigan that wasn't exactly pristine before I was knocked unconscious and transported who knows where. I don't even want to think about my hair.

But even though the women in this room all carry the same gorgeous, effervescent grace, it's not a beauty contest. And I'm not a crowd favorite.

"Do you know why you're here?" the British woman asks me.

"No. But evidently it's not because of all the assassins who keep trying to kill me. I gather this group is more or less indifferent to assassins."

No one thinks I'm funny. Not even me.

The British woman is anything but deterred. "You are here, Ms. Blakely, because you violated the sanctity of our sisterhood. You betrayed your heritage and our trust. In short, *you told*. And that was not very well done of you."

I find the PM in the crowd. I don't even try to hide my sarcasm when I turn to her. "So I've been summoned because I'm important, huh? You take care of your own, do you?"

"Grace," Ms. Chancellor whispers. A warning.

I'm not surprised the PM lied to me. I'm mad only at myself for believing her.

"Ms. Blakely?" the British woman prompts, and I spin on her.

"I'm sorry I had to tell my friends about the Society. It wasn't Ms. Chancellor's fault. People were hunting me. People were dying. Everyone I knew was in danger—they are *still* in danger. I didn't know why then, but I knew I had to try to stop it. If the people close to me were at risk, they deserved to know why. I didn't have a choice." I need this group of powerful women to

61

understand, to try to remember what it felt like to be young and afraid and powerless.

"And to tell you the truth," I say, looking down, "I'd do it again because they were my only chance."

This, at last, seems to make some kind of impression. I shrug. "At least they cared whether I lived or died. Or maybe I should say that they wanted me to *not* die, since it seems like maybe you ladies aren't indifferent at all."

"Grace, please," Ms. Chancellor tries. "The elders just need to discuss what happened."

"It's not her fault!" I say, ignoring Ms. Chancellor, speaking directly to the British woman and the others who seem least sympathetic to my cause. "Ms. Chancellor told me the situation. She warned me not to tell a soul. She did everything but tie me up and duct-tape my mouth shut." I give a sad, involuntary laugh. "Even that probably wouldn't have stopped me. I'm kind of hard to protect—even from myself, if you haven't already figured that out."

The woman in the sari leans toward me. "What do you know, Grace?"

I know I'm tired. I know I'm hungry. I know it feels like I've eaten roadkill and still have the taste in my mouth.

But, most of all, I know this started centuries ago.

I know it will never, ever be over, so long as my brother and I are alive. No wonder these women aren't overly concerned about the people who want to kill me. They're smart enough to know that's probably the only way this nightmare ends.

That doesn't change the fact that it's *my* nightmare.

"I know there was a coup in Adria two hundred years ago, and a baby named Amelia was the only member of the royal family to survive. I know the Society hid her among their members and she grew up. And I know that my mom and her friends spent years trying to figure out who Amelia's descendants might be. And when Mom figured out *she* was Amelia's descendant—her heir—then someone ordered her murder."

But I'm the one who pulled the trigger, I think and the memory comes in a wave, crashing over me. I bear myself up against it. Let it pass, and go on.

"I know whoever wanted my mother dead three years ago is hunting down her children now."

"So you are aware, then, that your brother, James, is the rightful king of Adria," the woman in the sari asks.

"He doesn't want to be king!" I yell, the truth flying out of me. "And I don't want to be a princess. I mean . . . I can hardly even say that with a straight face. Can you imagine?" I look down at my wrinkled clothes. I'd laugh if it weren't so painfully sad.

"What *do* you want?" the woman in the sari asks, her voice soft and kind.

"I want my mother back," I say without thinking. I shouldn't let the elders see so far underneath my protective shell. But it's too late. They're all smart enough to know that I am broken. "Since that's not possible, though, I guess I'd settle for not losing my brother, too."

"But that's not all, is it, Grace?"

63

I turn to the prime minister, who looks so sleek in her red suit. She knows me well.

"No." I shake my head. *"I want to make them pay."*

The PM smiles and leans back, her point made.

The woman in the sari looks at me. "The Society is not in the business of revenge, Ms. Blakely."

"That's okay," I tell them. "I am."

"The past was in the past!" The British woman seems to be on the brink of shouting or crying—I can't tell which. "It would have been safely behind us all if your mother had simply let it be. If *you* had let it be."

Now the hypocrisy is just too much.

"I thought you people wanted to chronicle history—to register the truth because it always repeats itself and it's almost always written by men. I thought you were founded so that you could guide the world and keep it from doing things that are stupid." I stop, take a breath. "I thought you were the good guys."

"This Society has not endured for a thousand years by taking on the pet projects of every one of its members. We work toward the common good," says a woman in the back. Murmurs fill the room. And then something hits me.

"Who knew what my mother found?"

My question silences them.

The PM is the one who answers. "We were unaware of the extent of her search. We—"

"Who knew what she found?" I shout.

"We don't know," the PM says.

The Society always seemed invincible, omniscient. I don't believe for a second that there's something they don't know. I have an even harder time believing they'd admit it.

"Maybe," I say. "Or maybe you're just not willing to tell me."

The PM straightens, bristles. "I do not appreciate being called a liar."

"And I don't appreciate being constantly lied *to*. I suppose we are both destined for disappointment."

I expect her to lash back, to lock me in some kind of dungeon until I learn not to sass my elders. But the woman only laughs. "You have spirit, Ms. Blakely. I will give you that. You would have made a magnificent queen."

"I will settle for being safe," I say as I study the assembly of women—the compilation of power. And the truth seeps into my bones. "But you all don't really care about that, do you?"

No one answers. But that's okay because at least it means that no one lies.

"Where is it?" A woman in the corner is now looking at me. Tension radiates off her. She is tired of this little dance and thinks it's time to get down to business.

"Where is *what*?" I ask, and look to the prime minister.

"Presumably, your mother had some kind of proof—something that would link your family to Amelia. Where is it?"

But I'm shaking my head. "No. I mean, I don't know. I don't have any idea what you're talking about."

The tension in the room is growing. I can feel it pulsing around me. "I don't know!" I say again.

65

"We will not help you overthrow the king of Adria," says the woman in the corner.

I spin and study her. Can she not see me? My wrinkled clothes and messed-up hair? Do I look like someone who is trying to overthrow a king?

"I'm not going to do that," I mutter.

"Adria is a pivotal cog in the wheel of the world, and we cannot have it destabilized."

"I don't want it destabilized! I don't care about your . . . cogs," I blurt.

I feel Ms. Chancellor's hand on my elbow, a soft and gentle touch. A reminder. I'm not *entirely* alone.

But I'm here, in this unknown room in an unknown city, and the faces staring back at me are not smiling.

"I don't want to overthrow the king! I want to . . . graduate high school!"

"You understand our concern," the woman with the British accent asks.

"No," I snap, sarcastic and afraid. "I *really* don't."

"A stable Adria is a stable Europe, and . . ."

Now Ms. Chancellor eases into the fray. "No one is trying to make it otherwise."

"Her very existence threatens that stability," the British lady says with a disgusted point in my direction. "The War of the Fortnight brought Adria a new king, a parliament, and a prime minister. Revealing Amelia's existence a few months or years after the coup could have destroyed that new government. What

66

damage do you think Amelia's heirs might do today? Centuries later?" She seems to consider it anew. "No. No. The risk is too great. It cannot happen."

I'm not Adrian.

I'm not ambitious.

I'm not political.

I'm not interested in attention. I've already had enough of that for a lifetime.

But the Society doesn't care about what I'm not.

They only care about what I am. And I *am* a threat. My very existence—my brother's existence—is something they can't control. And it scares them.

So, suddenly, they terrify me.

These are the women who covered up the shooting of Adria's last prime minister. They all but staged a coup in one of the most pivotal countries in the world. And now here I am—the sister to the rightful king of that country. What would they do to me?

Worse.

What could they have done already?

The PM lied to get me here. Lied and kidnapped and . . .

I can't help myself, I stumble back. Ms. Chancellor's hand falls away, and I'm alone again in my too-cold skin.

"Is it you?" I'm still backing away, shaking my head. "Did you kill her?"

The British woman rises. "This sisterhood is stronger than its sisters, Ms. Blakely. We do not exist to serve the best interest of ourselves. We exist to serve the greater good."

If she thinks her words are going to calm me, she is incredibly mistaken, because her words catapult me forward.

"Did you kill her?"

Ms. Chancellor lunges in front of me, holds me back. I look over her shoulder to where the British woman has retaken her seat.

"Of course not."

Ms. Chancellor must feel the rage slip out of me because she loosens her hold.

I pull away, study them all. "Okay," I say, even though I don't believe them. But I've recently learned not to believe myself, either.

"Maybe you just want to kill *me*," I say, and I know in my gut it might be true.

"Grace." The prime minister is moving closer. The British woman is staring. Even Ms. Chancellor is looking at me oddly, as if maybe I've started speaking in tongues, spontaneously combusted, turned green.

I don't stop to analyze their faces, to make sense of all the things they do and do not say.

There's a table nearby. On it rests what looks to be an antique candlestick. It's made of cast iron and heavy and looks more like a weapon than a way through the darkness, and I don't even think. I never think. I just pick up the candlestick and throw it over my head as hard as I can. I hear the crash, feel the rush of fresh air and falling glass, but I don't stay to watch them bleed.

I can hear chaos behind me, cries of pain and fury and fear. But I'm already running down the dark and twisty hallway.

Running to *where,* I have no idea. I learned a long time ago that sometimes it's enough to just be running away.

"Someone stop her!" one of the women yells, but the voice is distant, echoing. When I turn, there is a staircase, and I hesitate a second before climbing, taking the steps two at a time into the shadows.

I don't know where I am. I only know that this building is old, but modern. A product of this century, or maybe the last. And I know I have to break free of it. I have to get out of here and then, after . . .

I don't let myself think about after.

I'm running up the stairs, faster and faster. I can hear movement up ahead. Someone is running down. Soon, others will be rushing up behind me. I'm trapped here. I know it. But the darkness isn't quite so thick, and I ease around a corner, closer to the light of a window. It's tall but slender, and the glass is wavy. I can see darkness outside, punctuated by patches of light, and I know the sun is going down. If I can just make it outside, perhaps I can disappear into the darkness. Perhaps I can once again run away. But this time I won't stop running.

I pull off my cardigan and wrap it around my fist, over and over. It's achingly familiar, this gesture. And I know I've been lucky so far. Or as lucky as someone who lost her mother and is now being hunted by an unknown number of international assassins can possibly be.

"Up here!" someone yells. There are feet pounding on the stairs, and I stop thinking.

I stand to the side of the window and, with my covered fist, pull back and hit just like my father taught me. I shift my weight and drive through with my legs. It feels like my fist is going to shatter, but the glass gives, too. Pieces fall onto the stone floor and out into the night.

I'm climbing onto the ledge, staring down at what looks to be a rooftop twenty feet or so below me. Maybe I'm wrong. Goodness knows, I usually am.

But I'd rather be wrong than be here.

"Grace, wait!" someone yells, and I turn to see Prime Minister Petrovic on the stairs below me, looking up at where I sit perched on the ledge like a bird with clipped wings.

But I just shake my head.

"I'm sorry," I say.

And jump.

CHAPTER SEVEN

If there's one thing I've learned in my life, it's how to fall.

My feet are square as I hit the surface; my knees are soft. And my first thought is that, this time, my leg didn't shatter.

My second thought is that I am *still* falling.

It must be another roof because I can feel myself slip; my purchase on the slick tiles is precarious and fading.

I try to right myself, but it's no use. I turn to my stomach and feel the slide of tiles against my belly as I slip, faster and faster, and then drop, kicking to the ground.

It takes a second to adjust. To catch my breath. But I don't have a second. I land and crouch, feel the stones against my feet, damp and uneven. There are streetlights and narrow, twisting alleys. I can hear the sounds of traffic. The shouts of people.

I pull myself upright and run.

When I pass a man and woman holding hands, I don't ask for help. When I turn onto a wider street, I don't stop and look in any windows. I just keep going, curving, turning, backtracking, and twisting through the city with one goal in mind: getting lost. Because if I can't find me, then maybe no one else can, either.

I run until I can't run anymore. And then I stop in the middle of a large square. It's dark now but I know it's not as late as it seems. People walk arm in arm. They carry sacks of groceries or ride bicycles. So many regular people just living regular lives. I envy them. And I know I'll never belong—not here. Not anywhere. I will never be safe.

But I have to be somewhere.

My breathing slows. Standing still at last, my feet and legs start to shake. And my hand hurts. I think some bones might be broken, but I'm lucky, and I know it.

I really should be dead.

I let myself draw in a deep breath, then turn, taking in the darkness and the light, the sounds of whispered conversations in a language I recognize but don't really understand.

And, finally, my eyes catch the sight that, deep down, I've been expecting to see since I first perched on the edge of the window.

The Eiffel Tower glows in the darkness, smaller than I thought it would be, shimmering like a lighthouse, warning me that danger's near.

"Paris."

Turns out there's an advantage to being drugged and hauled to the other side of the world. If you're kept unconscious for a day or two, it's easy to stay awake. I'm not exactly rested. But my feet keep moving. My mind stays alert.

I can feel the cash and passports that I keep wrapped around my body. They're still there, itching, scraping. But present. And that is all that matters. The PM and her goons must not have searched me. They must have underestimated me. Again. That might be the only thing I've got going for me—the fact that I'm not quite as stupid and careless as everyone believes.

I'm not without resources. I'm just without . . . everything else.

It must be getting later. The people on the streets around me are fewer. Somewhere a clock chimes midnight in the City of Light, but I can only see darkness.

I hear laughing, talking. A group of twentysomethings are walking down the center of the cobblestone street, singing too loudly, arms thrown over shoulders and around waists. They're drunk. That much is obvious in any language. And I can't help but remember another night on another street. The color of fire and the smell of smoke and the crowds that grew thicker and thicker the closer they got to the flames.

I had my brother with me then. And Alexei. And my friends. But now I am alone.

I press against the stone wall of one of the buildings. Light seeps out of closed shop windows. The street curves, and I am like a rat in a maze, not sure whether to go forward or turn back. But that's not true, I realize. I can never, ever go back.

I jerk and bang my good fist against the wall at my back. "Stupid," I tell myself. Now both hands hurt, but it's what I deserve for believing the PM, for thinking I might be able to trust the Society.

I can't trust anyone.

And that's the one thing that makes me want to cry.

I miss Alexei and Jamie and Dominic. I'd give anything to see my friends or my grandpa—to know that Ms. Chancellor is okay. But anyone who might help me might also get hurt by me, and there's no way to know exactly who my allies are. The Society has taught me that much.

If there's one thing I'm sure of, it's that I have to keep moving. So I keep walking. There's a café up ahead. A few small tables dot the sidewalk. Couples sit too close on the same side of the table, sipping coffee or drinking wine. No one notices the too-thin, too-hungry, too-scared American girl with the wild hair and the even crazier eyes.

A woman's handbag hangs off the back of her chair, unzipped and daring me to do something about it. She and the man are kissing. Too absorbed in each other. Entirely too in love.

When I see her cell phone peeking out of the top of the bag, I don't stop to ponder that I'm about to commit the second crime of my life. I don't worry about the stain upon my record or my soul. It's too late for that.

Murder is hard to top, after all.

So I pull the phone from the woman's purse and keep walking. I don't let myself run. I just move smoothly away.

Maybe I should find a hotel or a youth hostel, some place where I can eat some food and take a shower and think. I know I need to *think*. But thinking has never done anything but get me into trouble.

So I dart into a dark and twisty side street. There's a dim doorway, and that's where I stand, hidden in shadow as I dial and wait for the voice at the other end of the line.

I don't want to hear it.

And I don't know what I'll do if I don't.

I just stand, shaking, listening until I hear: "Hello."

"It's me," I blurt. Even my whispers are too loud in the silence. I put my hand over my mouth and the phone. "No. Don't say my name," I say. "I'm . . . I'm in trouble. I don't know who to trust anymore."

My voice cracks, and maybe I'd even cry if I still had tears. But I don't. So I just crumble to the ground, my back sliding against the heavy wooden door until I reach the dirty stoop. I pull my knees up and rest my head against them, the phone still pressed to my ear like a lifeline to another world.

"I don't know who to trust. I don't . . . I need help." Probably the hardest three words in the English language, so for good measure I say them again. "I need help. Will you—"

I listen. I breathe. And in the end, I find some tears after all as I say, "Paris. I'm in Paris."

CHAPTER EIGHT

Tourists are the same everywhere—every city, every language. It's a crazy thing that I've started to realize: that the very act of seeing other cultures can make the see-*ers* so the same.

That's why it almost feels like home the next morning as I stand in the long line of people waiting to board a big red bus. There are fancy cameras and backpacks and sensible shoes.

It's a good place to hide, I learned long ago. Teenagers are supposed to be dragged along behind adults, sulky and sullen. No one looks or wonders or worries about me here. Everyone just assumes I'm someone else's kid—someone else's problem.

So the driver takes my ticket and looks at my Eiffel Tower sweatshirt and the hair I washed in a bathroom sink this morning. I practically feel like a new person. It's a shame it isn't true.

I walk alone down the center aisle, then up the twisting stairs that lead to the top deck. It's open, and the cool air hits me in the face, jolting me fully awake. It's a good thing. I can't be sloppy now, not tired or slow. I need to stay moving just a little while longer. If I don't, I might never move again.

The driver speaks in heavily accented English, but I don't care about the sights. I just needed to get on a bus. Now. I needed a ride and a good place to rest. To wait. To think.

Paris really is a beautiful city. Maybe someday Jamie and I can come here together. Someday when he is healthy and strong and we're both safe. He'd like it, I think. The history, the food. Jamie likes everything. He is always able to see the good. Even in me. And that is maybe his only weakness.

"If you will look to our left," the guide says, "we have turned onto a street where you might find your own countries, but here, in the heart of Paris. Many call it *Embassy Row*."

I turn my head and watch the buildings streak by, but I don't try to recognize the flags, read the signs. I've only had a croissant to eat, and the cup of coffee that I forced down an hour ago rebels inside my stomach. I want to be sick. But I'm surrounded by people taking pictures and smiling and enjoying the cool air and warm sun. I'm in one of the world's most beautiful cities, but I'm not lucky. When we pass the Eiffel Tower, I don't even see it.

The bus is almost at a bridge. We're slowing down. Some people will hop off here, I know. Others will hop on. Tourists will make this loop all day around the city. My ticket is good for twenty-four hours, but I have to get off. I can't stay here, sit here. Wait. I'm through waiting.

I have someone to meet.

So I bolt out of my seat and down the twisty stairs. The bus is just starting to move again when I jump, landing on the sidewalk.

There's an intricate railing along the bridge. Tourists and lovers lean against it, looking down at the river below. It really is a beautiful day, I have to admit. The wind blows through my hair, a slight chill to the breeze, but I feel cozy inside my new cheesy sweatshirt.

Maybe that's why, when I hear the voice, I don't immediately turn. It's like I'm hearing it in a dream.

"Grace?" the voice comes again, and that's when I know it's true. But even so, I'm not quite sure it's her.

It has to be, though. This is the time. The place. So I force myself to look beyond the plain denim jeans and sensible shoes—the lightweight trench coat she wears belted around her tiny waist. She's in a ball cap and dark glasses. No makeup. And still people look. Some even stare. No matter what, she is an absolutely beautiful woman.

Right now, she looks like a movie star, but even I don't really think she looks like a princess. Ann's one of the most recognizable women in the world, and yet no one here seems to recognize her. It just goes to show how people always see what they want to.

After all, who would expect Princess Ann of Adria to be standing on a sidewalk in Paris, absolutely alone? It's what I asked,

78

but even I didn't think she could do it—would do it. But she was my mother's best friend. And now she's one of the few people in the world who I might bring myself to trust.

"Are you . . . ?"

I look up and down the sidewalk, eager and afraid.

"It's safe, Grace." She takes a step toward me, then stops, as if she's afraid to move too fast, as if she already knows how far and how fast I will run if given any excuse.

"I'm alone," the princess says, but I've already seen them, the two men who linger at the end of the bridge. I spin and spy two more on the opposite side. I turn on Ann, glaring.

"I'm as alone as I can be," she clarifies. "I have men with me, it's true. They are my personal guards, Grace. They're Dominic's men. He trained them. He trusts them. I literally trust them with my life. Please let me trust them with yours." I wait a minute. Silence. "There's no way I could come alone. It was bring them or not come. So I brought them. I thought it would be okay to bring them."

She seems so sincere, so sad and so . . . scared. She's one of the most important people in Europe and she's afraid, I can tell. At least I'm not the only one.

"Trust is harder than it used to be," I say, and Princess Ann slips closer.

"And it never was easy. Was it, sweetheart?"

My mom used to call me sweetheart. Ann doesn't have the right, but I can't say so. When I brush away a tear I didn't know I'd cried, I'm just surprised that I still can.

"Grace." She's closer than I realized. She's almost touching me. "Are you okay? Are you hurt?"

I shake my head and take a step back. "I'm okay," I say, bristling. I need to make myself as small as possible. Even here. Even now. I vow to never be a full-sized target ever again.

"Grace," she snaps, pulling me back. "Are you sure you're okay?"

"Yes," I tell her. It's like she's asking me if I'm sure I don't have any homework. But no one ever asks me that. Ever. They're too busy inquiring if I might need any more stitches.

"I'm fine," I say again, but Princess Ann doesn't look like she believes me. Maybe my bathroom hairstyle isn't quite as convincing as it seemed at the time.

"And Jamie?" the princess asks. "Where is he?"

She looks up and down the length of the bridge. She scans the river's banks.

"He's not here," I say, and I can see she's honestly surprised and . . . something else. Disappointed?

"Then where is he?" she asks.

"Not here," I say again, as if that really should be answer enough.

"Grace—" There's a tension in Princess Ann's voice as she steps forward. She isn't the smiling, docile doll that the world assumes her to be. She's practically humming with tension—a string that has been pulled too tight. "Where is he? Take me to Jamie, Grace."

"He's . . ." The wind blows my hair in my face. It sticks to the corner of my mouth, and I pause. I think. I had a plan, but for a second I wonder if I should change it. I wonder . . .

"Grace?" Ann snaps.

"He's dead," I blurt. I don't even have to try to make my voice crack. It's a scenario that I've imagined too many times. It's far too close to the truth to have to make believe.

Ann physically recoils. "Is that . . . is that true?" she asks, then yells, *"Is it?"*

The guards at the end of the bridge fidget, wondering if she needs them, but they don't move any closer. She and I are still alone when I say, "Mom found Amelia. Did you know?"

The change of subject startles her. She shakes her head, almost stumbles. "What?"

"Princess Amelia," I say, as if people bring up two-hundred-year-old dead princesses every day in conversation. "You and my mom and Karina Volkov were looking for her, weren't you? Well, Mom found her. Or who she *was*, I guess I should say. The name the Society gave her after the coup. The name she grew up with." The princess's eyes are shielded behind her dark glasses, but I swear that I can see through them.

I can see straight into her soul.

"Mom learned the names of Amelia's *descendants*."

Ann shifts and glances back at the guards who linger at the mouth of the bridge. She's starting to shake in frustration. It's something that happens a lot to the grown-ups who have to deal with me, but with Ann there's something more.

"Grace, the last time I saw you, your brother was bleeding all over the palace floor. Now tell me, *is Jamie okay?*" She's not quite shouting, but her voice carries on the wind.

My words are almost a whisper. "Did *you* know that Mom found Amelia?"

Ann shakes her head. Frustration comes off of her in waves.

"Grace, your mother and I were obsessed with that as *girls*. We hadn't talked about it in ages. I haven't thought about it in—"

"Stop lying. I know she told you what she found. She probably couldn't wait to call her best friend. Were you surprised? Was she? Or did my mother always think she might be Amelia's descendant?"

"Your mother and I hadn't really spoken in years. We were very close as girls. And even in adulthood for a while, but then I became . . . but then I married, and she had you and your brother, and life took us in different directions. It was nothing specific. It was just life. It is simply something that happens. I wish I had known what she was doing. I wish I could have stopped her or helped her or—"

"Stop lying to me!"

People don't shout at princesses. I can tell as soon as the words are free, but I don't want to take them back. They are out. And they are almost magic.

It's like a spell is broken. Ann is still smiling, but her expression is morphing somehow. It's more a smirk when she asks, "Have you been to the tomb? Have you seen it?"

Numbly, I shake my head. They took my mother's body to Adria, but I've never been able to bring myself to visit her grave.

"Answer me, Grace!"

"I . . . I've never been there!" I snap, and I don't have to act confused and clueless. Lately, that's my natural state.

"Don't play coy, Grace. Tell me what you know so I can help you."

This whole conversation must be another figment of my messed-up mind—like a dream where your English teacher keeps asking you why you didn't bring a rhinoceros to the picnic. It doesn't make any sense.

People change. I know it. I've seen it. *I* have changed, that much is true. But people don't change this quickly. In a matter of minutes, she's morphed from meek to worried to outraged.

Something isn't right with her.

No.

Something isn't *right*.

The people who are looking at the touristy knickknacks on the vendor's cart haven't made a decision since we've been talking. They haven't moved.

The policemen who were wandering through the crowds haven't wandered on. There's a woman with a baby in a stroller. But that baby is too quiet—its mother too still.

No one on this bridge is as they seem. Especially the woman before me.

Now I don't even try to hide it. I ease away, moving until my back hits the rail.

"Who did you tell?" I demand of her. I'm tired of playing pretend. "Who knew you were meeting me here?"

Ann shakes her head. She actually takes off her dark glasses, looks me in the eye. "No one. My husband doesn't even know where I am. Or who I'm with."

"What about your father-in-law, the king?" I ask.

Ann shakes her head, her eyes impossibly wide. "No, Grace. No one knows. I'd never tell . . ." She trails off, thinking. Recognition seems to dawn. "Grace, do you think *the royal family* would try to harm you?"

I shrug. It's all I can do not to laugh. The whole thing is so preposterous—too crazy even to be a dream.

"Who else has so much reason to make Amelia's heirs disappear?"

"The Society!" she shouts, as if she's held it in too long. "Sweetheart, there is so much that you don't know. Your mother and I . . . They didn't want her to dig into it. They wanted Amelia lost. They needed her to stay lost. Please tell me they don't know where you are."

I don't know what to say—who to trust—so I don't say anything at all, and my silence is enough to make Ann panic.

"Grace, come with me. I have Dominic's men. I can keep you safe. Tell me where Jamie is so I can send some guards to help him. Grace?" She inches closer and closer.

Closer.

"Tell me!"

"Like I said," I say, moving along the railing toward the center of the bridge. "He died. Someone stabbed him outside the palace

84

that night. You saw him. He was bleeding so much. I tried to stop it, but . . . he's gone."

Ann squints against the sun. "I wish I knew if you were lying," she says.

"That's okay." I shrug. "I *know* you are."

And then the mask is gone completely, thrown away. It might as well be floating down the river below because the illusion is never, ever coming back.

"You need to come to the palace, Grace." Ann is pleading. "You're one of us. You belong with us."

"I'm not going anywhere with you!"

"I can help you!" she cries. "Maybe something can be done. The royal family has vast resources. You could—"

"No."

"Grace, your mother was my best friend. You know you can trust me."

At this, I finally do laugh, but there is no joy in it, no love or happiness.

"No." I shake my head. "I really don't know that." Then I stop laughing. I am just as serious as the situation when I say, "But there was one way to find out."

A cloud passes over the sun and for a split second there is shadow as Ann speaks, seemingly to no one.

"Get her."

• • •

Everything happens at once. The clouds shift. In the distance, a siren sounds. And the guards at the ends of the bridge start toward Princess Ann and me. She doesn't even try to stop me as I bolt away. That's not her job. She has people for that, and the people don't look happy. Two of the men are tall and strong. Even in their dark suits I can practically see their muscles rippling. I know they could sprint five miles without even breathing hard. I know because they're like Dominic. Like my dad. Like Jamie.

Or like Jamie used to be.

With that thought I feel a fresh rush of anger and adrenaline. I don't want to run away anymore. I want to turn and fight—to kick and claw until the whole world bleeds as much as my brother did.

A few tourists are being ushered from the bridge, and the woman with the fake baby has left the carriage behind and is easing closer. She's trained, I know. She wouldn't be here—have this job—if she weren't. But I'm trained, too, in my own way. I grew up wrestling on the living room floor with an Army Ranger, and I have the advantage of surprise and sheer unadulterated rage.

The man who couldn't choose a souvenir is on my other side. When the woman reaches for me, I sidestep and grab her arm, spin and whirl her toward the man who has no choice but to catch her.

And then I run. I'm almost to the center of the bridge when I realize that the men on my right are no longer moving toward me. There is a blur of action—fists and kicks. Someone is spinning, yelling, "Gracie!"

And then Alexei is here. Alexei is free. One of the men is falling over the edge, landing in the water below, and Alexei's almost to me.

He grabs my hand and yells, "Come on!" But I don't move.

"What are you doing here?" I ask him.

Alexei turns on me, disbelief in his eyes. "What do you think I'm doing here?" He sounds like someone who is perfectly willing to fight me, too, but he'd rather not have to.

The guards are closer now. I can feel the bridge getting smaller and smaller, almost like it's burning from both ends. I've burned bridges before; I should know what it feels like.

"Come on," Alexei says, tugging me in the direction he's just come from.

"No," I say, pulling back and holding on.

"Grace, we've got to get you out of here!" he shouts.

But I just calmly drop his hand and step closer to the center of the bridge that arches high over the water. I'm almost to the highest part. To my right, I can see two guards charging toward us. To my left, I see more men coming and, of course, Alexei, who stands dumbfounded, as if wondering if the pressure has finally broken me. If maybe I'm crazy after all.

"Grace!" he yells again, but I just hold out my hand.

"Do you trust me?"

This is it, I can tell. The big moment. I can hear the guards' cries on the wind. There is no one on the bridge but these people who would take me away and this boy who only wants to protect me from anything—everything—especially myself.

My hand is still outstretched, and I can almost read Alexei's mind as he looks at me. Am I a screw-up? A kid sister? A killer.

A princess?

Am I someone he can trust, he wants to know.

But time is running out, and I shake my outstretched hand. Instantly, Alexei takes it. I step onto the railing, and Alexei joins me, standing high above the water running below.

His hand is warm in mine. So sure. So strong. For a second, I just feel it—feel him. He looks down into my eyes. Blue staring into brown. Neither of us blinks as we stand atop this bridge in the center of Paris.

Maybe it's the fatigue, the fear, or the sheer force of the adrenaline that is pounding in my veins, but I'm not thinking anymore. I just bring my free hand up and weave my fingers into Alexei's dark hair, pull him close, and kiss him. Like maybe it's the last thing I'll ever do.

And maybe it is.

That's the thing that this whole mess has taught me. My mother was a young woman, strong and healthy right up until the moment she died. My brother had most of his life in front of him, and he came within an inch of having it all slip away.

I may never get off this bridge. I might die in Paris. Right here. Right now. But I won't die alone, and for that I will always treasure Alexei.

When we pull apart, there is a question in his blue eyes—fear and confusion and . . . hope? I don't know. And it's far too late to ask because there's movement in the corner of my eye.

The guards are almost here. Someone is yelling in French, words that feel like "Stop! Police!" My gaze is on the water. It ripples and flows like freedom, running out toward the sea. And then, I see it, the bow of a boat peeking out from beneath the bridge, running underneath us.

It's red and two stories, the boat equivalent of the bus that brought me here. I can actually hear a woman on the loudspeaker, explaining in rapid German the historical significance of the bridge they are passing under.

They have no idea.

And hopefully no one will ever know that this is the place where the rightful princess of Adria escaped from the usurper.

I drop Alexei's hand. When his eyes go wide, I say, "Thank you."

And then I jump, falling free, crashing to the roof of the ship below.

A second later, Alexei follows.

And then the boat is gone, too far from the bridge for anyone else to jump. As if anyone else would be that crazy.

I barely catch my breath before I roll off the side of the little roof, grab the edge, and dangle for a moment, then drop lightly onto the deck below.

Somewhere, the guide must have missed all the action, because she's still talking. But the people on the deck gasp and scream at the sight of the windblown American girl who seems to have fallen from the sky. When a slightly confused Russian drops to the ground beside her, people scatter.

"What was that?" Alexei practically screams.

He doesn't notice the tiny blond who is left standing alone on the deck once the tourists flee.

"That was my plan," Rosie tells him. "And it worked, I'll have you know. My plans always work."

She's got a cocky gleam in her eye. This is Rosie's proudest moment, I can tell.

She pauses for a second, listens to the woman on the speaker. "Okay," she says. "We're clear."

"Rosie," Alexei says, trying to summon all of his calm, "what are you—"

"Well, hello, stranger," Noah says, and Alexei spins. "Enjoying Paris?" Noah asks as if we've all just bumped into one another outside the Louvre.

Alexei looks at him and then glares at me. It's a look that is the same in every language: I have some explaining to do. But I'm too worried to stop now.

I turn to Noah. "Did we get it?"

He shrugs. "There's one way to know."

Then he and Rosie turn and start toward the stairs that lead to the lower levels. The steps are narrow and slick as I follow Noah, Alexei on our heels.

Somehow, Alexei doesn't seem surprised when we find Megan sitting by herself behind a laptop in the boat's tiny café. Really, there's just a couple of tables and a vending machine. No one else is here. The day's too nice, and they didn't pay good money to sit in a tiny room with only a sliver of a view.

"We were right," I say when I reach her. Megan barely looks up.

Noah is tall enough to glance out the high windows, almost at the same level as the water. "Grace, what are the odds they're going to follow us?"

"Very, very good," Alexei answers. He's trying to control his worry and his anger. Trying. But failing.

Megan has barely looked up from the laptop. Her fingers practically fly across the keys. "Did you get it?" I can't keep the impatience—the fear—out of my voice.

Megan pulls a cord out of the headphone jack. In the next instant, Princess Ann's voice comes through the laptop's speakers.

"Grace, do you think the royal family *would try to harm you?"* Ann's voice says. Then, a few moments later: *"Get her."*

It's not a confession, but it's not nothing. I'm not sure what this means. Is it leverage? Is it proof? Is this a recording that might guarantee my freedom and my brother's safety?

Not even close.

But it's a start. And it's more than I had an hour ago. Most of all, now I know. Not everything, but the list of people I can trust just got a whole lot smaller. The good news is that the list of people I can depend on is growing, too.

CHAPTER NINE

The train is almost empty. At least it feels that way as I sit in a forward-facing seat, looking out on the French countryside that is slowly going dark.

The sun will be down soon, but it's giving one last burst of light, and the countryside practically glows. It's almost like the golden aura that is so well known in Adria.

Almost.

But not quite.

I'm still hundreds of miles from Embassy Row, and I need for it to stay that way.

I'm barely aware of movement, the feel of heat when Megan slides a steaming cup of tea into my hands. Only then do I realize that a woman is pushing a cart down the aisle, handing out fruit and coffee and bottles of water. I cup my hands around the warmth and start to thaw, but part of me feels like I will always be a little bit frozen.

"Thank you," I tell her.

Megan shrugs. "It's complimentary," she says, but that's not the point.

"I wasn't talking about the tea, you know."

"Yeah." Megan slides a little container of honey in my direction. "I know."

My mom always took honey in her tea. Princess Ann knew that. She guessed that I would, too, when I went to see her at the palace last summer. Should I have known then what she was? What she would do? But Past Me has made so many mistakes that I can't quite bear to add another one to the pile, so I force myself to look away.

Megan also brought me a change of clothes. The jeans are soft, the sweater baggy and starting to fray, and I feel like maybe it's her favorite—the comfortable, easy, carefree thing that she throws on for rainy afternoons when all a girl has to do is curl up in her favorite chair and read. I know without asking that this is the sweater equivalent of macaroni and cheese—comfort food. I know my friend Megan somehow guessed that I would need it.

"Thank you. For answering when I called. And for coming. And for . . . believing."

"Of course," she says, as if it's easy. Traipsing across a continent and setting up a sting operation on one of the most beloved women in the world. All on the say-so of a thoroughly messed-up teenage girl.

"Thank you for believing me, Megan."

"Yeah, Grace." She's looking at me differently now. I think she can hear the tears I don't dare cry. "Of course I believe you."

It's a mistake, I want to say. I want to tell her how wrong I've been and for how long. For years, no one believed me. And the worst part is that they were right. I shouldn't have been believed. Not then. Maybe not even now. There has been so much crazy inside of me for so long that I no longer have any sense about it. I'm the last person whose opinion on this subject should ever be trusted.

But Megan trusted me. Trusts me still.

And trust is like an invisible tightrope. Only a true friend dares to take a step.

Megan is my true friend.

I know that now. And I swear that I will never, ever forget it.

"Are we really not going to talk about this?" Megan says.

"Talk about what?" Rosie asks as she slides into the booth.

Outside, it's more dark than light now, and the countryside has all but disappeared from view. We could be anywhere. Anyone. In any time. It would be so very, very easy to get lost. But the people in this car won't let me.

I turn and stare out the window, but there is no missing Noah's reflection in the dark glass, staring back. He catches my gaze and I know he never intends to let it go.

"You disappeared, Grace," he tells me.

I look down at my hands, at the tea that's growing colder by the second. In a moment it might freeze over. "I know."

"Seven weeks," Noah says. "Seven weeks! Do you know how long that is?"

"Yes. It's just longer than six weeks—not quite as long as eight."

Noah slides into the seat across from me. The train is smooth and sleek and modern, but this car seems to vibrate with Noah's rage. "Do you know how long it is when you have no idea if your best friend is dead or alive?"

He's got a point, and I hate it.

I hate everything.

"I'm sorry, Noah. We couldn't tell anyone. We—"

"We?" he asks.

"Yes." Without meaning to, I glance at Alexei. "We."

Noah says his favorite Portuguese swearword and pushes out of the chair again. He puts his hands on top of his head, long fingers threading through jet-black hair as he paces down the aisle of the train car.

"Noah, we had to leave. No. That's not quite true. Jamie and Alexei and I . . . we had to *run*."

My voice breaks and he hears it, turns very slowly, and says, "Why?"

This is it, of course. They have the right to know. More than a right. They *need* to know. But I can't . . .

"He kinda has a point, Grace," Rosie says, as if she thinks I'm getting ready to argue. What can I say, she knows me well. Rosie shrugs her small shoulders and goes on, "You disappear for weeks and then call Megan out of the blue and the next thing we know

95

you're acting like James Bond and having secret meetings with princesses. Not to mention that none of the stuff that Ann said on that recording made any sense."

"It makes sense. I mean, it *will* make sense," Alexei tries to explain.

"Grace, what happened?" Megan asks. "I mean, one moment we were all at the bonfire and then you were *gone*. You never came back to the embassy. Your grandfather and Ms. Chancellor wouldn't even say your name. What happened that night?"

"The Night of a Thousand Amelias?" I ask, as if there could ever be any mistake. Megan nods, and I turn back to the dark glass. Outside, the world is just a dark, blurry shadow. It's almost fitting as I say, "They stabbed Jamie."

"What?" Noah lunges back to sit across from me.

"That night. Outside the palace. Remember, you and Megan saw me, and we got separated somehow. It was so loud and crowded and . . . smoky. There was so much smoke. I hate the smell of smoke. I always have, ever since . . ."

The fire.

Mom died.

I killed her.

"I hate the smell of smoke," I say again. "But there I was. At the bonfire. And then I saw Jamie. But at first I didn't think that it *was* Jamie. I thought it was Spence. Or Spence's ghost," I say, then give a sad little laugh. "See? Told you I was crazy."

"You're not crazy," Rosie says. From her, it's a little of a pot-kettle situation, but I smile anyway.

"Thanks," I say. "Anyway, I saw someone who looked just like Spence, walking through the smoke and the firelight. You know how all the men were wearing masks and the women all had on those white dresses? It was . . ."

"Creepy," Rosie says. "It was incredibly creepy."

"Yeah. But I thought I was seeing Spence, and then when he got closer and took off his mask, I realized it was Jamie. And that's when it occurred to me that if *I* thought Jamie was Spence, then maybe——"

"Spence's killer thought Spence was Jamie," Megan fills in.

I nod. "Exactly."

For a second there is only silence and darkness and the smooth, swift motion of the train.

"Grace . . ." Noah prompts, and, finally, I find the words.

"They stabbed him. They stabbed Jamie. I mean, one minute I was trying to tell him that he looked like Spence and that maybe someone had confused the two of them—that maybe someone wanted *him* dead. And Jamie was looking at me like —he was looking at me like I was the world's most screwed-up little sister, and then . . ."

I turn and stare out the glass.

"Jamie's fine," Alexei says when Megan, Noah, and Rosie turn to him.

"Jamie is *not* fine," I say.

"Jamie is recovering. He will be fine." Alexei sounds so certain.

"At first, I thought maybe he'd been shot. Except I didn't hear a shot. I didn't see anyone stab him, either, but . . . There was so

97

much blood. Alexei found us then, and he helped me carry Jamie to the palace."

"You took your bleeding brother to the palace?" Noah asks.

I nod. "Ann was our mom's friend. I'd just been to see her, to ask her if she knew what my mom was working on when she died."

"So you were with Ann and then a few minutes later someone tried to kill your brother?" Megan asks.

"Yes."

"And then you took your almost-dying brother back to the palace?"

"Yes!" I say. I'm not mad at my friends. I'm mad at myself. "It was dark and the streets were so crowded. I didn't know who'd hurt him. I didn't know what to do, so Alexei helped me carry him to the palace."

"How did you get out?" Rosie asks. "I mean, if the royal family wants you both dead and all."

"Dominic," I say. "He told the guards that he was there to arrest Alexei, and then he dragged the three of us out of the palace and back to the embassy. Grandpa called in a favor from a general he knows and he sent a helicopter to get us. They flew us to an army hospital in Germany and rushed Jamie into surgery. He lived. Barely. And as soon as he could be moved, Dominic took the three of us on the run."

"Took you where?" Megan asks.

Alexei and I share a look, and I shrug. "Everywhere," I say. "We kept moving. But Jamie wasn't getting better. Jamie was never going to get better if they kept chasing us, so I . . ."

"So you what?" Now it's Alexei who is making demands.

I stare him down. "So I gave them someone else to chase."

That's the truth, isn't it? It's why I'm here. Why I'm not somewhere safely under the Scarred Man's watch. Or as safe as I possibly could be. No one seems to argue my logic. Not because I'm right, I know. Just because the people in this train car know there's never any use arguing with me.

"Grace." It's Noah who breaks the silence. He's not pleading, not blaming. He's just honestly confused as he says, *"Why?"*

I should answer. I owe him that much. More. I owe them all more than I could ever, ever repay. But for some reason I just look at Alexei.

"How familiar are you all with the story of the lost princess of Adria?" he says, as if super hot Russian guys are often obsessed with princess stories.

"You mean the baby?" Megan says. "Amelia? The one who was killed in the coup?"

"She wasn't killed," Alexei tells them.

"Awesome!" Rosie exclaims after a moment. "I mean. It's true? Really? Because I've been calling that for weeks, haven't I? I mean, that has always been my own personal theory."

"No," Noah says, shaking his head. "That's crazy."

"Yeah. It's true," I say. "A nurse smuggled Amelia out of the palace, and then the Society hid her among their own babies. Some Society member took her home that night and raised her. No one ever knew which baby girl she was. They just brought her home and kept her safe until she grew up and had a kid of her own.

And then that kid had a kid. And so on and so on, and then my mom . . ." I take a deep breath. "My mom found out that she was one of those kids. My mom was Amelia's direct descendant. *I* am Amelia's descendant."

"So you're a . . ." Rosie starts, a mischievous gleam in her eye.

"Yes, Rosie. I'm a princess."

Noah can't help himself. He laughs. And then Rosie bursts out laughing, too. Even Megan can't hide a giggle, and the pressure that Alexei and I have been living under—the constant worry and fatigue and stress—it's too much. And we both snap. Laughter pours out of us. For a second, I feel young.

Noah is trying to take a deep breath. He's trying to speak. "Do I need to bow?" he asks. "I really think I should bow."

He tries to stand, but I grab his hand. "If you get out of that seat, I'm going to kick you really, really hard."

"Fine. Your Highness."

And just that quickly, the laughter fades. The truth of the matter settles over us like a fog.

No one is laughing anymore.

"So the royal family tried to kill Jamie," Rosie says, so matter-of-fact that any other theory sounds stupid. "Right?"

Everyone is looking at me. "I think so. I mean . . . probably. It's just . . ."

"What is it, Gracie?" Alexei slides into the seat beside me. I can feel the warmth that radiates off him, centering me.

"The Society," I say.

"What about them?" Megan sounds almost afraid, almost like a part of her knew this might be coming.

"When I was with the Council of Elders, I thought they might help. They're the ones who saved Amelia after all. But they didn't want to help. In fact, they seemed to think that my existence—that Jamie's existence—might severely threaten the stability of Europe. And they are *very* committed to a stable Europe."

"So you think the Society might want you dead, too?" Noah asks me.

For the first time I wonder if Noah's mom was there. At the meeting of the elders. I might have just called Noah's mom a killer, but he doesn't look concerned.

"So, long story short, there are a whole lot of people who might want you dead," Rosie says in an entirely too-cheerful summary of my situation.

Megan is too quiet.

"What?" I turn to her. She's maybe the smartest person I know, and something in her silence scares me.

"That explains it." Megan's voice is almost a whisper, part awe and part fear.

"Explains what?" I ask.

"The embassy," she tells me. "That night, The Night of a Thousand Amelias . . . the embassy was crazy. No one would tell me why, but it was obvious something had happened. My mom wouldn't let me near the residence, but everything was insane. I've never seen the marines like that. It was like a war zone."

"What's it like now?" I ask. For the first time I let myself remember that all my family wasn't evacuated that night. Grandpa is still there.

"How is it different?" I have to know.

But Megan just shakes her head, almost like she's slowly waking from a dream. "I don't know. It just is. I mean, for one thing, Ms. Chancellor is never around. At least, I haven't seen her. I think she might be gone. Moved. Transferred or something. I don't know. And there are way more guards posted. My mom has been working like crazy. I tried to snoop around and figure out what's up, but they're using next-gen encryption, and protocols like I've never seen. I do know that your grandpa brought in a bunch of security experts to revamp the cameras and gates and fences and everything. The passage that opens up into the basement? That's long gone. They put up wire around the walls! Oh, and all the Adrian citizens who work at the embassy? They're gone."

"What do you mean, gone?" I ask.

"I mean fired. Or farmed out, given jobs at other embassies on the row. Replaced. No one gets in unless they're a US citizen who has been through all kinds of CIA background checks and/or is on a very short leash."

Megan takes a deep breath.

"The place you left, Grace? The building where your mom grew up and you spent your summers when you were little? It's not an embassy anymore." Megan looks me in the eye. "It's a fortress."

I never had a home. Not really. Or that's what I liked to say—liked to think. We moved so many times and so often that I never even tried to put down roots. But that's not true, I've come to realize. My mother's roots were always on Embassy Row. And she planted mine there, too. It's more than a building, more than my grandfather. More even than the secret, ancient heritage of a grandmother I never knew. Like most things, I didn't know it until it was gone. And Megan's words make me miss the only home I've ever known.

I look back out the window. When I speak, my breath fogs against the glass.

"So . . . someone is trying to kill me. And Jamie. They want—no, they *need*—us dead. We're a threat. And as long as we live . . . as long as our entire bloodline lives, we will always be a threat."

"But, Grace . . ." Rosie stumbles over her words, she seems so confused, so lost, as she asks, "Do you *want* to be a princess?"

That this is a question people now seriously ask me is something I can't quite comprehend.

"No, Ro, I most certainly do not *want* to be a princess."

"Well, maybe if you explain that to everyone," Rosie says. "Maybe if you just tell them, then maybe . . ."

I'm just starting to speak, to protest, to try to explain that no one has ever taken my word about anything, when Megan beats me to it.

"It doesn't work that way," she says.

"Yeah. They're never going to believe me," I say, but Megan is shaking her head.

"No, Grace. You don't understand. Adrian law won't allow it."

Megan reaches into her bag for her laptop. In a flash, it's open and connecting to the train's Wi-Fi. We all sit in silence as her perfectly manicured fingers fly over the keys. Then Megan is spinning the laptop around.

"I'm talking about this."

It's a website devoted to Adrian history, specifically the history of the government.

"After the War of the Fortnight, all kinds of people still believed that Amelia was alive," Megan says. "Or maybe they just hoped she was. Anyway, it was a rumor for a long time."

"Okay," Noah says, as if it's not okay and he doesn't understand at all. He's not the only one.

"Think about it," Megan tells us. "The country had just been through a *war*. A bloody, bitter revolution. Adria was fractured and broken. And they needed to move on. They brokered the peace treaty under the condition that the dead king's brother would assume the throne but that there would also be a new parliament. Peace depended upon that. But there were still all these whispers—all these theories—that Amelia was alive, and as much as half the country wanted the war to be over, the other half didn't want Amelia's throne taken away from her if she was still alive—that if she really did survive, they owed it to her to keep her throne intact."

"So?" Leave it to Rosie to cut right to the heart of the matter.

"Amelia never was put on the throne. And then, presumably, she died. Unless she became a vampire. Did she become a vampire?"

"No," Megan says quite simply. "But they wrote the constitution as if someday she might come back, and"—Megan turns to the laptop and then begins to read—" 'In the event that our lost Amelia should be found, she *or her heirs* shall return to the throne of the country that is rightfully theirs.' "

Megan's words are still echoing around the train car, but my thoughts are racing by as quickly as the landscape outside.

"Don't you see?" Megan sounds like she's losing patience with us. "If Amelia had returned— if her *heirs* return—then it all goes away. The prime minister. Parliament. Not to mention the current king. All gone. Amelia's heirs—that's you, Grace. That's Jamie—would reclaim the throne and then Adria would, by law, revert to the government it had before the coup."

"That can't be right." I'm shaking my head, retreating farther and farther back in my seat as if it can also send me back in time. "They wouldn't have written the constitution to a country like that. Not to pacify some crazy conspiracy theorists."

"But they weren't crazy, were they?" Noah asks.

And that, of course, is the problem.

"It's in the constitution," I say, suddenly defeated.

"I'm not saying the Society is right, Grace," Megan goes on. "But, according to this, Jamie doesn't have a choice."

I'm sixteen years old and short for my age—too thin and unstable for my own good. But I've never felt truly powerless before. Even strapped to a bed, medications and guilt pounding in

105

my veins, I had the power to keep yelling about the Scarred Man. I had a mission, a cause. A vigilante's surety that someday the world would see that I was right.

But that day has come and gone, and now I know that there is absolutely nothing I can do to change it.

"Grace?"

The window is so black now. How is that possible? Outside, there aren't even any lights. No distant towns or lone farmhouses. It's like this train has carried us far, far out to sea.

Maybe that is why it feels like I am drowning.

CHAPTER TEN

You should probably wear a hat or something."

It's easy to forget—with all my crazy and my drama—that Alexei is still a wanted man. They still think he killed that cadet in Adria. There's still a price on his head. And now he's come back to Europe—to the belly of the beast.

Because of me.

And, suddenly, it scares me.

"You need to go back, Alexei."

"*I* need to go back?"

The train car is empty. It's supposed to be the café, but it's too late. There is no one working behind the tiny bar. If a person wanted to buy a stale sandwich or bag of greasy chips, they'd be out of luck. Alexei and I are all alone.

There's no Dominic looking over our shoulders, no Jamie lingering nearby.

"You shouldn't have come to Europe."

"*I* shouldn't have come to Europe?" Alexei shouts.

"You can do something besides repeat everything I say, you know."

"Oh, can I? Because what I want to do is strangle you. I want to tie you up and throw you over my shoulder and jump out of a moving train. I want to take you to the coldest place in Siberia, to the darkest part of the moon. I want to keep you safe, Gracie. So the question is, why are you so determined to stop me?"

"Is Jamie okay?"

His fingers are sliding into my hair, holding me still and keeping me close. *I'm not going to run anymore,* the gesture tells me. *We are bound now. From this moment on . . . together.*

"Gracie." My name is like a breath, and I'm not sure Alexei even knows he's said it.

"Is Jamie okay?" I remind myself that he's the only thing that matters.

Alexei smiles, a wry expression that's somehow lacking any joy.

His fingers massage my scalp, and I wilt against him.

"Jamie isn't my primary concern at the moment."

"You know what I mean, Alexei," I say, pushing away. "Are they still on the run or are they someplace where Jamie can get better?"

Alexei steps back. It's almost like he can't face me anymore.

"You ran away."

It's not an accusation. It's a fact. And that's why he hates it.

"I ran so that the rest of you could *stop* running."

Alexei spins. "You left!"

"Yes." I somehow choke out the word, swallow hard. "And I'd do it again."

"Not without me." In a flash, Alexei has me. His arms are tight. "Never without me. Never again. Say it, Grace. Say it."

"Okay."

"Say it!" He stares down into my eyes.

"Never again."

"I was so scared. When I woke up and you were gone . . . And then when I found you and those men were there . . ." He curses in Russian. "I was so scared."

"Alexei."

There's no thinking after that. No worry and no fear. I'm aware only of the warmth that is radiating off Alexei, the rocking of the train.

And then Alexei's lips are on mine, and I'm not aware of anything anymore. It's different from the kiss on the bridge. There's no urgency now. This isn't about the heat of the moment and the danger. This is about now—right now. No future and no past.

"*Ahem.*"

Megan's voice breaks through the fog that fills my head, and I stop the kiss, but there's no pulling away from Alexei. Not now. Maybe not ever.

"Sorry to interrupt," Megan says, then picks up a remote control and turns on the television that hangs behind the bar. "But we thought you'd like to see this."

I know those buildings and those streets. I know that world. And I know I'll never quite escape it.

Even if I wasn't fluent in my mother's native tongue, I'd know the meaning of the words that fill the screen.

A newscaster stands outside the police station while uniformed officials lead a man in handcuffs through the doors.

Then the picture changes.

"Alexei——" I start, but what comes next feels so surreal I can no longer say a thing.

Does Grandpa look older to everyone, or is it just me? His hair has been white all my life, but also thick and wavy. He's always been the quintessential elder statesman. But he's never looked elderly before.

Seven weeks Jamie and I have been gone—but my grandfather has aged ten years.

Megan turns up the volume in time to hear him tell the press, "We are extremely pleased that the perpetrator of this terrible, random crime has been caught and that Alexei Volkov's name has been cleared. Our relationship with our neighbors is very important. Ambassador Volkov and I have spoken, and I look forward to everything returning to normal as both of our countries get back to the important diplomatic work for which we are here."

When Grandpa glances behind him, I recognize the stoic man who stands watching, partly because the younger, only slightly less stoic version of him is in front of me.

If Alexei feels any emotion at seeing his father, he doesn't show it. His dad was willing to throw him to the wolves, after all. The man on the screen doesn't look relieved to have his son's name cleared. He looks like a man who will never be truly pleased about anything ever again.

"Alexei!" Rosie is running, practically throwing herself into his arms. He has to release his hold on me to catch her. "It's so great! You're cleared! You're free. You didn't do it! I mean, we always knew you didn't do it, but now everyone knows, and you're free!"

But Alexei doesn't look free. He looks furious.

He turns on me. "What did you do, Gracie?"

"Alexei, you can come home!" Rosie says, blissfully unaware of the storm that's brewing in Alexei's blue eyes.

It's only when Noah peels her from Alexei that Rosie begins to realize something is wrong.

"It's not that simple, Ro," Noah says.

"But . . ." Rosie starts.

She looks from Noah to Alexei, then to me.

"Gracie, what did you do?" Alexei asks again.

"I got you cleared," I say, as if the details don't really matter. They shouldn't. But they do.

"Grace?" Now Megan's sounding worried.

"I asked the prime minister, okay? When I turned myself in to the Society, I said that I had some conditions. Clearing your name was one of them."

"And you didn't think to tell me this?"

"I didn't think it mattered! Or, well, I didn't think they'd do it. I kind of ran out on them. Literally."

"You bargained for my freedom?" Alexei says, as if it's a bad thing.

"You didn't do it, Alexei! You were the most wanted man in Europe for something you didn't do."

"And what of that man they arrested, Gracie?" Alexei points to the screen. "What did *he* do?"

"I'm sure he did something," I blurt, but I'm far from certain.

"Most of the world was sure that *I'd* done something."

"Maybe he really is the killer. We don't know. We may never know. And now you . . . you can go home."

"I'm not going anywhere."

"You have to," I snap. But when I look around, I know arguing is futile.

"You seem to think we're giving you a choice," Megan says.

She isn't especially tall. She's not obviously strong. But right now—in this moment—I know it would take half the NATO forces in Europe to drag her off this train. She isn't just with me; she's *with me*. And there's nothing I can do to stop her.

"Fine." Noah shrugs, then turns to me. "Where do we start?"

It's a great question—really the only question. And for all the hours and miles that this truth has been chasing me, the finish line remains elusive. I honestly have no idea what to say. But when I look at Alexei I see a spark there. Well, not a spark, but something . . .

"What?" I ask.

Alexei runs a hand through his hair. It's thick and black and too long at the moment. It ripples through his fingers like black waves.

"I was afraid you were going to say this, so . . ."

"So what?" I ask.

He eyes me. "So I didn't come alone."

Instantly, terror grips me.

"If Jamie and Dominic are in Europe, then—"

"Not your brother," Alexei cuts me off, then reaches for the backpack he's been carrying. There's a duffel bag, too, which we picked up at the train station. I'd just assumed they held clothes, shoes. Weapons. But I was wrong. I know it as soon as Alexei clears off a table and upends the backpack over it, sending papers and Post-it notes, tiny leather-bound books and photographs scattering below.

"I'm confused," Rosie says, hands on hips. "How is a bag full of junk going to help us?"

But I'm reaching for the pile. I run one finger along the glossy surface of a photograph as I say, "It's my mother's junk. She kept it in a secret room beneath her shop."

I seem to have Rosie at "secret room" because she leans closer to the pile and mutters what I assume is the German equivalent of *awesome*.

"My mother collected all this. She collected it, and she kept it hidden."

Megan meets my gaze, finishes my thought. "And you only hide the things that matter."

She turns her attention to the pile. Noah, too. Soon, four sets of hands are shuffling and sorting. I stand a little apart. I hurt everything I touch, after all. I'm half-afraid that my fingers might make it catch fire.

"Grace."

Megan's voice brings me back.

I don't know how long I've been standing, staring but seeing nothing.

"Grace, you need to look at this. Do you recognize it?"

The small book is a soft brown leather, and I can't help but remember standing in a store with Jamie, running my hands along its cover, thinking I couldn't wait until Christmas morning to give it to my mother.

"It's a calendar," I say without having to look.

"Do you want to . . . ?" Megan tries, but I'm already shaking my head.

"No." I can't read my mother's careful notes, her perfect penmanship. I can't look too closely because that's one way to never see a thing. "You do it."

Megan nods as if she understands.

The train keeps going, flying through the night. But inside the car, all is quiet as Megan scans the pages, speed-reading, taking it all in.

"When was it?" she asks, and I know exactly what she means.

"November," I tell her. "Mom died the first week of November."

She nods and flips through the pages until she sees something and makes a face, flips back, then forward again, as if something doesn't quite make sense.

"Grace, what do you remember about . . . before? In the days leading up to the fire?" Megan says, and I'm grateful for it. I don't think I could stand to hear *her death* or *when she was shot*. My nerves are like live wires. My insulation is all gone, and it doesn't take much to make sparks.

"Was your mom acting differently? Did she say anything?"

I've spent so much time trying to remember that night. And I've spent the rest of my time trying to forget. I can't believe I've never really considered Megan's question before. What was Mom like in the days or weeks leading up to what happened? I have to think now, recall. It hurts, but I push forward.

I remember dressing up for Halloween and making caramel apples, playing in big piles of leaves and talking about a Thanksgiving that never came.

I remember . . .

"She was gone," I say, honestly surprised by the words, by the memory. "She left. The week before, she left on a buying trip for the shop. Or for the Society, I guess. I don't know. She was gone for a few days. She said it might be longer than usual because if she was going all the way to Adria, she should spend some time with Grandpa."

But Megan is taking the book, turning the pages again. She points to something. "This says she went to Binevale. Do you know where that is?"

"No." I shake my head, look at Noah.

"I've never heard of it," he says. "And Adria's not that big."

"Megan, can you get online and see if you can find out where this town might be and what—"

"It's not a town." Alexei's voice is flat and even, almost like he is remembering a ghost. When he turns to look at the distant lights of the countryside, I can see his face reflected in the darkened glass. He presses his palm against it, like he's trying to push his way back in time.

"And it's not in Adria."

CHAPTER
ELEVEN

Valancia isn't a large city, and Embassy Row is even smaller. But there's an advantage to having best friends who each, technically, reside in different countries.

It only takes a few phone calls and a couple of well-placed lies for Rosie and Noah and Megan to all have "sleepovers" that are going to go on a little longer than their parents initially expected.

Then we get to work.

We put away our credit cards and hide our real IDs. Those things are lost to us now. Alexei and I have the fakes that Dominic gave us, and they are the only ones we dare to use. Luckily, borders are porous in Europe, and largely unpatrolled. A person can drive through three countries in a day and have no idea where one ends and another begins. So time is the only thing that stands between us and where we're going.

And, eventually, time runs out.

"Alexei, are you sure about this?" Rosie asks when we reach the tiny nation of Dubrovnia. "I mean, I know the Soviet Union was big and stuff, but that was a long time ago. Maybe . . ."

"It was not so long ago if you are Russian," Alexei says.

The car we rented at the train station is small and loud, and the transportation system here isn't exactly state-of-the-art, so we rattle and roll along a two-lane highway that's more trail than road.

The mountains are growing steeper around us, and change is in the air. In a lot of ways.

"Turn up the heat, will you?" Megan asks. She and I are shivering with Noah in the backseat. Alexei's driving; Rosie's riding shotgun. At first, she was disappointed to learn that an actual shotgun didn't come with the position, but she's made her peace with it, and now she and Alexei share a glance, as if to say that we're all wimps. And I suppose we are. But we're wimps who have been raised in much warmer climates.

It's only early autumn, but already the terrain is cold and hard. The sky is a steely gray, and I can't even imagine what it must feel like in the middle of winter. Dubrovnia hasn't been a part of the Soviet Union since well before any of us were born, but Alexei seems at home here. We aren't that far north—I think this country even shares a border with Adria at some point. But the little bit of sunshine that is seeping through the overcast sky feels precious, a fading, fleeting thing. For a moment I wonder if it really is as cold outside as it feels. Or maybe the cold is just radiating off Alexei.

"How far?" Noah asks.

Megan checks the phone she stole from her mom. She swears it's untraceable, unhackable, and generally unbeatable. We're choosing to believe her.

"It should be close, but I don't see anything."

Alexei pulls off the narrow road. There's no one coming for miles, but we park near a bunch of trees.

"What is it?" I ask. "What's wrong?"

"We walk," he says, and no one argues. We're on Alexei's turf, in a place that speaks Alexei's language. My body aches as I crawl out of the backseat of the car, but I know better than to complain. Alexei's already up ahead. His long legs eat up the ground and the rough terrain as he climbs a steep hill, and the rest of us follow, leaving the car behind.

"I thought we were going to Binevale," Rosie says, trotting alongside Alexei, not even a little bit winded.

"We are. We're here."

We crest the hill—and that's when we see it, a building on the horizon, nestled into the valley below. But it's not a building, really. It's a complex—a large, three-story structure made of cinder blocks and stone. It's as cold and gray as the sky, surrounded by a few smaller buildings and a tall chain-link fence. Though where anyone would run to, I can't really tell. It seems like an island set down in the middle of an ocean of cold, hard land.

"Is it a prison?" Megan asks as she reaches into her backpack, removes a camera with a huge telephoto lens, and starts snapping pictures.

"Of a sort," Alexei says.

"This can't be it," I say. "Why would my mom come here? It doesn't exactly scream *antiquities*."

"Technically, it's *not* here." There's a look in Alexei's eye as he studies the compound below.

Rosie and I turn back to the building as if maybe it was some kind of mirage that was going to flicker and fade before our eyes.

Noah just studies Alexei. "Girls like it when you're cryptic, don't they?" he asks, then turns to Megan. "Should I start being cryptic?"

But Megan shrugs him off. "Alexei, what is this place?"

Alexei gives a sad smile. "It's where you send the people you want to disappear."

I can feel him looking at me, blue eyes honing in like lasers, but I can't take my gaze off the building. It feels too big. Too eerie. Too familiar.

"I'm not sure what it is," he says. "Not exactly. It was built by the Soviets not long after the Second World War. Many believe it is a prison . . ."

"Of course it's a prison," Rosie says with a roll of her eyes. "I mean look at it. What else could it be?"

I've often wondered what Alexei knows about me—what stories Jamie's told. How many of my brother's worries has he passed

120

on to his best friend? I'm almost afraid of the answer. But as I stare down at the cold, institutional buildings below us, I know.

"A hospital," I say, and, suddenly, instead of a chilly fall, it feels like the middle of winter. "It's a hospital."

"No way." Rosie is shaking her head. "Look at that place. How are people supposed to get better in there?"

"They aren't," I say, but everyone looks at Alexei.

"People who go into Binevale do not come out."

I only notice that I've started rocking back and forth when Noah puts an arm around me, pulling me in like I've just made a game-winning goal or something. I'm grateful for his steadiness, for his warmth.

"Are you sure, Alexei?" Megan takes a break from her camera and looks at him. "I've never heard of it. And, I don't like to brag, but I read a lot. I mean *a lot*. And most of it is classified."

She's perfectly serious, but Alexei gives a cold, dry laugh. It's like the joke's on us, like we've never been more un-Russian in our lives.

"I'm sure," Alexei says, then looks at the gray building in the distance and says something low, under his breath, and in Russian.

"What does that mean?" Rosie asks.

"It is hard to translate, but it basically means *Troubled children take a train. They take a train to Binevale*." He laughs again, then shrugs. "In Russian, it is very clever. And it rhymes."

"What is it? What does it mean?" I ask.

"It's something parents say to naughty children. It is the Russian version of *Be good or the boogeyman will get you*."

"I don't get it." Rosie throws her hands up. "Why would bad kids get sent to a hospital? That doesn't make any sense."

"It does. If it's a mental hospital," I say. "You don't have to be bad. You just have to be crazy."

Saying the words is enough to make my wrists burn, my legs twitch. I want to move—to run—just to prove that I can. I have to remind my body that I will never get strapped to a bed, restrained, or held against my will ever again.

"I never knew it was real," Alexei says. "Even driving here, I kept thinking that it couldn't possibly be real. But there it is."

"I hate to say it, but Rosie's right," Megan says.

"Hey!" Rosie spins on Megan, but Megan isn't deterred. She just clicks through the images displayed on the little screen on the back of her camera, showing the place close up for the first time.

"It doesn't make any sense," Megan continues. "Why would Grace's mom come here?"

"I—" I start, but I can't finish once I see Alexei's face. He's staring at the back of Megan's camera, at the image there.

"Because that's my mom," he says.

CHAPTER TWELVE

When we leave, Megan drives. Noah sits with her up front, while Rosie and I sit in the backseat, Alexei beside us. But he's not here. Not really. Alexei is a million miles away.

I don't ask where we're going. To be perfectly honest, I don't care. I only know that Alexei is too quiet, too still, and there is far too much that we don't know.

"I think . . ." Megan says, turning the car down a dirt road, slowly moving until the dim headlights flash over a small house that looks like it has grown right out of the earth. "Yeah. We're here."

Only Noah asks, "What is this place?"

We get out of the car and gather our things, follow Megan onto the porch. Somehow I'm not surprised when she knows exactly where to find a key.

"When we moved to Adria, my mom sat me down and made me memorize fifty phone numbers and twice as many addresses. This is one of them," she says, then opens the door.

I watch her pause on the threshold, like she's half-expecting to be shot on sight. Or at least to hear the roaring of an alarm. But nothing greets us but silence.

"What is it?" Noah asks.

"It's a safe house," Megan says.

"But what *kind* of safe . . ." Noah trails off when Rosie turns on the lights. The bulbs crackle and hum, like they haven't been used in a decade or two. An eerie glow fills the room, but there's no mistaking the row of guns that lines one wall, the computers and monitors and maps that cover another.

We all look at Megan, stunned.

"What can I say?" She shrugs. "Safe. House."

Megan's mom works for the CIA, and that fact has never been more obvious to any of us as we all spread out, carefully opening doors and examining cabinets.

"Is that a shower?" Noah asks, peeking into one room. "Please tell me that's a shower."

But I can't let myself relax. "Megan, should we be here?"

"Do you have someplace else to be?" she asks, which is an excellent question. And the obvious answer is no.

"What happens now?" Rosie says what everyone else is thinking.

Megan got us to this place, but she's not in charge; I can feel it as everyone turns in my direction. They're looking at me like

I'm supposed to lead, but all I really want to do is take a hot shower, eat whatever food we can find in this Cold War kitchen, and then sleep until it's time to meet my mom in Heaven.

I'm so relieved when Noah steps forward and says, "Now we sleep. And we eat. And we try to figure out what comes next."

"Yes!" Rosie sounds entirely too chipper. "Exactly what is the best way of breaking a woman out of a former Soviet mental facility? Explosives? I think it might be explosives."

Luckily, Alexei doesn't roll his eyes. "There can be no explosives, Rosemarie."

"Of course there can be," Rosie says, undaunted. "I saw some in that cabinet over—"

"My mother is in there for a reason!" Alexei's practically shaking now. Not with rage, with something else. It's like another Alexei is inside of him, trying to break out of this calm, cool shell.

I'm seeing cracks, and I don't like it.

"She is in there for a reason," he says again, his voice full of a calm I can tell he doesn't feel. "That is where we found her. And that is where she will stay."

"Alexei—" Rosie starts, but his eyes are like ice.

"This is not a debate. Whatever she did, she should stay there. People get sent to Binevale for a reason. She deserves it."

I don't realize I'm rocking. I don't even know I'm speaking until the words are free. *"I deserved it."*

It's like Alexei has just remembered where I am. What I am.

"We should get you back to Dominic," he tells me, then turns to the others. "You need to return to Adria now. Forget about us. Stick to your routines and your embassies. There are no answers here."

Alexei grips me tight. It's supposed to comfort, to soothe, but it just reminds me of another time when I was held too tight and for too long.

"No," I say, pulling away from him and stalking to the other side of the room.

"Grace?" Noah eases toward me. "Are you okay?"

"No!" I snap again, then wheel on Alexei. "My mom came here. And if there's a chance that your mom knows why, then I am going to take it."

"You don't understand, Grace. People do not get sent to Binevale by accident. Whatever she did to end up in that place . . ."

"Oh, and no one has never been imprisoned unjustly?" I ask. "Besides, criminal or not—crazy or not—I don't care. I have to talk to her. I am going to talk to her. I don't care what it takes."

They know that I mean it. It's not hyperbole or exaggeration. I'd cut off my own arm if it was the only way inside those gates. And Rosie would find me the knife.

When I turn to Megan, she's already shaking her head, carefully considering the question I don't have to ask.

"It didn't look that secure," she says. "I hate to say it, but I think Rosie might be right."

"I'm standing right here," Rosie says, but Megan isn't fazed.

"It's old. Unless they've spent a lot of money upgrading it, then the walls should be fairly breachable. And there weren't a ton of guards. If we watched for a few days and mapped their

126

patterns, then there might be a window of opportunity. Of course, there might also be a fortress and an army hidden underground or something, but . . . I kind of think we could do it."

A part of her hates saying this, I know. And another part is itching for the challenge.

Noah shakes his head, almost as if he can't believe what he's about to ask. "Just to be clear, by 'it' you mean break someone out of a Cold War–era, former Soviet facility that is so infamous and scary and generally feared that it has become a bad nursery rhyme that people use to scare children? Also, though I hate to point this out, *we* are children."

"Nursery rhymes usually start with the truth," I say, thinking of the song my mother used to sing to me about Adria's lost little princess.

"That doesn't make me feel better," Noah says.

"I'm just saying that I don't think it's *impossible*," Megan says, throwing up her hands. Noah's starting to fire back when Alexei laughs. It's a cruel, cold sound.

"What is it?" Megan asks him.

"People don't get sent to Binevale because they're dangerous. They get sent because they're the kind of people no one is going to come looking for."

As this settles over us, that a woman's own son would say such a thing, Rosie nods thoughtfully. Then she asks, "So explosion? Or helicopter. Because—"

"We don't have to break her out," I say.

"But we could," Rosie says.

"We have to talk to her," I say. "I have to talk to her."

"Grace, I don't think they're going to let you walk up to the gates and schedule a meeting," Megan points out.

"No." I turn to the boy beside me. "But they might let her son do it."

"She no longer has a son."

He's out the door before I can catch him.

Sometimes, when I was a kid, Dad would go away. We wouldn't know where. We wouldn't know for how long. We just knew that—if we were lucky—he'd come back eventually.

And, eventually, he always did.

Sometimes, in the days or weeks after, I'd wake up to the sight of light flickering in the hallway. I'd crawl out of bed to find my dad sprawled on the living room couch, some show on the TV that he wasn't really watching.

"I'm too tired to sleep, Gracie," he'd say. He'd be bruised, scarred, and alert at all hours of the night. He was home, but his mind was still off in some faraway war zone, struggling to stay alive.

That's what it feels like now. My body knows that it should rest, but my head just won't let it. I trust Megan when she says this house is secret and secure. I'm sure that we're as safe here as we are anywhere. But that isn't saying much.

Finally, I close my eyes, and my mind drifts. I hear my

mother's voice. I see her sitting on the stairs. The beautiful box is on her lap.

"See, Gracie, it's a puzzle box," she says.

"Open it for me," I tell her.

But Mom only laughs. "That would be cheating, sweetheart. Besides"—she runs her hand along the wood—*"I don't know how. Yet."*

I sit upright in bed. Sleep, I know, will never come. So I ease out from beside a snoring, kicking Rosie and start toward the main room.

The box is sitting on the table, atop the pile of papers and photos from Mom's shop. It's cool and smooth as I run my hands across the surface.

"What's that?"

Megan's voice makes me jump. I whirl and take in her form standing in the shadows. Slowly, she comes forward.

I look back at the box. There's a single light on in the kitchen, a bare fluorescent bulb that burns low, casting the box in its yellow light.

"It was my mom's," I say. "I think it was a puzzle box."

All Megan really needs to hear is *puzzle*, and then she's standing beside me, fully intrigued.

"Do you know how to open it?" she asks as she leans down and eyes it at table level.

"No."

Megan has never turned away from a challenge. "Do you mind if I try?"

I hold my hands out, as if to say, *Go ahead.*

For a moment, she just looks at it, studying the different pieces of wood that blend together in a gorgeous mix of light and dark.

Then, carefully, she reaches for it, running a fingertip along the strips of wood.

"I saw this once," I tell her. "When I was a little girl. Mom told me that I'd figure out how to open it when I needed to."

"I don't see anything," Megan tells me, standing upright again. "But it's beautiful. Do you mind if I work on it for a while?"

"Go ahead," I say. But I'm not optimistic.

CHAPTER THIRTEEN

This is a mistake."

I've seen Alexei cocky and scared and worried, but nervous is a whole new look on him. I'm not sure if it's the Soviet-era institution that scares him or the woman we hope to find inside.

No, I realize then. I do know. And I can't blame him for what he's feeling.

The morning air is cold, and a heavy frost lies on the ground around us. The night was long and winter is coming, and I want to get out of here before we all start to freeze. But it's too late for the boy beside me. His heart froze over ages ago.

I try to make light of it. "I know this whole plan seems a little crazy. But crazy is kind of normal for us these days, isn't it?"

"We should leave her in there," Alexei says.

"We *are* going to leave her in there. We're just going to talk to her—find out what happened."

"We should leave her in there. Alone."

I've known love, and I've known hate. But I've never seen how easily one can morph into the other. Alexei's mother left him. She didn't just hurt him; she changed him. And I know the boy beside me is proof of what happens when you grow up knowing you're the kind of person who can be left behind.

"Alexei, don't you wonder how she ended up in there? I mean, do you think your dad had her committed? Because if he didn't . . . If my mom got killed, maybe your mom got locked up? Maybe she didn't leave you."

When he turns, he's almost a stranger. "My mom left long before she went away."

"Alexei, we don't know what happened. We don't know why your mom is in there or why my mom went to see her. We don't know anything."

Alexei's voice is cold. "Maybe it's better that way."

He takes my hands in his. They're big and warm, and I let myself savor that feeling. I let myself feel safe.

"Sometimes it's better not to know," he says.

No one knows that better than I do. I think back to before I knew. About who killed my mom. About why. Would I go back if I could? I don't know. And it doesn't matter. Time only runs in one direction.

"Promise me something," Alexei says, pulling me closer.

I look up. "Anything," I say, and I mean it. I actually do. I don't stop to think about why that scares me.

"If something goes wrong today, I want you to run."

"I'm not going to leave you."

"You're too important," he says, then pushes a strand of hair out of my eyes. "To the world. To me." Then Alexei looks at me—I mean *really* looks at me—and says, "Promise that you'll keep my girlfriend safe."

I can't help myself. I pull back, look into his too-cool, too-blue eyes. I almost choke on the words. "I'm your girlfriend?"

"No." Alexei shakes his head, then pulls me to him again, holds me closer. "There's not a word in either of our languages for what you are to me."

And then he kisses me, soft and sweet, and for one brief second I actually let myself think that maybe—someday—it is all going to be okay.

When Noah clears his throat, Alexei and I pull apart. I jerk back, but he's so calm and sure. He's not ashamed to be seen kissing me, and that's the first sign that maybe he's not entirely sane, either.

"We ready?" Megan asks as she walks from the house to the car.

Alexei and I look at each other, equally unsure of the answer.

"Are you sure you want to do this?" Noah asks, pulling me aside.

"I have to do this."

"No." He shakes his head. "You don't have to go in there."

Noah is my best friend, so maybe that's why he sees what the others don't, why he hears what I don't say.

Noah doesn't want me to rethink my plan because the compound might be filled with guns and guards. Noah wants me to stay here because it might be filled with ghosts.

"Don't go in there, Gracie. Don't do that to yourself. Let Alexei go. I'll go with him. I'll ask your questions, just . . . don't go."

"I have to."

"No!" Noah snaps. "You don't. We can help you. Let us help you."

Noah is smart and kind and right—there's no denying that he's right. I'm the last person who should walk into Binevale, but you don't end up in a place like that in the first place if you always make the smart decision.

"She saw my mom," I say, because, really, it's the only thing that matters. "She saw my mom and then my mom died. I have to go."

Alexei and Rosie are loading the cars, both the one we got at the station and the one we found in the garage. We won't come back here, I know. No matter what happens today, tomorrow we'll move on. We have one shot.

When Megan comes up, I'm half-afraid of what she's going to say. "Can I talk to you?"

"Sure." I brace myself for another you-don't-have-to-do-this pep talk. Only Rosie seems to think this is an excellent idea.

But when Megan turns back to me I don't quite recognize the worry in her eyes.

"Alexei's going to have to give his real name," Megan says, and the words knock me off guard. "He'll have to give them his real name and then maybe—maybe—they'll let him in. He can't hide in there. He's going to be on the grid. And you're going to be with him."

I wasn't expecting this particular argument, and maybe that's why I stand for a moment, totally unsure what to say.

"I have to go," I reply, because it's a reflex now.

"They might not let you in anyway," Megan says. "I mean, if the place is as legendary as Alexei says, then we don't know what to expect. But I'm gonna see if I can hack in and make it seem like you've got clearance. That is, if their systems are hackable. I mean, that place looks pretty analog, but I'm gonna try. Don't worry. About getting in, I mean."

I've never heard Megan talk so fast or look so worried. I know she hasn't even gotten to the good part.

"But, Grace . . ." she starts slowly. "If Karina is . . . I mean, since she's in there, there's a chance she might be . . ."

"It's okay, Megan," I say, taking pity on her. "I'm fluent in crazy."

"That's not what I mean. It's just . . . she could be one of them—the royal family or the Society or whoever is behind this. Or she could be in there *because* of them. We don't know. But we do know that your mom came here and then she died, and I don't think that's a coincidence. That's why I'm saying one more time that you don't have to go in there."

I look across the yard at where Alexei stands, waiting by the car. "That's why I'm saying that I do."

The car is older than we are. By a lot. I imagine the CIA probably stashed it here about the same time the Berlin Wall came down. But it's ours now, and we're grateful to have it.

Alexei is silent as he drives. The stick shift is rusty and the gears grind as we crest the hill and look down at the stark gray building that lies in the small valley.

He's stoic and calm, utterly competent in all that he does. Even this—driving a car that's twice as old as he is, down a beat-up road, on his way to confront the woman he used to love—seems natural for him. I almost wish he'd mess up, skip a beat. Times like this it would be nice to have proof that he is human.

But we both stay quiet as we reach the valley and drive toward the chain-link fences.

The guards meet us in the road. We're still thirty feet from the gates, and these guys are excited. I guess they don't see a lot of action. Today is special, I can tell. They're going to replay this interaction for years, or so it seems, as Alexei slowly cranks down the dirty window on the driver's side of the car.

"*Zdravstvujtye*," Alexei says.

The guards rattle off something in Russian, the words like a blur I can't even start to understand, but I nod and smile and try to act like it's also my mother tongue.

Alexei makes a terse reply, but I tell myself that doesn't mean much. Everything sounds terse in Russian.

Then one of the guards snaps something, hand outstretched, and I know he's asking for our papers, our IDs. I know this is the point of no return. I could tell Alexei to turn around. We can still pretend we're just a couple of kids out for a drive, lost and looking for a thrill.

We can still turn back.

Alexei looks at me, our gazes lock, and I know what this is costing him. I also know he's not here for himself or his mother. He's here for me.

The guard grunts something and holds his hand out again, so I nod at Alexei.

Alexei hands him his passport. It's a black one, but these guys don't know the significance of that, that Alexei is important, protected. They just look at each other as if they're not quite sure what to do.

They stop arguing after a minute and just stare at us.

Alexei rattles something off—I'm pretty sure it's the Russian equivalent of *Well, what are you waiting for?* But the guards just snicker. One of them leans down, rests an elbow in the open window, and eyes the two of us. When he speaks again, I don't have to be fluent in Russian to know what he's saying.

I know exactly what I'm doing as I pull a wad of cash out of my pocket and shove it in the guard's direction.

He straightens and counts it, smiles as he hands Alexei back his passport, then waves at his friends to let us in.

"Do I want to know how much that just cost us?" Alexei asks under his breath as we drive through the gates.

He doesn't know that there is no price I wouldn't pay for answers.

"Did he believe who you were?" I ask.

"He didn't care."

Alexei parks, and we start toward the doors. The steps are cold and hard—just like the building. Just like the sky. I don't even know that this place needs walls. Anyone who lives here probably gave up the will to fight ages ago.

"Gracie?"

It's only when Alexei speaks that I realize how long I've been standing on the threshold. Alexei's holding the door open, but I haven't moved a muscle.

"I can go alone," he tells me. He knows.

"No." I shake my head. My hands tremble. Then my hands are caught by Alexei. He holds them tight, sandwiching them between both of his, warming my fingers, then bringing them to his lips.

"I have you," he says.

He should be the one who is shaking. I should be telling him that he doesn't have to do this. I shouldn't make him go. Through these doors waits the mother he hasn't seen in ages. I can't quite blame him for not wanting to face her. Some things are better left as secrets. Some people are better off as ghosts.

But I smile up and step inside, wait for the slamming of the door, the ominous click.

"Alexei?" I ask.

"Yes?"

"What did they tell you? When your mother went away."

Alexei puts his hand at my back, urges me forward. "They told me men don't cry."

I stop and spin on him. "You were just a kid."

Blue eyes find mine. "I am Russian."

When Alexei starts down the hall, I'm by his side. There is no sense in arguing, in telling him that it's okay to cry. It's not okay sometimes—I know that. After all, one time I cried so hard and for so long that I ended up in a place like this.

I'm trying not to think about that when a man appears in the doorway in front of us, a smirk across his face.

He wears a gray suit and has a very thin mustache and looks like the villain in an Agatha Christie novel. I half expect him to swing a greatcoat around his shoulders and try to kill us both with a sword he keeps hidden in an umbrella.

I ease closer to Alexei.

"I was told that we had guests," the man says. I don't know how he knows that we speak English, and I don't ask.

Or care.

"We are here to see Karina Volkov," Alexei says. He doesn't say *my mother.*

The man with the mustache looks like he finds this amusing. "I am Viktor Krupin. Welcome to Binevale. I am the director of this facility. It is not often that people drive willingly through our gates."

"We would not have come were it not important. My mother is Karina Volkov. I need to see her. Please."

"Oh, I'm afraid we have no patients by that name." He eyes us skeptically. "And we have no patients who receive guests."

"I'm her son," Alexei says. It feels like this admission costs him, like it's something he's spent years hiding, even from himself.

Viktor shakes his head. "You will not find your mother here."

When I look up at Alexei, I can see the truth of those words reflected in his eyes.

Alexei's mother *isn't* here. She is a dream of his that has been dead for a very long time. But the Karina who lives here has answers. It's that Karina I'm desperate to see.

"This woman." Alexei takes out a phone and shows Viktor the picture Megan took. It's cropped, and even through the fence the woman's face is clear.

"We need to see her," Alexei says.

But Viktor shakes his head. He lets his gaze slide onto me.

"That is impossible."

I don't miss a beat. I just ask, "How much?"

"Excuse me?" Viktor almost succeeds in acting confused.

"How much to speak to the woman in that picture?"

"There is no amount of money that would make such a thing possible." He sounds smug and indignant, but it's an act. I can tell.

Alexei must think so, too, because he rattles off a string of Russian that I can't hope to understand.

Viktor's gaze narrows. He practically glares. *"Nyet."*

Alexei is just opening his mouth to reply when I step forward. "Who is she?" I ask.

Viktor seems confused by the question. "Excuse me?"

"If that woman isn't Karina Volkov, then who is she?"

There's a glimmer in Viktor's eye, as if one of us has finally stumbled upon the right question.

I watch him weigh it, considering. I have no idea what he wants to say, because at just that moment, a woman's voice asks, "Viktor?" Her accent is thick.

"If you will excuse me," Viktor says, then turns and goes to her. They whisper low and close. I look at Alexei, but even he can't understand what's going on.

I don't recognize the look on Viktor's face as he turns back to us. "It seems I was mistaken. If you will come this way . . ."

I can imagine Megan sitting behind a laptop somewhere, easing her way into whatever ancient system keeps this place running, telling them to let us in.

Alexei must be imagining it, too, because he whispers, "Megan?"

"That's my bet," I say as we climb the stairs.

When we reach the second floor, the lights are harsher, the smell of chemicals stronger. The floor beneath us is white-tiled and ancient, and our footsteps echo down the long, cold hall.

When Viktor reaches a pair of heavy doors, we pause. Thick, filthy windows show a blurry outline of life on the other side. Viktor looks through a slot beside the doors and says something in Russian. A few seconds later, they open with an ominous creak. I don't jump until we're on the other side and the doors slam shut.

I already know what life is like on this side.

Megan was right. This place was built like a fortress, but everywhere I look there are signs of decay. Floor tiles are missing and water stains cover the ceiling like a dingy patchwork quilt. There's cardboard duct-taped over a part of one grimy window.

Somewhere, someone sings a song in Russian. It sounds sad and off-key. Water drips from a pipe, an ominous, rhythmic tick that feels almost like a bomb.

But the thing I notice most—the thing that makes me tremble—is the screaming.

"Gracie?" Alexei asks.

"I'm okay," I tell him.

He turns, and I know he's hearing what I'm hearing. I'm pretty sure he's thinking what I'm thinking.

"I would not blame you if you left. I can ask your questions."

"No," I say, and walk on, following Viktor past an empty room. The door is open and the sheets are mussed. Restraints dangle empty from the headboard, waiting for someone to return.

"You are not okay," Alexei says, taking my shoulders and turning me from the room.

"I am," I say. "I will be."

"You don't have to be strong for me," he says, and he's sweet to think it. But he's wrong. I have to be strong for *me*. It's a lesson

142

I learned three years ago. It's a lesson that someday—just for an hour or two—I'd love to be able to forget.

He takes my hand. "I have you," he says again.

I look up. Smile.

We have each other.

As we start down the hall again, I admit, "It wasn't like this. I mean, it was. But nicer. Cleaner," I say as, in the distance, someone screams.

"It wasn't like this," I say, and I know it's not a lie.

There, I was the one who was screaming.

When we reach the end of the hall, Viktor pauses beside a door, takes a key from his pocket, and turns the lock. He gestures us inside.

There's no bed in this room. No dresser. Just a table and a few chairs.

"You may wait here," he says. "I'll go see that she is escorted to this room."

He closes the door behind him but doesn't lock it.

I'm not sure how long we wait. There's no clock in the room, and the sky is so gray there's no use tracking the sun.

"Maybe she's sleeping," I say. "Or having therapy or something."

"Do you honestly think this place offers therapy?" he asks.

I don't, but still I shrug and say, "Well, maybe—"

Alexei gets up so quickly his metal chair crashes to the floor. "We should go."

"We just got here," I say.

"We've been here for more than an hour. Something isn't right. We should leave. Now."

In my mind I know he's right, but in my heart I can't bring myself to move.

"Something is wrong, Gracie. This feels wrong. My gut is telling me . . . Jamie says to trust your gut."

Mentioning Jamie is a low blow, but it works. I'm turning toward the door when I hear . . .

"Hello, there."

There's a woman in the doorway. I know her from Megan's photo, but I would never have recognized her as my mother's old friend. She wears a dirty, threadbare robe over some kind of nightgown. On her feet are army boots. Her hair is dirty and pulled back in a pink plastic headband. But the most surreal thing is the expression on her face. She is smiling, bright and wild. She's like a child on Christmas morning, getting her first look under the tree.

"They said that I had visitors." She brings her hands together. "I love visitors!"

Her voice is high, with a singsong lilt. I doubt she's had a visitor in years, but now isn't the time to say so, because she's rushing forward, exclaiming, "I never dreamed it would be you!"

I expect her to hurl herself across the room and into Alexei's strong arms. I think she's going to cry big fat tears of joy to finally be back with her only child. But Karina rushes right at me instead.

"I thought I'd never see you again. I . . ." She eases closer, looks at my face like I'm a painting in a gallery, as if every brushstroke matters. "It's really you."

I look at Alexci. Worry grows inside of me but turns to panic when his mother dips into a clumsy curtsy and says, "I am beyond honored, Your Highness."

CHAPTER
FOURTEEN

I know I'm not crazy. Not really. Dr. Rainier says that I was trau-
matized, confused. I was hurt in both body and soul by what
happened three years ago. And I'll be better someday. Maybe. I
spent years not knowing what was real and what was imagined.
Truth and fiction are a spectrum, you see. And I am slowly,
surely, trying to crawl back to the other side.

But that's not true for Karina.

It's not just the glossy look in her eyes, the vacant smile and
messy hair. She's entrenched on the wrong side of reality. She's
been too deep for too long, and I don't know that there is any way
to get her out.

She's rising from her shaky curtsy, her smile too bright as she
exclaims, "The heir is here! The heir lives!"

"I'm . . . no!" I exclaim, partly because it isn't something I like being reminded of. Partly because the last thing I need is for the rest of the world to hear her.

"Amelia—"

"No!" I snap, and grasp her by the arms. "I'm not the heir. Mrs. Volkov—Karina—I am Grace. Grace Blakely. Do you know who I am?"

Alexei's mother goes silent and still. It's scary how drastically she changes. She tilts her head, as if studying me. It's like I'm a noise in a distant room, trying to pull her from a dream.

For a second, she sees me. I can tell by the tilt of her head, the look in her eye. Then her gaze shifts onto Alexei, and the curtain falls again.

"Karina," I try, but she reaches out for both of my hands, makes me twirl around like we're a pair of girls playing outside on the first pretty day of the year. But we're not outside. We're surrounded by four dirty cinder-block walls and there are bars on the windows. The sky outside is dull and gray.

But Karina doesn't notice, doesn't care. She just starts to sing.

" 'Hush, little princess, dead and gone. No one's gonna know you're coming home.' "

"Karina, please. I need to ask you about Caroline."

" 'Hush, little princess, wait and see. No one's gonna know that you are me!' "

"Karina!" I yell, but it's like she doesn't hear me. I risk looking at Alexei. I expect disappointment, maybe fear. But his face is frozen, like he's incapable of feeling anything anymore as his mother keeps dancing.

"Karina, I need to talk to you, please. We came a long way to talk to you."

She leans close, as if to share a secret, then sings, " *'Hush, little princess, it's too late. The truth is locked behind the gates.'* "

This stops me. I know this song. My mother used to sing it when I was a little girl. It's the "Ring-Around-the-Rosy" of Adria—everyone knows it; all the children sing it. It is the chorus of my childhood.

There are lots of different versions with minor changes— different words used here or there. But I have never in my life heard this verse.

I stop and look at Alexei.

" *'Hush, little princess, pretty babe. The sunlight shines where the truth is laid! Hush, little—' * "

"Shut up!" Alexei's shout fills the room, and Karina stops singing. Slowly, she turns to her son, almost like she's just now realized that he's here.

She stands up a little taller, smiles a little brighter. "You are very handsome," she says. Then she turns to me, whispers, "Isn't he handsome?"

I glance at her son. There's no denying the truth. "Yes. He is."

"Is he yours?" Karina asks, and I can't help myself. I look at Alexei, not quite certain of the answer. I almost miss the tear that falls from the corner of her eye as she says, "I used to have a boy who was handsome."

Is she thinking about Alexei? About Alexei's father? There are so many things I want to know, but I feel like answers are precious and Karina will only grant a few.

I'm just getting ready to ask about Alexei when he says, "Do you know her?" and points to me.

The dreamy smile is back. Karina starts to curtsy. "The heir has risen. The heir has returned."

But before she dips down again, Alexei grabs her arms.

He's being too rough, and she's too fragile. Her mind and her body. Alexei has never really known his own strength.

"Do you know her?" he demands. "Did you talk to her mother?"

"Alexei," I reach for his hands, try to pull his fingers free of his mother's arms.

"Do you know her?" he asks, and Karina smiles up at him, at me.

"Of course." She stumbles back as he lets her go. "It's so good to see you again, Caroline. I have missed you so."

I didn't realize that she could move so fast, that she might be so strong. But before I can really process what she's said, she lunges toward me, pulls me into the world's most awkward hug.

And somehow I know it's the first touch of kindness that she's felt in years. I let myself sink into the hug, trying not to think about how rare they are in a place like this.

"I missed you," Karina whispers.

"I . . ." I pull back and glance at Alexei. "I missed you, too. You know, I was trying to remember—when was the last time I saw you?"

Gently, Karina pulls away, like a child trying to keep from having to admit she hasn't cleaned their room. She goes to one of the grimy windows, looks out at the gray sky and barren land.

Softly, she sings, " *'Hush, little princess . . .'* "

I don't want to look at Alexei. I don't want to take the chance that seeing this might break him, too.

"Karina, I need to talk to you about the last time I was here," I say, but she doesn't turn.

" *'Hush, little princess . . .'* "

"Karina!" I say, louder, sharper. I need her to turn, to focus, to *think*. "Karina, do you——"

"That's peculiar," she says when she stops singing.

Her gaze is locked on the filthy window, but I'm pretty sure Karina's looking into the past.

"*Posmotri na menya!*" Alexei blurts.

His mother turns. Her words are so fast and so frantic that I can't hope to follow.

"What?" I ask. "What did she say?"

Alexei shakes his head. "She's talking crazy."

"What did she say?" I have to know.

Alexei looks defeated, and for the first time I realize that I wasn't the only one who had come here looking for answers. He just hadn't realized it himself.

He takes a slow, deep breath, almost like the words hurt. "She said they're going to storm the gates and kill the heir. She thinks it's two hundred years ago, Gracie. And she thinks you're your mom. We should go. She can't help us."

Alexei's already turning, starting for the door, when it opens. Viktor's standing there, an orderly right behind him.

"She just got here," I say. I can't let him take Karina away, not when all we've gotten so far are more questions. "You can't make us leave yet."

Karina is still at the window, singing, " 'Hush, little princess . . .' "

"We're not leaving," I say again.

"I quite agree," Viktor says. "You're not going anywhere."

Maybe I'm just too stressed—too tired—but what happens next happens in a flash, and yet it also feels like slow motion.

The man behind Viktor is massive. He wears dingy gray scrubs, and when he pushes past Viktor, toward me, it's almost like a tornado bearing down. But he never reaches me. Alexei blasts across the room, leaping and catching the massive orderly in midair, the two of them crashing to the floor in what feels like a blur of hits and kicks.

The man is strong. He's huge. But Alexei has something to fight for. And I realize with a start that the something is *me*.

I watch him twist, launching himself over the bigger man, and in a flash Alexei has his arms around his neck and he's squeezing.

"Alexei!"

Just a few weeks ago, most of the world thought Alexei was a killer. I never thought it possible—never thought him capable—

until now. Jamie told me once that Alexei's father was some kind of Russian special forces—that Alexei was the only kid who could ever keep up with the son of an Army Ranger. Only now do I see what he meant. He's not the perfect boy next door anymore. He's the guy my grandfather warned me about as he staggers upright, the orderly's head and neck gripped too tightly in his grasp.

"Alexei, no!" I snap. Alexei sees me, and a new terror fills his eyes as his gaze shifts.

"Gracie!" he shouts, and I turn to see Viktor behind me. There's a syringe in his hand, and a new terror fills me.

I don't know what drug it is, but my body can feel it long before the syringe touches my skin. I know the foggy haze that it will bring, the sense of floating, distant and free. And I know that it's not right—not real. I know that whatever peace that syringe might bring me would be a lie—would be worse. I know that I don't belong in a place like this. Not anymore. I may be crazy, but I'm not insane, so I lash out, kicking and clawing like a fiend.

Like a madwoman.

The orderly slumps as Alexei cuts off his air, but I can't stop to think about that. Viktor swings his arm down, wielding the syringe like an ax. I throw my hands up, catching his wrist with both hands, pressing up as he presses down.

Viktor mutters something under his breath. I don't speak the language, but I know what he's saying. That I'm reckless. That I'm dangerous. That I should just shut up and be the meek little girl that would make the world so much more comfortable for the likes of him.

But I'm not that girl. And I never, ever will be.

I'm the lost freaking princess of Adria, and I'm not going to take it anymore.

The orderly's on the ground, and Alexei's jumping the man's body, coming in my direction, but I don't wait. Viktor lunges toward me, one last-ditch feat of strength, and I use his force and his weight against him, spinning like my father taught me long ago, twisting Viktor's arm back until the syringe lands in his own leg. I hear his cry. I see the pain in his eyes. But I just reach for the plunger and push until that pain is erased by a mindless, empty bliss.

Slowly, he slumps, falling to the floor.

I look down but don't have time to think about what's just happened. Alexei grabs me, makes me look into his eyes.

"Are you okay?" he asks. I could ask him the same thing. There's a scratch on his face, a growing bruise. But we're both still here and we're still breathing.

Then I remember the bad part: *We're still here.*

"I told you they were storming the gates," a voice says from the window, and I look at Karina.

Alexei moves to the window and lets out a Russian curse when he see what's going on outside.

I already know even before I look out and see it for myself. Dust clouds fill the road, kicked up by a convoy of SUVs.

"Well, I guess now we know why they changed their minds and let us in," I say.

"Yes. And why they insisted that we wait so long," Alexei says, but he's not waiting anymore.

He grabs my hand, tugging me toward the door. "We must leave. Now!"

"But, Alexei—" I turn back to his mother, who is running her hand along the cinder-block wall.

" 'Hush, little princess . . .' "

"We must leave her," he says.

"But . . ."

I don't get to argue. There's no time to fight. Because just as I open my mouth to speak, a blast shakes the room, throwing me off of my feet and into Alexei, who grabs me and then presses me to the floor, shielding me with his body as dust and debris cloud the air. I'm choking, gagging, as I hear a familiar voice say, "I told you there were explosives."

Rosie looks larger than usual as she stands silhouetted against the gray sky, surrounded by a cloud of dust. She's a conquering hero. And she's not taking any prisoners.

"What are you two waiting for? We've got to go. Now!"

The caravan of SUVs is at the gates, but the guards are nowhere to be seen. The gates are wide-open and they're coming in fast.

"Now!" Rosie shouts again, and then jumps. I run to the hole in the wall only to notice for the first time that there's a roof not far below. There must be a single-story section of the hospital because Rosie is running across the roof, then climbing down a ladder that leads to the back of the facility.

"Go, Gracie. Now." Alexei is trying to push me outside, but I look back at the woman who is still behind us, singing and swaying in the dust.

There's no time to argue. Alexei just spins and walks toward his mother, sweeps her up into his arms, and runs in my direction, climbing through the hole in the wall that Rosie left in her wake.

As they pass I hear Karina say, "Your boy really is handsome."

And then I climb through the hole in the wall and join them.

There are shouts from the hired guns that fill the courtyard. Echoing cries fill the halls, and I know that some of the men are already inside, racing up the stairs.

They'll reach us soon, see the room is empty and follow, so I run faster. Alexei is guiding Karina down the ladder when I see the huge SUV that is waiting for us.

"We borrowed it," Rosie says, and I don't ask any questions. We all just run toward the doors that are already open. The engine is running and Megan is behind the wheel.

"Hold on," she says once we're all inside. If they're surprised by Karina's presence, no one says so.

The SUV spins out, kicking up rocks and dirt and gravel, then fishtails as it pulls around the side of the compound.

The guardhouse is empty. The yard is abandoned. Four huge SUVs surround the tiny car that brought Alexei and me here, blocking us in. The men must all be inside, and a clock in my head is counting down the seconds until they realize that we're gone.

We're going to have to go fast.

We're going to have to go far.

We're going to have to keep running until we run out of earth. That's the only way.

"They'll find us," I say, the words spilling from my mouth. "They'll chase us and they'll find us and—"

"They're not going to chase us," Noah tells me.

"Of course they are!" I shout. "They will never stop chasing me. You guys have got to leave. It's too dangerous. I'm too dangerous. You've got to—"

"We have a Plan B," Megan says.

"What's Plan B?" I ask just as, behind us, a huge boom rings out. When I turn, I see black smoke filling the air. The little car that Alexei and I arrived in is now an inferno. Flaming debris fills the yard. Windshields are smashed. Tires are flattened. The smoke is blinding anyone who might be running out the front door. Even the roof of the little guard shack is starting to burn.

I'm almost numb as I turn to Rosie.

"That's Plan B," she says, and Megan keeps driving.

CHAPTER FIFTEEN

Sometime after midnight we cross the Adrian border, or so Megan's super secret spy phone tells us. I can also tell because that's when I start shaking.

We're still hours from Valancia, and the countryside around us is vast and empty. We should be safe here. There's no Internet, no cameras. No nosy innkeepers or customs officials asking us for papers. I swear none of us will ever use our real names ever again if we survive this.

I don't stop to think about how big that *if* really is.

There's a big barn up ahead, but no farmhouse. No town. There's not a single telephone pole in sight. Bright headlights slice across an empty field when Noah steers the SUV off the road and pulls up to the barn's big double doors.

"Wait. What are you doing?" I ask, leaning up between the two front seats.

"We're stopping," Noah says.

"No," I tell him. "We can't stop. Ever. We have to keep driving."

It's late, and we're all tired. It takes Noah's last ounce of patience to calmly ask, "Okay. Where are we driving *to*? And what are we going to do when we get there?"

He's got a point, and I'm too tired to disagree. But that doesn't mean I have to like it.

"Megan?" I don't even have to ask the question.

"If the royal family is after you, then we should be okay here. Adria is more into tourism than national defense. They don't exactly have a bunch of satellites they can reposition on a whim to track us down. So . . . we *should* be okay," she says again.

"And if it's not the royal family?" Alexei asks what everyone else is thinking.

Megan gives a sad, almost hopeless shrug. "I have no idea what the Society is capable of."

None of us do, and that's the scariest thing of all.

Inside the barn, we find bales of straw stacked on one end and park the SUV on the other. It doesn't take long for us to spread out—we've been too confined for too long. At least Noah loaded up some canned food from the safe house, and now he and Rosie are trying to build a small fire in a ring of stones just outside the barn's double doors.

I watch them work together in silence, in peace. We're all getting way too comfortable with life like this.

Noah catches me looking and grins. Then he stands and wipes his dirty hands on his jeans and sidles toward me. He turns to see what I see—Rosie and the flickering flames, a dark night under a blanket of thick clouds, lightning striking in the distance. Wordlessly, he settles in beside me, leaning against the SUV.

We feel the rain before we see it. The wind turns crisp in a second and water falls to the dusty ground in fat, wet drops. Dust bubbles up, then turns to mud before our eyes. The storm rages and the wind blows and I breathe in the cool, fresh air. For a second, I relax, lost inside the thunder.

Maybe Noah feels it, too. Maybe that's how he finds the strength to say, "So I was going to ask how Alexei's mom was, but . . ." Noah gestures outside to where Karina is standing, staring up at the dark clouds, rain streaming down her smiling face.

"She thinks I'm my mom. Or she thought that earlier. I don't really know what she's thinking now, to tell you the truth."

Noah nods. "I can see that. About your mom, I mean. In every picture that I've ever seen, you look alike. I can see where that might be confusing to . . ." He motions to the woman who's outside, dancing in the rain.

"I doubt she even knows what year it is," I have to admit. "I dragged everyone across half of Europe, and she doesn't know anything about my mom." I look up at Noah. "She doesn't even know Alexei."

I'm pretty sure Noah curses in Portuguese, but then he eyes

159

me. "Don't worry about Alexei. He's worried about *you*. He doesn't care what happens to him."

I look at Noah, cock an eyebrow, and he knows I'm not buying it. "Would you care if your mother didn't recognize you? If she acted like you never existed?"

Noah stares into the distance. "I'm not Russian."

I don't argue with Noah's logic. It makes as much sense as anything.

"At least now he knows she didn't leave him—that she was sick and had to go away," I say, almost hopefully.

Noah is spinning on me, though, a disbelieving look upon his face. "Is that really what you think?"

"What?"

Noah turns back to the woman who's holding her arms out wide, turning in circles in the rain. "Maybe she went to that place because she was crazy. Or maybe ten years in that place *made* her insane. What do you think?"

He's not asking my opinion about Karina. He's asking about me. What would have happened if my dad and Jamie hadn't decided to stop fighting with me—if they hadn't gotten tired of reminding me day after day that I was the one who pulled the trigger? Would I have gotten better there? Or would my last sliver of sanity have slipped further and further away with every passing day? It's something I've never really considered. And, frankly, it's an answer I don't really want to know.

Noah can tell. So he just nods again in Karina's direction and asks, "Is she okay?" When I don't answer, he turns back to me. "Are you okay?"

But no one really wants the honest answer to that question, so we just turn back to the rain and the woman dancing in it.

"What comes next?" Noah isn't asking about tonight. He's asking about tomorrow. And the day after that. And the day after *that*. It's *the* question, and everyone but Karina gathers around, listens.

"Tomorrow, I'll drive you guys to the train station, and you'll go back to Embassy Row."

"What are you going to do?" Rosie sounds almost hurt—like I'm throwing a party and she hasn't been invited.

"On the bridge that day, Princess Ann kept asking me if I'd found it—if my mom had told me where it was."

"What did she mean by *it*?" Noah asks, and I shake my head.

"I'm not sure. I thought that maybe it was something Mom found on that last trip. I thought maybe . . ." I trail off but can't stop myself from looking at Karina. She might have had answers. Once. But they're locked away in some dark recess of her mind now. I know better than anyone how easy it is for a memory to stay buried.

"I have to find it," I say. "Whatever *it* is."

"Which means you have to come with us," Megan says. "You've got to go back to Valancia."

"No." I shake my head. My hands tremble and my blood pounds. "No. I can't. It's not safe there. No."

"On your mom's last trip, she saw Karina and she saw your grandfather," Noah says. I hate him for his calm, cool logic. "If there are answers, they're in Valancia."

"No. I have to keep moving." Because as long as they're chasing me, then Jamie's safe. Jamie's resting. Jamie is somewhere under Dominic's watchful eye, getting stronger every day.

They all want to argue. They want to fight. I want to climb into the SUV and start driving.

"Let's get some sleep now. Perhaps an answer will present itself in the morning," Alexei says, and we're all too tired to argue. As the others drift away, he pulls me into his arms. "You're not going anywhere without me," he whispers too low for the others to hear.

"Your name's been cleared," I say, but I don't pull away. "You can go home."

He squeezes me tighter. "I am home."

Alexei's mother is twenty feet away from us, but he never even glances her direction. He just pulls my head to his shoulder and holds me. I could cry now. I could break down—allow myself a little weakness. No one here would judge me. But I would judge myself. So I don't shed a single tear.

Alexei holds me until the fire dies and the barn seems to go to sleep around us. Even the storm seems to be drifting away, but then I hear a sound like thunder coming closer. The low rumbling is followed by the flash of headlights through the open doors, and I'm already pulling away from Alexei. I'm turning. I'm getting ready to yell for my friends to run when a car door slams and a single word slices through the storm.

162

"Grace?"

I know the voice, but I can't believe what I'm seeing when a woman steps from the shadows. Her suit is dark. Her heels are high. And the brown eyes behind her glasses are rapidly filling with tears.

"Ms. Chancellor?"

Then I realize that she's not alone. At the first sign of movement, I pull back. In a flash, Megan is running past me, rushing into the other woman's arms.

"Mom!" Megan cries, and her mother swallows her up. Megan and her mom look alike. They both have the same sleek black hair and huge brown eyes. But Megan's mom wears her hair in a sleek bob. When she tucks a strand of hair behind her ear just like I've seen Megan do a thousand times, something about it makes me want to cry.

My mom will never hug me again, never worry about me or whisper in my ear or tell me everything is going to be okay. Things will never be okay again, and I have no one but myself to blame.

So I blame everyone.

"What are you doing here?" I say.

"Grace . . ." Ms. Chancellor starts toward me slowly. She knows me well enough to know I'm looking for a fight. I don't care where it comes from. That's probably why one always finds me.

"It's my fault." Megan moves out of her mother's grasp. "I called them. I . . . We need help."

163

Megan isn't wrong, because Megan isn't stupid. But that doesn't mean I have to like it.

"No. I . . ." But I honestly don't know what I'm supposed to say. That I'm sorry. That I'm wrong. That I am the thing that goes bump in the night and they'd all be better off far, far away.

My voice cracks. My eyes fill with tears.

And then Ms. Chancellor can't be held back anymore. "Oh, Grace." She rushes toward me and pulls me into her arms. It's almost like a mother. It's almost like I'm loved. Even if I don't deserve it.

"Let me look at you," she says, pushing me gently away and eyeing me from head to toe. "Are you okay? When you ran away in Paris . . ."

"I'm okay."

"Where did you go, sweetheart? What did you—"

"Hello." Alexei's mother's hair is still wet from the rain. Her eyes are big and blue, just like her son's. But when Ms. Chancellor turns and takes her in, it's like she's looking at a ghost.

"Karina?" She's not entirely wrong. Alexei's mother is thin and pale, and the nightgown she wears beneath one of Noah's jackets is an eerie, dirty shade that probably used to be white. "Karina, where . . ."

Karina looks at Ms. Chancellor, and for a moment, there is a light in her eyes. Recognition is starting to dawn, but then it fades away again, like a sun that can't quite find the strength to rise.

Ms. Chancellor turns on me. "What have you done?" she asks, and I snap.

164

"Do they know you're here? Is that why you came?"

"Grace—"

"Is the Society trying to kill me?"

At the word *Society*, Karina shivers like someone just walked over her grave. Noah goes and slides an arm around her, leads her to the other side of the barn.

"Are they?" I persist when Ms. Chancellor's silence is too much.

"The Society is not why I'm here. Or not precisely."

"Then why?"

As soon as I've said the words, I regret them. I can see it in Ms. Chancellor's eyes. Good news never brings anyone to my door.

"Grace, your grandfather . . ."

The barn doors are open, but it's like her words suck all the air from the room. I can't stop myself from swaying, unsteady. Alexei's arm slides around my waist, anchoring me to him while Ms. Chancellor goes on.

"Sweetheart, he went to the palace, and . . ."

"They killed him," I finish for her, but Ms. Chancellor hurries to shake her head.

"No! He's alive. But they say he had a heart attack. He can't be moved, or so they claim. I haven't seen him. They won't let me see him."

Ms. Chancellor is always calm, always cool. But it's like her chocolate-colored eyes are starting to melt, and for the first time I realize what I'm seeing. This isn't a concerned member of my grandfather's staff. This is the woman who has been with him for

165

decades, working by his side, living under his roof. This is the woman who loves him, and my heart breaks just a little more.

"Why are you here?" I ask again, my voice softer.

"The Society has brokered an . . . arrangement."

The last time I saw the Society, the central question seemed to be whether they should kill me or just step aside and allow the royal family to do it. I don't have to hear about their arrangement to know that I won't like it.

"There may be a . . . solution," Ms. Chancellor says. "The Society would like for you to return to Valancia. They would like—"

"To kill me?"

"To end it," Ms. Chancellor says. "I told them where they could shove their offer, but then your grandfather . . ."

She can't finish, and I can't blame her.

"What kind of arrangement?" Alexei asks, and for the first time Ms. Chancellor seems to realize we're not alone.

"I'm not certain of the details, but Prime Minister Petrovic assures me that they have arrived upon a . . . compromise. They consider it something of a truce."

"This is the same Society that was perfectly willing to let me die just to keep the status quo in Adria," I remind her.

"Yes, dear. I know." Ms. Chancellor sounds like a woman who knows entirely too well—who'd give anything to forget.

"I don't trust them," I say.

"Oh, neither do I," Ms. Chancellor agrees.

It's too hot in the barn. There are too many people watching, too much riding on one more-screwed-up-than-average teenage girl. I want to go back to when my biggest worry was whether I could trust the Scarred Man. I want to go back in time, but I can't. So I settle for going outside.

The rain has turned to a hard, wet drizzle. Water's not really falling from the sky anymore; it simply fills the air. It's like walking into a cloud—or a fog. In a way, it's how I've been feeling for ages.

Megan's jacket is hanging on a nail by the door, and it's the most natural thing in the world to pick it up and slip it on. Outside, water clings to me, soaking my hair and chilling me to the bone, but I barely feel it. It's like I'm already numb as I ease farther and farther from the open barn doors and the light inside. I stand under the overhang of the barn's roof, staring at the wet night, thinking. And then I want to scream. I want to fight and kick and claw until the rest of the world hurts as much as I do.

I want to make it bleed.

But I can't. So I do the next best thing.

Megan's phone is heavy in my hand when I pull it from the jacket's pocket and dial the number that I wish I could forget.

As soon as the voice says hello, I know it's a mistake. But I've always been my own worst enemy, and that, of course, is saying something.

"Where is he?"

Princess Ann's cold laugh fills the line. "In a hurry, Grace? I suppose that makes sense. It's foolish of you to call, you know. This can be traced. You're being careless."

My carelessness is the least of her problems, and of mine.

"If you hurt him, I will kill you," I say. My voice is calm and even. "And, just so you know, that's not a threat. This isn't the frantic ranting of a delusional girl. I'm not talking crazy, Your Highness. *I am crazy.* And if you harm my grandfather in any way—if even one snow-white hair is out of place, I will hunt you for the rest of my life. And I will kill you."

At the other end of the line, Ann giggles. For a moment, she sounds like the girl who used to be my mother's best friend. She seems like the person in the photos that my mom kept all those years. But just that quickly, that girl is gone.

"Oh, Grace—" she starts, but I don't let her finish.

"And then I'll kill your son."

A different kind of silence fills the line now. Ann isn't laughing anymore.

"We want the same things, Grace," she tries, but I shake my head. Finally, it's my turn to laugh.

"I find that incredibly hard to believe."

"We both want you to be safe and happy. We want you to be able to stop running."

"You're right," I tell her. "I do want to stop running. Maybe I should just go ahead and kill you, hurry this process along."

"Oh, Grace. What good would that do? I'm not in line for the throne, and you're no killer," Ann tells me, but she's wrong.

I *am* a killer. And I know it. What I did to my mom was an accident, but does that make any difference? My soul is already charred, my moral account overdrawn. Would one more death really matter? Would two? Maybe I should set Valancia on fire—burn the whole world down. Maybe then I could stop running.

"You people are going to let him go," I tell her.

"Oh, are we?" Ann says.

"You are if you don't want the world to find out that you aren't the rightful rulers of Adria."

I don't want to be a princess. I don't want the spotlight and the chaos and the duty. But more than that, I want the people I love to be safe, and I'll do whatever it takes to make it happen. Even this.

"That would be a very hard thing to prove," Ann tells me.

"But not impossible." Even as I say the words, I know they're true. "If it were impossible to prove, then none of this would be happening. My mother *found proof*, and you're terrified I'm going to use it to expose you all."

"Do you have it?" Panic fills Ann's voice.

"Release my grandfather and you won't have to find out."

A long pause fills the line until Ann laughs again. "Oh, Grace. You always were a bright girl. Foolish, but bright."

"You're right. I am foolish. But the truth is, it doesn't matter if you trace this call. I'm through running, but you might want to hide. You took my grandfather, and now I am coming for you."

"Oh, Grace. Why would you do that when there is a far easier solution?"

I'm pretty sure that's how the serpent sounded in the Garden of Eden. I'm starting to feel a lot like Eve, and yet I can't help but snap, "What?"

I don't believe her. I'll never, ever trust her. But I'm not going to lie awake all night, wondering what she might have said. I've had enough what-ifs for a lifetime.

Still, the last thing I expect is for Ann to say, "Come home, Grace. Come home and meet me and we'll discuss it."

It takes a moment to be certain that I haven't misheard.

"I might be crazy, but I'm not stupid," I tell her.

"Talk to Ms. Chancellor, then. Ask her what you should do."

"Gracie?"

Alexei is standing in the rain that's falling harder now.

"Gracie, who is on the phone?"

I don't say another word to Ann. I just hang up. She doesn't deserve a good-bye.

Alexei inches closer to me. He's afraid, I can tell. But I don't stop to explain.

"Ann," I admit. "She said there's a solution." It's supposed to give me hope—the thought that there's a way out—but it doesn't. I'm too numb to feel anything anymore. Hope isn't an option for me.

I can hear Alexei breathing; I can almost hear him thinking. It's like he knows I'm standing on the threshold of a very bad idea.

"Grace, they can't be trusted," he says, and he's right.

But I can't help smiling when I look at him. "Neither can I."

CHAPTER SIXTEEN

The wall that circles Valancia is a thousand years old, still tall and wide and solid. They call it one of the Wonders of the World, and it brings tourists here by the thousands. Ironic, considering that once upon a time it was built to keep people *out*.

Guard towers peek up at regular intervals. In a place or two, tourists can pay to climb to the top and stand with the sun on their faces as the wind blows off the sea. I know exactly how that feels, rising like a bird above the city, nothing between you and the horizon.

When I was little, I used to spend my summers chasing Jamie and Alexei up onto the wall.

When I was twelve, I jumped off, just to prove I could.

And now I'm back, wind on my face, sun at my back, on the verge of doing something stupid.

"You're gonna be fine," Megan says. We're standing on top of the German embassy. From here, it's literally a hop, skip, and a jump onto the wall itself. This is as far as my friends can follow.

"I wish you'd let us come with you," Megan says.

"I'm supposed to go alone," I say, just like I've been saying for the past twelve hours.

Once again, Rosie rolls her eyes. "Yes, and *that* has never ended badly."

"Guys." I look around at the group: Noah and Alexei both seem ready to start a fight; Megan and Rosie seem ready to end one. "I'll be fine. And if I'm not . . . then at least it's over."

"Don't." Alexei grabs my hand before I can turn and jump onto the wall. "Don't joke about that," he says, pulling me into the safety of his arms.

I don't dare tell him I'm not joking.

"I'll be fine," I say again, and then I reach up and kiss him, lingering a little longer than I should, savoring the feel of his freshly shaven cheek against my lips. I want to stay here and breathe him in, pretend that I'm the kind of girl who gets a happy ending. But I can't, so I make myself pull away.

I don't look back, but when I jump onto the wall I know that I'm alone. I should get bonus points for following directions. It goes against my very nature, after all. I don't want to be here; I don't want to do this. But, most of all, I don't want any more blood on my hands, so I keep walking, and when the wall curves, climbing up the hill, I know I'm out of sight.

I am entirely alone when I hear her.

"Hello, Grace."

The prime minister is in black today. I wonder if she's come straight from a funeral. Or maybe she's dressed for mine.

"Thank you for coming," she tells me. It's all I can do not to roll my eyes.

"I didn't come for you."

"Of course." The PM smirks, as if she's allowing me the indulgence of my indignation. "I'm sorry about Paris, Grace. I should have explained the situation to you more clearly."

"You mean before you drugged and kidnapped me? Don't bother."

"This situation affects us all. It, in fact, affects the world. And the stability of that world is no laughing matter."

"Do I look like I'm laughing?" I snap back.

"We only want to help," she says, and now I do laugh.

"You mean the kind of help that might keep me from being hunted down like a rabid dog?"

Her gaze hardens and she talks on. "I'm glad you're here. We have a solution that will make this problem go away and please everyone in the long run, I believe."

"Everyone?" I don't mask the sarcasm that I feel.

"Yes," the PM says. *"Everyone."*

Just as she says the word, a figure appears over her shoulder.

I don't know who arranged to close the wall today, but it's totally free of tourists. We're alone when Princess Ann speaks.

"Hello, Grace. Thank you for coming."

"Sure," I say. "I mean, we all have to die sometime, don't we?"

I hope she remembers my vow, but she doesn't show it. She just nods at the PM, and it's clear the two of them have already talked this through. The only problem is me.

What else is new?

"But that's just it, Grace." Ann steps closer, as if she has to make me see. Instinctively, I step back, and she halts. The last thing either of them wants is for me to start jumping off walls again.

Ann shakes her head. She almost looks like Mom's best friend. "Nobody wants you to die."

I almost believe her.

But then I remember.

"The men who attacked my friends yesterday in Dubrovnia didn't seem to agree. Were they yours?" I ask Ann. Then I turn to the PM. "Or maybe they worked for the Society."

"You're at risk, Grace," Ann says. "Your brother is at risk."

"Jamie's dead," I say, the words automatic now. But neither of the women on the wall are fazed. I'm not surprised they don't believe me.

"It doesn't matter." Ann gives a shrug. "As long as Amelia's descendants survive, there remains a . . . problem."

"And you think killing me and my brother is going to solve it?" I want to laugh. "Amelia lived two hundred years ago. There have got to be other descendants. Probably dozens. Maybe hundreds. Are you going to kill us all?"

"Wars have raged since then, Grace. Time has passed. Perhaps there are other descendants. Or maybe you and your brother are the end of the line."

"Jamie's dead," I repeat.

"For your sake," Ann says, studying me, "I almost hope that's true."

Suddenly, I'm too hot. The sun is too bright. I don't want to be here. I want to turn and run all the way around the great walled city. I want to jump into the sea and swim away.

"What do you want?" I ask.

At this, Ann and Prime Minister Petrovic share a look.

"Your mother was the only child of an only child of an oldest child. We know this. We can trace her line back to Amelia. What we want is for *your* oldest child to sit on the throne of Adria," the PM says, as if it is the most obvious thing in the world.

"I thought the Society wanted to maintain a stable Europe?" I challenge.

But the PM is undaunted. "That is precisely what we want. And we intend to have it."

They're talking crazy, and I'm losing patience. "Say what you came here to say or I'm going to go ahead and kill you no matter what."

I'm not prepared to hear Ann laugh. "Oh, Grace. You do have spirit. I hope my grandchildren inherit that from you."

For a second I just stand atop the wall, stunned. And even as the words sink in, they still don't quite make sense.

"You're crazy," I tell her, then turn to the PM. "She's crazy. I'm serious. I think she is insane. And I'm something of an expert on the topic."

"I assure you, Grace," the PM says, "this matter is utterly serious. Hear her out. *Please*." She almost chokes on the word.

"Amelia's heir belongs on Adria's throne, Grace," Ann tells me, stopping only briefly to push her hair out of her face as the wind blows harder. "I've always wanted that. When I was a girl I wanted it more than anything. I still do. For a time, it seemed that *I* was Amelia's heir, and I started trying to right this wrong then. I met the prince. I married the prince. Your mother and Karina and I . . . we thought we'd solved the problem. But I was the wrong princess." The words are so surreal, so . . . crazy. I can't quite believe this is happening when she says, "You are the *right* princess, and I want to end this. Now."

"End it how?" I ask.

Ann smiles and shakes her head as if the answer should be the most obvious thing ever. "If Amelia's heir marries the crown prince, then we are one generation from Amelia's bloodline returning to its rightful place. All we need is a marriage. And a baby."

"Baby?" I look at the PM. "Did she just say *baby*?"

"It is a tidy solution," the PM says.

"You're both crazy."

"Grace, wait!" PM Petrovic calls out to me before I can leave. Or fight. Or . . . jump. The wind is in my face now, slapping me awake.

"Ann married the prince to put Amelia's heir upon the throne. Now it is up to you to do the same."

I know that she's not joking—Prime Minister Petrovic doesn't tease. But the earnest expressions that greet me don't belong here. Someone's playing a joke. Even if it is God.

"Please, Grace," Ann says. "Let us end it."

I look at the PM. "It would be best for everyone. For you. For your brother. For whatever children either of you might have," she says.

"And the line in the constitution about what would happen if Amelia or her heirs were to show up? We're supposed to forget about that, are we? If I'm right, your job would go away, wouldn't it?" I ask the PM.

"Do you want anarchy?" she asks. It's almost like a dare.

"I want a nap, Ms. Petrovic. I want a shower and the chance to wake up in the morning not terrified that someone's gonna try to kill me. Again."

She nods. "This plan gives you that, Grace. We can draw up papers. Your brother can abdicate the throne. And within a few years the succession will be secure. Amelia's bloodline will be merged with the current royal family, and this will never be a problem again."

"Okay. Fine. Then draw the papers up for me. Let *me* abdicate, too!"

"No." PM Petrovic shakes her head. "As you said, there may be other heirs. There no doubt *are* other heirs. This needs to end,

Grace. You need to end it. Put Amelia's bloodline back where it belongs."

"Bloodlines! You're talking to me about bloodlines! As if I'm . . . livestock. How can you both stand there and talk about *breeding* me as if that's all I'm good for?"

Ann actually smirks—she smiles—but there's no joy in it. "Welcome to life as a princess."

They're serious, I realize. They're crazy, but they are also 100 percent serious. And I should be, too.

Two hundred years ago rebels threw open the palace gates and massacred a family and changed the kingdom. The world. Somehow, that's brought me here, two centuries later. I think about the king and queen whose bodies hung from the palace windows, a cautionary tale. And then I think about my mother, about my brother's friend. And Grandpa.

Centuries have passed, and people are still dying.

But if these two women are to be believed, I may be the only one who can stop it.

I should feel high on power, but I just feel sick with grief. For the people who are already gone and for whatever future I might have had right up until this moment.

"If I take your deal, it will be a trade," I say. "I'll move into the palace just as soon as my grandfather leaves. Not before."

The PM and Ann share a look. Then the PM smiles. "That is acceptable."

"You are a monster," I tell her, but she isn't insulted. Not even a little bit.

"I'm the monster who just guaranteed that you and your children and your children's children will never have to worry about this bomb going off ever again."

She seems so proud of herself as she and Ann turn to leave.

I hate them. I hate them so much.

Mostly because they're right.

CHAPTER SEVENTEEN

I wake up early. Well, that's assuming I sleep at all. Which I don't. Not really. I know the marines are outside 24-7, keeping watch and standing guard. But my ghosts are already inside the embassy. My mother's bed creaks beneath my weight. Shadows dance across my walls. The tree outside my window is gone now, chopped down and hauled away, partially to keep people from crawling in, partially to keep me from crawling out. And I know it doesn't matter. There's no place left for me to run even if I tried.

I don't have a panic attack. Dr. Rainier should be proud of me. I just sit in the middle of my mother's canopy bed, my arms wrapped around my legs. Rocking. But I don't scream and I don't cry. I wait quietly for morning, for the nightmare to be over. But some nightmares never end.

The sun isn't up yet, but the sky's getting brighter when I grab some clean clothes and pull my hair into a ponytail.

The embassy's still asleep.

The lights are off and the phones are silent.

But I know I'm not alone.

There's one room downstairs with the door cracked. A little light seeps out into the hall, and I'm quiet as a mouse as I creep close and look inside.

"Gracie?" the voice is low and weak, but it's the only sound, and it echoes in the stillness of the halls.

The room used to be the formal parlor. It's where Megan and Ms. Chancellor wrestled me into my first puffy pink dress. But now there is a hospital bed near the window. The antique rugs have been rolled up and the floor is so sterile it shines. But it's the man I can't stop looking at.

He is smaller than I remember—frail. His white hair doesn't shine like snow. His skin is the color of ashes.

But he is alive.

And he is home.

"Gracie, come here. Let me look at you."

I ease toward the bed.

"Grandpa, I—" I start, but he shushes me and glances toward the corner.

There, curled up on one of the most uncomfortable couches in the embassy, is Eleanor Chancellor. There's a crocheted blanket across her lap and her high heels lie discarded on the floor.

"You'll wake the guards," Grandpa says with a smile and a wink in Ms. Chancellor's direction.

He tries to laugh. It makes me want to cry.

When I reach the bed, he takes my hand and pulls me closer. The Tennessee is thick in his voice when he says, "Oh, Gracie, what did you do?"

"I . . ."

"Tell me you didn't agree to any craziness for the sake of this old man."

"Jamie's okay," I say, because it feels like the only thing that matters. It seems like ages since I've seen my brother, but I know this in my gut. "Jamie's okay now." I run my hands through Grandpa's hair, push it off of his cold forehead. "And you're okay. And now everyone is going to be okay."

"What about you, Gracie?" Grandpa asks.

I lean down and kiss his cheek.

When he drifts off to sleep, I don't bother telling him the rest: that I forfeited the right to be okay three years ago.

Only the marines and the sky are awake as I head out onto Embassy Row.

The buildings are all dark. A few delivery vans and police cars pass, but I keep walking, head down, certain of where I have to go.

As I walk through the gates, the sun starts to crest the hills that circle the east side of Valancia. The light is the color of gold, and the whole city shines. My mom's hometown looks so beautiful, here at the top of this hill. Now I understand why Dad and Jamie had to bring her back here—why this is where she was laid to rest.

Adria isn't just where this story started; it's also where it has to end.

"Hi, Mom."

My mom isn't here. This is just a slab of stone with her name on it, some remains that share my DNA. *Caroline Blakely, beloved daughter, wife, mother.* Her tombstone doesn't say anything about her being a princess—that that's the reason why she's here.

No.

I'm the reason why she's here.

I remember this, and just that quickly my breath goes away. I fall to my knees. The grass is damp with a heavy morning dew that seeps through my old jeans. Suddenly, I'm not on a hilltop in Adria; I'm on a dark street in the US, looking through a window, about to make the biggest mistake of my life.

"*Grace, no!*" my mother yells, and I close my eyes, refusing to see the scene that fills my mind.

My breath comes too hard. It's like my lungs don't work, and my body wants to draw in on itself. I'm aware only of the damp ground and the cold headstone and the utter emptiness that is left when all your hope is gone.

But hope's not gone. Not really. Jamie is alive. And I have the power to make sure he stays that way.

Slowly, breath fills my lungs. My heart slows. And the sun climbs higher, turning the city into gold.

"I'm sorry, Mom," I say to that piece of stone. "I'm sorry I haven't come before now. I guess it never felt like you were really here. And you aren't, are you? It's not over yet, but it could be. They say it will be—that this will end it. They're probably lying. They're probably going to kill me, too. But . . ." My voice cracks. My vision blurs.

"But maybe that wouldn't be so bad. Then I'd be with you."

I don't cry. Crying is tears and grief coming out of you in equal measure. I'm too far gone for that. For me, grief is almost all that's left, and it pours out of me, the anguished screams of someone who has finally hit rock bottom.

I don't know how long I stay crumbled before my mother's grave. She's not there, but that doesn't matter.

Nothing matters anymore.

"I'm doing it for Jamie," I say after a while. "And for you. And for Amelia, too, I guess. Someone has to do it. And I have to pay for what I've done. Dad and Grandpa would never let me go to jail, but I have to pay. I *deserve* to pay, so . . . I'm going to the palace instead. I'm going to be a princess. At least that's what they tell me."

It's almost time now. I can feel it in my bones. So I put my hand on the cold stone and push myself upright. My eyes are no doubt puffy, my face red. There's no hiding that something's wrong. Or, more like, nothing's right.

Embassy Row is waking up when I reach the city's wall. There are more guards on the street, some locals heading into work. Part

184

of me half expects to see Jamie coming around the corner, sweaty and breathing hard after running ten miles around the city. Then I have to remind myself that my brother *is* running. And I've just made a deal with the devil so that he can stop.

"Gracie!" Alexei isn't chasing after me. He's standing, staring. And I have to will myself not to turn around and run away. I have to remind myself that he'd run faster.

"What's wrong?" he asks as soon as he can see my eyes. They're still puffy and red, I'm sure. And I realize that Alexei probably hasn't seen me cry that often. For too long I was out of tears.

"Gracie, what has happened?"

"I went for a walk," I say. I want to push past him, head for the US and our walls, but Alexei is so big and strong. He has too much gravity, and right now I'm too weak to pull away.

"Gracie, what did you do?"

He's not talking about three years ago. If he hasn't learned the truth already, he surely doesn't want to hear it now. Maybe he sees it on my face. Or maybe he just knows me too well. But Alexei isn't fooled for one single second.

"What happened yesterday? What happened on the wall?" he asks.

"The princess and the Society had a proposal. It's the best for everyone, so I took it." I force a smile. "It's over, Alexei. Now everything can go back to normal."

"What kind of normal?" He prowls toward me. I'm afraid that he might pounce.

"They're going to stop chasing Jamie. They're going to stop chasing me. It will be okay. I swear. It will be over."

"Gracie—" He reaches for me, and I try to dodge, but he's too fast. Or maybe I've been running for too long. He's the only person I want to catch me.

Alexei's hands are warm, his fingers gentle as they brush my hair out of my eyes and tip my head back to look up at him. He places a gentle kiss on the top of my head, then holds me close.

I can feel as much as hear him say, "Tell me, Gracie. Please."

There's a choice now. I'm like the sand on the beach, and I can either slip through Alexei's fingers or turn to glass. Either way, I know I'll never feel like this again, so I close my eyes and breathe him in. And then what I have to do hits me. Like lightning. I'm practically brittle as I pull away.

"I'm going to move into the palace."

It's like Alexei hasn't heard me, like someone put this moment on pause. But then my words sink in.

"No," he says. "You're not."

I shrug and try to laugh. "It's the palace, Alexei. Why wouldn't I want to live there?"

"What did they say to you yesterday?"

"It was like Ms. Chancellor said. They had a plan, and it's a good one. I'm going to do it."

"What plan?"

"Well, see, to start with, I'm going to move into the palace and then . . . in a few years . . . I'm going to marry the prince. It's all been decided."

Alexei looks like maybe I've hit him. Like maybe he wants me to.

"What are you talking about?"

"It's really genius when you think about it. They know Jamie is the rightful heir—the oldest kid of the oldest kid and so on. So they could kill us. But there are probably other heirs, you know, and they probably can't kill us all, so—"

"What are you talking about?"

I look at him and bat my eyes, shake my head like the pretty girls in movies always do. "I'm going to marry the prince, and then our oldest child—Amelia's rightful heir—will be on the throne eventually. Our own little coup, and the country never has to know. Everything is back the way it should be and the region remains stable and . . . everyone is happy."

I smile, but Alexei scowls. It's like a part of him is starting to believe me. "Are *you* happy, Gracie?"

Now it's time to laugh and smile and tell him that every little girl dreams of growing up and marrying a prince and living in a palace.

But this is Alexei. He knows I never was a typical little girl.

"Princess Ann did it—when she was a girl. She and my mom and, I guess, your mom thought that Ann was the heir, so she married the prince. Now *I'm* going to marry the prince."

"You don't even know him!" Alexei's shouting, but Embassy Row doesn't care.

"We're not getting married tomorrow. I'm just going to move into the palace for now. The official story will be that Ann was

187

my godmother, so I'm living with her. And then the prince and I will get to know each other, and in time, I'm sure—"

"Do you think I care about time?" Alexei shouts, but I want to tell him that he *should* care. We're running out of it, after all.

"Gracie, you don't have to do this. Jamie would never want you to do this!"

He reaches for me again, but this time I manage to pull away. I'm too cold and too hard to cling to. Maybe Alexei realizes that if he were to squeeze me, I might break because he doesn't reach for me again.

"Maybe *I* want this," I tell him. "Did you consider that?"

For the first time, he seems to wonder if it might be true.

"Do you?"

"It's my birthright," I say with a shrug. "I was born to be a princess."

Alexei laughs now. A cold, cruel sound. "You could have fooled me."

I talk on. "Really, there's no reason *not* to do it."

I've done things—terrible things for which I will never, ever be forgiven. But this is the first time I've been intentionally cruel. I see the words hit him, and as big and strong and stoic as he is, he actually stumbles.

The sun is rising, and I can feel Alexei's gaze on me, like he's looking for some clue that I've been drugged or replaced. I'm not Gracie, Jamie's kid sister. I'm not the crazy, reckless girl next door. I'm not the young woman he has been getting closer and closer to for weeks now.

I am a stranger.

And for the rest of our lives I'm going to have to stay that way.

"I can think of a reason." Alexei's arms are around me then, his lips pressing against mine. It's not like the kisses that we've shared before. This is stronger, deeper. This is a kiss that is going to have to last us both a lifetime, because the thing that we both know about this kiss is simple: It's probably our last one.

"You're a nice boy, Alexei," I say when, at last, I pull away. "I'm sorry, but this is for the best. You'll always be one of my very best friends, you know."

"Friend?" Alexei says, and steps away.

"I'm sure we'll see each other sometime. It's not like this is good-bye."

"No." He shakes his head. "That's not what this is."

He doesn't follow me down Embassy Row. I'm alone when the limo pulls up in front of the US gates and the uniformed driver comes around the car and opens a door.

I look up at the residence, but there's no use going inside. I can't bear any more good-byes, I tell myself.

So I give one last wave at Alexei and climb into the dark backseat. The windows are black and bulletproof. It's as good a place as any to shatter.

CHAPTER EIGHTEEN

I've been to the palace three times.

Once, when I was new to Adria and stuffed into a pretty pink dress. That night, I danced and I curtsied and I tried to make my grandfather proud.

Once, when I was adrift and needed Princess Ann to explain my own mother to me, to make the past make sense.

And once more when my brother was dying and the crowds were descending and I was desperate for fences and walls, anything to hold the tide at bay even if for just a little while.

But that was before I knew the truth. About my mother and Amelia and Ann—about the terrible, twisted fate that another mob set in motion on another night.

It's been two hundred years since the Society smuggled a baby girl through the palace gates.

Two centuries have past, but now it's like Amelia is finally coming home. I'm taking her rightful place and reclaiming her birthright. No one seems to care that that means turning my back on my own.

The car is quiet and dark, so I close my eyes and savor the last sounds of silence that I might ever hear. I have no idea what to expect when the gates swing wide and we pull onto the grounds. We drive up to a portico on the far side of the palace, a place sheltered by tall walls and heavy trees. We're in the heart of Valancia, but the rest of the world feels a million miles away when the limo stops and a man opens the door.

I have to squint against the sunlight as I slide to the edge of the seat and step outside. A hand in a white glove reaches down to help me, but for a second I honestly don't know what to do. I've never been one to ask for help—I don't even know how to take it—so I crawl out of the backseat by myself, study the man in the ornate uniform who stands before me, formal and surreal. It's like stepping into a dream. A bad one.

"Hello, Grace!"

That's when I turn to see Princess Ann coming down the stairs, walking past a long line of uniformed servants. A man in a full tuxedo follows closely behind the princess, carefully listening to every word.

"Welcome home, dear," Ann tells me.

She tries to pull me into a hug, but I recoil. It's instinct now. I can't help it. After all, home was wherever Dad was stationed. Home was wherever Jamie was in school. Home was where my mother was, but my mother is gone now and the woman before me is responsible. The thought makes me want to kill someone. Again.

But instead I just shudder and want to cry.

"Grace, may I present Henson. Henson is the butler for the family wing. He and his staff will take care of your needs, dear. Henson," the princess says, turning back to me. There's a sickly sweet smile upon her face. "This is my goddaughter, Grace."

The butler speaks. I'm pretty sure he bows. But I'm too busy looking at Ann, wondering how I'm supposed to live here with a woman I hate.

"As you know, Henson, Grace's grandfather, Ambassador Blakely, isn't well, and so we agreed that it would be best if she were to live here for a while. With me. I'm sure you and the staff will do all you can to make her feel at home."

At this, the butler bows again. "Of course, Your Highness," the man says in Adrian. Then he turns to me and switches to English. "Ms. Blakely, if you ever need anything—anything at all—you have only to ask. The staff and I are here to serve."

I'm supposed to say something, I know. But all I can do is mumble something like "Okay, sure," and then follow Ann down the long line of servants. Maids and footmen bow and curtsy as we pass. And soon we are in a dim, quiet entryway that bears almost no resemblance to the grand, main doors of the palace.

"Do you think people are really going to believe you're my godmother?" I say as Ann starts to climb the stairs.

"Your mother was my oldest, dearest friend, Grace. No one will question that."

"I'm questioning it," I say, and Ann stops. She's standing one step above me, looking down.

"We had a deal, Grace."

"The devil makes them all the time."

Something in her eyes makes me laugh. It's either that or cry.

"You have a choice, dear." Ann steps down to my level, glares into my eyes. "Life here," she says, then gestures up at the crystal chandelier, at the veritable army of servants who are filing in through the doors behind us, returning to their work. "Or a life out there, looking over your shoulder. No peace for you. Or your brother. Or whatever descendants either of you might someday have. Those are your options. Now choose one."

In my head, I know she's right—that this is true. But my mind has been too wrong about too much for too long. How am I supposed to trust it with something like this?

I think about my grandfather and my brother. I think about life on the run and the way Alexei held me close and said that I was home to him. But, most of all, I think about what Noah said—that whatever my mom found, she probably found it here. In Adria.

This was where she came. This was why she died. And if I'm going to find it, too, I'm going to have to stop running. It's time to keep my friends close and my enemies closer, and you don't get much closer than under the same roof.

Still, with every step, the reality becomes greater. Heavier. I stop and try to breathe, but there's not enough air here in this massive building. My vision narrows and my heart pounds, and it's not a beautiful day in Valancia; it's the middle of the night outside my mother's shop and my whole world is about to catch fire.

"I . . . I have to go back to the embassy."

Ann eases closer. "I thought you understood, Grace. There is no going back."

"I don't have my bags or my clothes or . . ." *My mother's boxes and journals and papers.* "I didn't bring my clothes."

"Is *that* the problem?" Ann asks, and then she throws back her head and laughs. It's like I've just made the best joke ever. "Your clothes? Oh, sweetheart, you won't be needing your clothes."

"Why?" I snap. "Am I going to be chained naked to a radiator or something?"

"You watch too many movies, Grace."

"I need to go back," I say as my gut fills with some unknown, unnamed dread. "I want . . . I need to bring my things."

"No," Ann says. "You don't."

Then she turns and climbs the stairs. My following her isn't up for debate or discussion. I have made my bed, I know. And now the most beautiful woman in Europe is going to go chain me to it.

"It'll never work," I call. "No one is going to believe that I belong here."

"They will," Ann says. "I do a great deal of charity work."

"Great," I say as I start to climb. I'm charity.

194

"This is your life now, Grace. And it can be a good life. Or it can be miserable. From this point forward, it is a choice. And the choice is entirely up to you."

For a second, tears well in my eyes. My throat burns, and I can't help it because, for a second, she sounds just like a mother.

Like my mother.

When Ann leads me down a long, wide corridor, I have no choice but to follow.

"The palace is comprised of many different spaces that serve many different functions. I believe you are familiar with the state ballroom and perhaps some of the more formal, public areas, but those are typically only used for functions of state. You've also seen the royal drawing room, if memory serves. As you might expect, there are a number of rooms dedicated to the royal family as well as individual apartments for those of us in permanent residence. In addition, there are guest quarters and entire floors reserved for servants. In total, there are, I believe, one hundred and seventy bedrooms inside the palace."

Ann stops suddenly. She places a manicured hand against a pair of wide, double doors. Then she pushes.

"This one is *yours*."

The lights are off, but the sun streams through floor-to-ceiling windows on the far side of the room, cutting through the darkness like a spotlight upon a stage. It's fitting, I have to think. This is my great role, and I'm going to have to become a brand-new person in every way that really matters.

"Do you like it?" Ann asks. Maybe my mind is playing tricks on me, but I could almost swear that she sounds nervous, like she actually cares about the answer.

"It's pretty," I say, and that much is true.

"Grace. Is that all you have to say?" She flips a switch, and light fills the room, falling from a crystal chandelier that dangles from a ceiling that's probably twenty feet tall. The walls are covered with silk. The bed is massive and canopied with lace. There's an antique dresser, a vanity table, and a mirror. Every surface is covered with fresh flowers, and the hardwood floor is so polished that it shines.

"It's the prettiest prison I have ever seen," I say. It's the only compliment I can muster at the moment.

Ann looks like maybe she wants to lecture me again, but she thinks better of it. I'm the textbook definition of *lost cause*, so she's quiet as I walk to the tall windows and look out on the world outside.

"I really do hope you'll be happy here, Grace. When I married the prince, I wasn't prepared for this life. You will have a huge advantage, you see. By the time you are in my place, this will truly feel like home to you. Someday soon you won't even remember what it felt like to live anywhere else."

I've lived a lot of places—that's the life of an army brat. None of them were a palace, and yet I'd trade this place for any of those in a heartbeat. But my deal has already been made and the devil stands behind me. It's far too late to look back now.

"Yeah. Sure." I force a smile. "Home, sweet home."

"Hey, Mom, have you seen my—"

The words are in Adrian, and it's a voice that I don't know, but when I turn, I'm not entirely surprised by who is standing in my doorway.

His feet are bare and his hair is mussed, and overall the effect is undeniable. If I were the kind of girl who reads magazines or gossip sites, I'd probably be panting right about now. But I'm not that kind of girl.

I'm the girl he's going to have to marry.

"Oh. Hello," he says, switching to English.

I expect some kind of sly smile, maybe a roll of the royal eyes or something to show what he thinks of my situation—of *me*. But he doesn't do any of those things. "So you're the goddaughter." He's grinning as he says it. He actually steps forward, offers me his hand. "I'm the son."

The prince, he means. The heir's heir. Someday, this barefoot boy will wear the crown of Adria. And he's the reason why I'm here.

"Darling, come in," Ann tells him. "There's someone I'd like for you to meet."

I keep looking at the prince, trying to read his thoughts, but I can't see anything in his eyes besides boredom. When he comes closer I realize that he and I are about the same height. He's a little younger than I am, I remember. And he's no doubt still growing. His hair is lighter than Ann's, more like his father's. But he has Ann's eyes—her smile. If he were a girl he'd be beautiful, but he's a boy and so that just makes him . . . striking. He's going

197

to break hearts, I know. I just hope that, someday, he doesn't break me.

"Welcome to Adria," he tells me.

"Do I curtsy?" I ask.

"I don't know. Do you?"

"I have before," I say. "I didn't like it."

When the prince laughs it's such a natural, honest sound that I have to look at Ann; I have to wonder what he knows and what he fears. Is he unaware of the bargain his mother has struck, or is duty so much a part of the royal DNA that he doesn't even register how weird it is to be meeting his future wife at the age of fifteen with his shoes off?

That's when I realize that I'm staring.

"Sorry," I tell him. "It's weird, though, right? I mean, I never thought I'd move into a palace one day and meet my future——"

Hurriedly, Ann steps between us. "Grace is going to be staying here with us, dear. I hope the two of you will become close."

The look on her face tells me that he doesn't have a clue just *how* close the fate of Adria needs us to be.

"I'm Thomas," he says with a broad grin. "They tell me I'm supposed to make you feel at home."

"Is that right?" I glare at his mother. "What else do they tell you?" I ask, but Ann is reaching for her son.

"Sweetheart, why don't you run along? I need to get Grace settled in."

"No," I tell her. "You don't."

"Yes. I do."

Prince Thomas looks between us. He knows girl drama when he sees it, so he starts toward the doors. "It was nice meeting you, Grace. I'm sure our paths will cross again soon."

We are going to share a palace. A future. A life. He gives me a cocky, silly bow, and I want to laugh. My future husband is funny, I realize. And handsome. And everything a literal Prince Charming is supposed to be.

He just isn't for the likes of me.

"Grace." Ann's voice cuts through the fog that fills my mind. "Grace, what do you think?"

The prince is gone and Ann is no longer in my bedroom. I start toward the open door into the hall but stop when I realize that another pair of double doors has been thrown open and Ann stands inside this other room. Except it's not a room. It's a . . .

"It's your closet!" she exclaims, as if something like that matters to someone like me.

Megan should be here. Or Noah's twin sister, Lila. Or Ms. Chancellor. The closet is twice the size of any bedroom I ever had on any base. It's full of dresses and neatly folded sweaters, row after row of shoes. But it's all lost on me. I know I'll just rip them, stain them, ruin them like I ruin everything else.

"See?" Ann sounds almost giddy. "I told you you wouldn't need your own clothes."

I walk to one of the racks of sundresses, finger the soft cotton and look at the pretty colors. I walk slowly past shoes with heels so high I'm pretty sure it's just a matter of time until I fall and break my other leg.

"I hope you like them." Ann actually sounds nervous, and I realize that she never questioned the order to have my mother's line exterminated, but choosing her future daughter-in-law's shoes seems to be keeping her up nights.

"They're beautiful," I say.

"I wasn't sure of your size, but we can always send them back. Or get more. The designers will love working with you. And the palace has a seamstress. Well, actually, I believe it has an entire staff of seamstresses and tailors. We can have anything altered—anything at all. It's really no—"

"You didn't tell him, did you?"

Ann doesn't even slow down.

"I want you to feel comfortable here, Grace. If these clothes don't suit, then we can get you more. Any designer will work with us. We will cultivate the perfect style for you. Soon—"

"What does Prince Thomas know?" I shout.

Finally, Ann turns to me. "He knows what everyone knows. You are the daughter of my best friend. You are troubled and alone and desperate for safety and some degree of stability. He knows *the truth*, Grace."

I wish I could tell her that she's lying—that she's wrong. But it *is* true, I have to admit. Every single word.

"It's going to be fine, Grace. You will adjust. You will accept this."

The scary thing isn't that Ann believes it. The scary thing is that, deep down, I think she might be right.

"Do try on some of the clothes. Good clothes are like armor, I've found."

"So I'm going into battle?"

Ann smirks and raises one eyebrow. "Women are always in battle. Your mother knew that better than anyone."

"Don't talk about my mother."

Ann stops fingering the dress in front of her and turns on me. "Why not? It was *her* idea."

Something about this stops me. It spikes my guns and tempers my rage.

"*What* was her idea?" I ask, my voice like ice.

"For Amelia's heir to marry the prince. Your mother was the one who first thought of this solution."

"I don't believe you."

"I'm not surprised that you don't believe me, but it's true. The only problem is . . . well . . . we got the heir wrong. It should have been her who married the prince."

"So you killed her."

"No." Suddenly, Ann's voice is hard. She's not the smiling, waving paragon of virtue anymore. She's anything but a princess as she steps closer. "I've never killed anyone. Can you say the same?"

I know that Ann walks away. From the corner of my eye I can see her at the closet's big double doors. I want her to close them, to lock me in here like a cell. Like a tomb. I want to do whatever time—whatever penance—I have to do to move on. But my mother doesn't get to move on. Not ever. So why should I?

"Grace?" Ann finally gets my attention. "We want this to work. We *need* this to work. You are the solution to a two-hundred-year-old problem, and I assure you your safety is our top concern."

"Forgive me if I don't believe you."

"That's fine." Ann smiles. She eases toward the doors. "But perhaps you'll believe *him*."

Ann steps away, but I don't follow. I'm too busy staring at the man who stands behind her, at his dark suit and broad shoulders, the all-too-familiar scar that marks his face.

"Hello, Grace Olivia."

CHAPTER NINETEEN

As soon as Ann leaves and the door closes, the panic is the first thing to hit me. I fly toward Dominic.

"Where's Jamie?" I practically yell.

"He is well."

"Where is my brother?"

Dominic had one job, one responsibility. If he left Jamie to be hurt in order to come find me, then I will never forgive him. Never forgive myself.

"Where is he?"

"He's safe, Grace." The Scarred Man's hands are on my shoulders, holding me tight before I can run away or lash out—hurt someone, especially me. "He is resting and recuperating with people I trust. He is fine. I swear to you. His only problem is that he is constantly worried about his little sister."

Instantly, I feel guilty. I never thought that worry for me might keep Jamie from getting better. But it has. Of course it has. Jamie is a good person. Good people worry. And even when I try to help, I hurt.

"Why are you here?" I pull back, calmer now, and Dominic lets me go.

"I am to be your personal security detail."

"But—"

Dominic brings a finger to his lips and looks around the room. For the first time, I look past the antique furniture and soft, silky draperies. I try to see the room through the eyes of a man who has spent his whole life looking in shadows, chasing down ghosts. And I know even the room around us can't be trusted.

"Come with me." Dominic starts toward the doors, and I follow. He never wavers as he leads me down wide corridors and narrow staircases. The halls of the palace twist and turn. It's not a building—it's a maze that runs horizontal and vertical. Maybe I'm the Minotaur, I realize. Maybe it's better for the world if I never find my way outside.

But Dominic doesn't have that problem. Soon, he's pushing through a door and leading me out onto the palace's grounds.

White gravel crunches underfoot as we walk along manicured paths, between tall hedges and beneath shady trees. I had no idea that the grounds were this large, this grand. But it shouldn't surprise me. It certainly doesn't surprise Dominic.

"You know the palace." I don't know where the words come from. It's hardly the most important thing. But the Scarred Man lived inside my mind for years, and now every piece of him I come across makes him less villain, more human. Dominic isn't a figment of my imagination anymore. He is flesh and blood and here to help me.

"I have had occasion to learn some of its secrets, yes," he says.

"But not all of its secrets?"

Dominic's eyes stare into mine. "The palace of Adria is five hundred years old—older in places. No, Grace, I don't know all of its secrets. I doubt any one person does. And it is better that way, I believe."

He's not talking about secret societies or lost princesses. Adria is a thousand years old. Even older in many ways. And that many secrets could press a person down, grind her into dust.

"What about you?" I ask.

"What about me?"

"Does anyone know all of *your* secrets?"

Dominic shakes his head. "You do not want my secrets, Grace Olivia," he says, and I don't doubt that it's true.

Eventually, the garden path leads to a massive glass house—a giant room that isn't like a room at all. Dominic opens the door and, immediately I feel the air change. It's hot and humid. The floors are tiled and damp, and everywhere I look there are plants and flowers. Bushy green ferns and orchids so fragile they look like I could crush them with the tip of my little finger. I tell myself not to touch a single thing.

"So now can you tell me why you're here?" I ask, spinning on him.

"I'm your protection detail," he says, as if I'm silly to have forgotten so quickly.

"Why are you *here*, Dominic? Why aren't you with Jamie?"

"Jamie is no longer in danger."

"Do you really believe that?" I can see on his face that he doesn't. Danger is a way of life for people like Dominic. He sees it everywhere and has for a very long time. He will for the rest of his life.

So the Scarred Man doesn't lie. He just says, "I am where Jamie wants me to be."

"Jamie doesn't know where you are." I shake my head, defiant. "And he definitely doesn't know why you're here."

Dominic eyes me. "What brings you to this conclusion?"

"Because I know my brother." I turn from Dominic, walk down a long row of flowering plants. "And I know that if the royal family doesn't kill me for taking this deal, Jamie will."

Dominic doesn't tell me that I'm wrong. "Jamie is fine. He is safe. He is getting stronger. And I am where I need to be."

I know better than to argue. I can't change anyone's mind, not even my own. So I just ask, "Do you know what my mom found here?" It's the only thing that matters.

I look around the plants. A few feet away, sprinklers spring to life, coating a long row with a very fine mist.

"Electronic surveillance doesn't work in here, does it?" I ask, and he nods, almost impressed. "That's why we're here. No bugs in the greenhouse."

"Grace—"

"Before Mom died, she took a trip. We know she went to see Alexei's mom at Binevale. And we know she came here—to Valancia. I think she found something, and the royal family found out, and that's why they wanted her dead. Did she tell you what she found?"

"Is that why you're here, Grace Olivia?"

The Scarred Man sees too much. The Scarred Man knows too much.

"Keep your enemies closer, right?" I shrug. "She found something, and they're terrified I have it. So if you know what it is or where it is or—"

"Have you ever seen the grounds before? The gardens of Valancia? They're quite famous for people who care about such things."

"Answer my question, Dominic. *Do you know what she found?*"

"Have you ever heard of this house?" Dominic looks up at the glass ceiling overhead. The pieces fit together like those in a puzzle, and the light that comes through is almost ethereal in its glow.

"It's a nice greenhouse. The nicest. But I don't care about greenhouses. I care about whatever it was my mother found!"

"Oh." Dominic laughs. "It's no mere greenhouse. This house was one of the last acts of King Alexander the Second. It was built right before the War of the Fortnight. The gardens, too."

For some reason, this is the fact that stops me.

"They built those gardens during a drought?"

Dominic's raised eyebrow is his answer.

"The coup was not right, Grace Olivia. But that does not mean it wasn't without cause."

I'd never considered this, but I should have. Nothing happens in a vacuum. There is a cause and effect to everything.

"And it was all built for the king's mistress." Dominic walks around a massive fountain that stands in the house's center. Once on the other side, he looks up through the wavy glass, and I realize that we are almost in the literal shadow of the national cathedral. "They say the king chose this place so that his mistress would be between his wife and the church. He liked the idea of mocking both simultaneously."

I shouldn't be surprised, but I am. And I'm not entirely sure why.

"He kept his mistress in a glass house?"

"She was said to be the most beautiful woman in the world. Helen of Adria, they called her. Fitting for a walled city, don't you think? And what's the use of possessing the most beautiful woman in the world if the world cannot see her?" Dominic walks on. "Originally the glass house was not on the palace grounds, but as a sort of revenge, the queen had the land annexed, the fences moved, hoping to drive the woman out. But the king only laughed and thanked her for making his mistress's house an official part of the palace."

I stop. Turn to him. "Why are you telling me all of this?"

"The royals who died in the rebellion consisted of two innocent children but also a king who openly mocked his queen and his church and a queen who built gardens so grand that before

208

they were even half-finished they had drained the city's reservoir. I am not saying they deserved their fate, but the war, the parliament, the prime minister—these things all grew out of that tragedy. The results were not entirely bad."

"What are we going to do, Dominic?" I snap, tired of history, of this walk down memory lane. "Are we going to look for evidence? Poison Ann's tea? Please tell me you have a plan."

"It's important that you listen to me, Grace Olivia." Dominic steps forward. He's so tall he looms above me, ominous and omniscient. "We are not going to do anything."

"But there has to be a way out. *There has to be.*"

"There is." Dominic reaches for me, takes my narrow shoulders in his large hands and holds me steady. "There is a way out. There is only one way for it to end."

"What is it?" I ask, but Dominic stays silent. It's like he doesn't want to tempt fate, like he knows that tempting me is the exact same thing. "*Tell me!* I'll do it." My voice cracks. My eyes water. "I'll do anything."

The whole world is a blur as the Scarred Man says, "You become a princess."

CHAPTER TWENTY

I don't remember sleeping. But that's silly, isn't it? No one ever does. Still, I'm surprised when I wake up, sun streaming through the tall windows of my pretty princess bedroom. I'm a little afraid to think that I might get comfortable here—that, someday, this might be routine. Normal.

I'm even more afraid to realize that I'm not alone.

"I'm sorry, Your Highness."

When I bolt upright I see a maid at the foot of my bed. Her Adrian accent is strong, but her English is perfect. Her curtsy is sure and straight.

"I do hate to wake you, but you have a busy day ahead."

"Oh." I want to get out of the bed, but I'm so twisted in the covers that I struggle, trying to break free. It's the story of my life, I have to think, but this girl doesn't want to hear it.

"Will you be wanting tea, Your Highness? Or coffee? The kitchen can prepare whatever you wish to have."

"I'm not . . ." *Hungry. Thirsty.* There are a lot of words that could fill in that blank, but I say, "Your Highness. I'm not . . . I'm just Ann's goddaughter. I'm not a member of the royal family." *Yet.*

I expect the girl to curtsy and apologize, go about whatever business brought her to my room. But she just drops her gaze and her voice.

"I don't believe that's true . . . *Your Highness.*" The girl leans over as she curtsies again, deeper this time, then pulls a gold chain out from the neckline of her uniform. She lets a small medallion dangle. It's the same symbol I followed through the streets and down into the tunnels last summer—the same image that's been haunting me for months. She isn't just a maid, I realize. She's a member of the Society. And I'm suddenly grateful she didn't try to smother me in my sleep.

"My name is Clarice, Your Highness. I am to let you know that you are not alone."

"Is that supposed to be a threat?" I blurt, and I mean it. "If the Society sent you to keep me in line, then tell them I get it. I made my bed. Now I'm sleeping in it."

I expect the girl to smirk like the PM, to scowl at me like the women in Paris. But she continues to look at me with something approaching reverence.

"There are those among the Society who have longed for this day—for Amelia's heir to finally claim her rightful place. Please consider me your loyal servant, *Your Majesty*." This time she doesn't act like I'm a princess; she's treating me like a queen as she bobs one final curtsy and dashes toward the door.

I'm throwing off the covers, chasing after her, but I don't know why. I only know I'm darting into the hallway and then . . .

Slamming to a stop.

"Hello, dear."

"Ms. Chancellor?"

How many hours has it been since I last spoke with her? A little over a day at most. But that feels like ages ago, and now she stands before me like a ghost from another life.

"What are you . . . ?" I trail off, then look down the hall behind her, behind me.

I need to know what kind of tragedy is looming on the horizon now. I want to know if she knows that the Society has moles within the palace. I want to ask what Mom was looking for—what she found. But, most of all, I want her to tell me that my grandfather is okay—that she's not here to break even more bad news.

"Grandpa?"

"He's fine." Ms. Chancellor eases forward. "He's getting stronger every day."

"Then . . . why are you here?" I ask.

"I came to see you." She opens her arms, but I don't go to her. If I let her hug me, hold me, I might cry. And if I start crying, I may never, ever stop.

Ann was right, I know. This is my path. My destiny. The one

212

and only way out. And the sooner I make my peace with it the sooner I can grow numb.

The sooner I grow numb the sooner it will all be over.

"Grace," Ms. Chancellor says, "are you okay?"

"Yes. I'm fine. It's just . . . I just woke up."

"Have you spoken with Dominic?" Ms. Chancellor asks, but I can only nod. "You aren't alone," she tells me with a smile.

I just shake my head slowly. Right now—in this moment—it feels like *she* is the young one, the naïve one, the foolish one. I don't have the heart to tell her that I am always alone.

"What brings you by?" I ask, my voice too casual, too light. And she knows it. But she never gets to answer because that's when Ann's voice comes floating over my shoulder.

"She's here to help, silly."

I spin. "Help with what?"

"Turning you into a princess, of course." She actually smiles when she says it. And I can't help it: I turn to Ms. Chancellor, eyeing her, wondering if I'm the only one who sees this moment as surreal.

But Ms. Chancellor is a born diplomat. If she notices anything amiss, she doesn't show it. Her brown eyes twinkle as she says, "Her Highness was kind enough to include me in today's fun."

Fun? Ms. Chancellor knows me well. I don't even have to say the word aloud.

"Now, Gracie . . ."

As soon as Ann uses my nickname I want to scream. I want to claw. But Ms. Chancellor shakes her head, a gesture so slight that only someone who knows her well would see it.

"I just live here now," I say. "I won't have to be *a princess* for a long time."

"Oh, but we have to start building you now," the princess says.

"Building me *how*?"

"Your perception. Your persona. Your personal style. If in a few years, people are to believe that the prince has fallen for you, then we will need you to be a bit more polished." She looks from my bare feet to the top of my bedhead and I want to recoil. This woman doesn't have the right to judge me. If anything, this woman should fear me.

"It will be fine, Grace. Parts might even be a little fun. That's why I'm here. To help you get ready for the party," Ms. Chancellor says.

And this stops me.

"What party?"

"My father-in-law has been on the throne for fifty years now," Ann says. "There will be a gala to commemorate the occasion in a few days, and this felt like the perfect time to bring you out, so to speak."

I look at Ms. Chancellor. "It is for the best, Grace," she tells me, and I hear what she doesn't say.

If I'm going to do this . . .

If this is going to be my life . . .

If I'm to keep my deal with the devil, then eventually I'm going to have to live up to my part of the bargain.

"So?" Ann claps her hands together. She actually bounces a little as she says, "Let's get started."

It wasn't that long ago that I stood with Noah in one of the formal rooms of the US embassy while Ms. Chancellor taught us how to dance. I remember trying on clothes with Megan, laughing in a limo with my grandpa.

It was only a few months ago, I realize, but it might as well have been another decade. I might as well have been another girl.

"No, Grace," the princess snaps. "That curtsy is far too low for a countess. Unless she is a duchess or higher, then you mustn't go below here." She holds her hand at my midsection, orders me to try again.

"Now. You cannot stand in the receiving line of course—"

"Of course," I echo, and Ms. Chancellor eyes me, a warning.

"But Thomas shall escort you in for the evening, and I assure you that as soon as you take your place on my son's arm, everyone will notice."

"Yay," I say.

Ms. Chancellor steps on my foot.

"My office is spreading it around town that I've taken you in. The optics are very good, you know. Orphaned girl taken from homelessness to the palace."

"I'm not homeless! I'm not an orphan. I have a father and a grandfather. I have people who love me," I snap before it hits me. Before I realize that it's true.

There *are* people who love me. But they are on the other side of these walls, and I can never go back again.

"We have to make you sympathetic," the princess tells me. "Otherwise . . ."

"Why would anyone believe that a prince would choose someone like me?" I fill in.

She just shrugs. She can't even be bothered to tell me that I'm right.

They shove me into dresses and heels. The royal seamstresses are summoned and I'm measured and poked and prodded until I bleed on something from a shop that's so exclusive there's a nine-month waiting list just to get in the door.

"You're doing well," Ms. Chancellor tells me as she unzips a gown that's worth more than most houses.

Ann is across the room, conferring with someone on her staff. They're always running to and fro, asking questions, getting approval. She isn't the queen, but that doesn't mean Ann doesn't have her own little empire. No wonder it doesn't matter to her that her best friend died in order for her to keep it.

"Don't."

I look up to see Ms. Chancellor's big brown eyes staring into mine.

"What?"

"Don't think about it, sweetheart."

216

I should tell her that she doesn't know what I was thinking, but that would be useless. Ms. Chancellor can read my face, my moods, my very mind. She knows me better than I know myself. And that's why she looks terrified.

"Don't think about your mother, Grace. It's too late to save her."

She doesn't say the rest of it—that it's not too late to save myself.

But, on this, even Eleanor Chancellor is mistaken.

I have one shot—one last mission. And I don't dare waste it, so I ease a little closer to Ms. Chancellor. I finger a gown and lower my voice. "Do you know what my mom was looking for? Does the Society know?"

"Don't do this, Grace."

It's all I can do to keep my voice down, my face placid. "Mom found something, and if I can find it, too, then——"

"Then they'll kill *you*?" Ms. Chancellor guesses. "Is that what you want?"

Suicide by secret. I hadn't really considered it, but that's Ms. Chancellor's deepest fear, I can tell. It's one more thing about which I can't help but feel guilty.

"No. It's . . . If I found it, maybe I could stop it—stop this."

"Grace, listen to me." Ms. Chancellor turns me to her and tucks a strand of hair behind my ear. Like a mother. And it makes me want to cry. "Even if you find whatever it is she found, it won't change what happened to her. It won't change what happened to Amelia. It won't change who you *are*."

What I did.

"Grace, if I could change this for you . . ." Ms. Chancellor trails off. "I know this isn't how you saw your life playing out, and if there were any other way . . ."

She doesn't have to finish. She's a smart woman. She knows how the story ends.

So I look back at the pretty dresses that fill the pretty room, the perfect accessories for my new, ugly life.

"How is everyone?" I ask.

"Your grandfather is doing very well. He's sitting up and speaking and feeding himself. The doctor said she expects him to make a full recovery."

I let out a breath I hadn't realized I was holding.

"And everyone else?"

"Noah and Lila's mother tell me that they're well. They are . . . concerned, but unharmed."

"Megan?" I ask.

"Aside from trying to hack into the palace's security feeds so that she can track your every move?" Ms. Chancellor raises an eyebrow and I know that she's not teasing, not guessing. "She's fine. Rosie, too."

I swallow and nod. I can't bring myself to say his name. Turns out I don't have to.

"Alexei has a . . . visitor." *Karina*, I think, but neither of us dares to say her name aloud. Ms. Chancellor eyes me over the top of her glasses. "I don't believe they're staying at the embassy, but I know that he is well."

It's supposed to give me comfort, let me rest. But all I can remember is the look on his face, the hurt that filled his eyes as I turned my back on my embassy and on him. They say if you love something to set it free. Alexei's free now. And I'll never love again.

Behind us, Ann is speaking in rapid Adrian, something about finding a picture of me where I look the right kind of ordinary and then leaking that to the press along with a story.

I turn and look at my reflection in the three-way mirror the seamstresses set up before they began their work. My dress is blue. Royal blue. Ann is certain that the people of Adria are going to see me in it and take that as a clue. The waist is narrow and the skirt is long. They've already decided to put my hair up and that I shouldn't wear too many jewels to the gala.

But I can't help thinking about another party and another time.

"Remember my pink dress?" I ask, and Ms. Chancellor meets my gaze in the mirror. Her smile is a little nostalgic. A little sad.

"It was beautiful."

Was being the operative word. It was beautiful before I saw Dominic and ran from the palace in a daze, before I stumbled down the streets of Adria and crawled through the rain. Before I set into motion this terrible sequence of events. Before I knew better than to leave well enough alone.

"I should have stayed home. If I hadn't seen Dominic . . . if I hadn't heard him with the prime minister . . . if I hadn't . . ."

"Look at me, Grace." Ms. Chancellor's grip is solid. "Look at me and listen closely. You did not do this. This is not your fault.

These events were set into motion two hundred years ago, and you are simply trying to bear this weight as well as you can." She tips my head up, makes me look into her eyes. *"This is not your fault,"* she says one final time.

I only wish I could believe her.

"Well, what have we here?"

A kind of panic fills the room at the sound of the deep voice. At first, I think it must be because a man has dared to invade such a feminine space, but all around us, seamstresses fumble and maids curtsy and even the air is changing.

As soon as I turn, I see why.

Even Ms. Chancellor drops into a curtsy—one far lower than the one I'm supposed to give a duchess.

"Grace," she whispers, and I realize I'm still standing atop the little stage the seamstresses use, looking out in my blue dress. I'm just starting to remember where and what I am when the king reaches me in two long strides.

"We meet again, Ms. Blakely."

"Uh . . ." I drop into my curtsy. My head is bent when I say, "I'm honored, Your Majesty."

"Stand up, girl. Let me look you over."

I do as the king says because . . . well . . . he's the king. But he doesn't seem like a king in this moment. His smile is too broad, his laugh too loud as he reads my bemused expression, then asks, "How's the old man? Pinching all the pretty nurses, I'd bet."

It takes me a minute to remember the camaraderie he shared with my grandfather the night we met.

"He is much improved, Your Majesty. I'm told he should make a full recovery."

"Excellent. Very glad to hear it."

Slowly, I force myself to look up, to meet his gaze.

He doesn't seem evil. He doesn't look like a monster who would see everyone with my DNA exterminated just to keep his place on the throne. But I know better.

No one in this palace is my friend.

"Is this for something special?" The king gestures at my new blue ball gown.

"You know it is, you big flirt," Princess Ann tells him with a laugh. "Now, shoo. No boys allowed."

"Even sovereign rulers?" he asks.

"Especially them," she says, playfully pushing him toward the door.

"Five decades on the throne and this is how they treat me, Ms. Blakely. Makes me wish I'd been a teacher." His voice drops. He almost sounds a little wistful. "I would have liked to have been a teacher."

And then the king of Adria is in the hall. He is walking away.

He didn't chose to wear the crown, I realize. But he has chosen to keep it.

It's all I can do not to take his head.

CHAPTER
TWENTY-ONE

The walls around the palace are at least twenty feet high. Higher in places. But they're short compared to the wall around the city. When darkness falls, I ease out my third-story window and drop onto the brick ledge below, but I'm not even a little bit afraid. I should be, I know. If I were normal. If I had good sense. If I were sane.

But I'm not any of those things, so it doesn't matter.

The gardens are surprisingly dark in the middle of the night, but it's not hard to find the big tree I saw on my walk with Dominic. Its limbs stretch across the top of the wall, and it's like I am on autopilot as I start to climb.

Part of me thinks I should warn palace security that they have some serious gaps in their perimeter. Part of me is just glad that they've spent all their time keeping people out. Makes it that much harder for them to keep me *in*.

The moon is high and the streets are empty. I was gone for weeks, I have to remind myself. It's like a part of me expects the Festival of the Fortnight to still be going on, to see hordes of tourists, to smell smoke and see fire. But the streets of Valancia are almost empty, almost still as I walk away from the palace.

I am almost alone.

Almost.

"Hey, Lila," I say, studying the girl before me.

She's like a shiny, sparkly specter as she steps out of the shadows. "I was wondering when the prodigal was going to come home."

She's Noah's twin sister, and they're both tall and thin with beautiful dark skin and jet-black hair. They have the same strange accent that's a blend of Portuguese, Hebrew, English, and Adrian. But, really, that's where the similarities end.

Noah would have made a joke by now.

Noah would have made me smile, made me laugh, made me forget.

Lila looks like she's here to make me pay.

"What did you do to Alexei?"

Has she been lingering outside the palace for hours, lying in wait? Is this some kind of coincidence? Or maybe Lila just knows me well enough to know that it was only a matter of time until I did something stupid.

"How is he?" I ask, even though I'm half-afraid of the answer.

Lila raises one shoulder, the chicest of shrugs. "How do you think he is? He's got a mother who is back from the dead, a father who wanted to hand him to the wolves, and a *whatever-you-are* who has dumped him for a prince. He's Alexei. He's Russian. He's fine. Except in all the ways he's terrible. You're a smart girl. You knew that."

"I—"

"What are you doing out here?" Lila asks me.

"I needed some air."

"There's plenty of air in there." She points toward the palace.

"I needed to see everyone and . . . explain."

"You didn't explain before you left?" It's not a question. It's an accusation. And I really hate how much she's right.

"I didn't want anyone to talk me out of it, okay?"

Lila eases closer. "What exactly is *it*?"

I look back at the palace, at the spotlights and the turrets and the walls.

"Running away," I whisper, but I don't explain and Lila doesn't ask for more.

"Where is everyone?" I ask.

Lila eyes me. "What makes you so sure they're all together?"

At this, I have to smile. "I know them."

She rolls her eyes and cocks a hip but goes ahead and says, "Come on."

• • •

Iran.

Of course they're in Iran. Lila freaked out the first time we brought her here, but I guess she's gotten over it because she doesn't bat an eye as we move out of the tunnels that run beneath the city and into the basement room with the hot-springs-fueled swimming pool and golden walls.

"They're up here," she says, starting up the stairs.

I've never been on the third floor, but that's where we find them.

Rosie is pacing. Megan and Noah are too close on the couch, so at peace and at home in each other's presence that I feel a little guilty for having seen it, having spied on what it looks like to be happy.

"Look who I found," Lila says, and everyone turns toward us.

"Grace!" Rosie is a tiny blond blur, hurling herself into my arms. "Where have you been?"

"You know where she was, Rosie." The accent is thick and the voice is deep and I know without turning that Alexei is angry. He closes a door behind him.

Heavy draperies cover the windows, pulled tight to block the light of the little camping lanterns that are scattered throughout the room. We're a long way from the cave in the hills where Alexei took refuge last summer, but we're still hiding, I realize. Alexei. And me. I just have to do my hiding in plain sight.

"How . . ." I start but trail off when I hear the singing.

"'Hush, little princess . . .'"

I look at the closed door, but I don't try to move past Alexei.

"How is she?"

"She's crazy," Alexei says, as if he can't believe that I forgot.

But Megan is up and coming toward me, pulling me into a too-tight hug. "Karina has started eating," she says when she pulls back. "And she's been sleeping, too. We've gotten her to take a shower and—"

"Now she smells good while she rants and raves like a crazy person," Alexei says.

It should hurt me. I'm pretty sure it's meant to. But I'm numb now. It's going to take a lot more than that to make me bleed.

"Has she mentioned my mom?" I ask. Megan shakes her head.

"But we haven't asked," she rushes to add.

"So, Grace." Rosie is practically bouncing. She's like a golden retriever puppy that has just been asked if it wants to go play. "What's the plan? I mean, you do have a plan, don't you? I know you have a plan."

"A plan for what?" I ask.

Rosie practically rolls her eyes. *"For vengeance."* She sounds more than a little bit evil. Then she laughs. "Or revenge or justice or whatever you're planning. So tell us. What. Is. The. Plan?"

I realize they're all looking at me now. This is supposed to be some kind of move in the chess game of my life. But I'm just a pawn who has already been sacrificed. I don't know how to tell them that the game is over.

"I . . ."

"Are we going to blackmail Ann?" Rosie guesses. "Kidnap the king? Ooh. I know. Palace coup!"

"A coup is how we got into this mess in the first place," Noah reminds her.

I have to shake my head. I have to find the words. You'd think I'd be used to it by now, disappointing people. I've certainly had enough practice. But there is something in the way Rosie is staring up at me. These people trusted me once. They trust me still. I've already decided to break my own heart. Not even I am cruel enough to keep on breaking theirs, too.

"There is no plan," I tell them at last. Maybe I've somehow given up on the dream of finding whatever my mother was looking for. Or maybe I'm just through letting other people get hurt.

Rosie rolls her eyes. "There has to be a plan. You wouldn't just move into the palace and—"

"I'm going to end it, Rosie. I just want to end it. And if I move in with Ann and let her groom me into whatever I need to be, it will end. Eventually."

"I don't understand," Rosie says. "How is that going to end anything?"

"It will end . . . when I marry the prince," I say.

I'm ready for stunned silence. I'm prepared for outrage and indignation. But I'm not expecting the sound of a voice I barely recognize yelling, "When you do *what*?"

CHAPTER TWENTY-TWO

No one bows. There are no curtsies. I don't know what is more unexpected—the sight of the future king of Adria standing in the lantern-lit room inside the Iranian embassy or the looks on the faces of my friends as they recognize the boy who is now screaming inside the sanctuary of Iran.

"Hi, Thomas," I tell him.

"Grace." He strides toward me, but he doesn't seem very prince-like. He just looks like a scared kid who snuck out looking for adventure and got so much more than he bargained for. "What were you talking about?"

I glance from the prince to my friends. "I should introduce you to everyone."

Then he seems to realize that we're not alone. He shifts from scared kid to future ruler in a heartbeat. "I am sorry to interrupt," he says, as if he's just popped by during high tea, unannounced.

"Thomas, these are my friends." One by one I make the introductions, but he doesn't care about the names, the nationalities.

"Hello, Rosemarie," he says to Rosie as I get to her.

"Hey," she tells him. When I look at her, she shrugs. "Thomas and I go way back." I must make a face because she throws up her hands. "What? I know people."

I'm just starting to realize that Rosie knows *everyone*, but that is hardly the point.

"What is the meaning of this?" the prince asks, turning back to me.

"These are my friends," I repeat like an idiot. "I'm allowed to have friends even though I live in the palace. Aren't I?"

"That's not what I was talking about, and you know it," Thomas snaps. "What did you mean when I came in, about marrying a prince. *This* prince?"

I look around the group, but they all just shake their heads, and I know I'm on my own.

"Your mother and my mother were friends."

"Yes. I know. But why should that mean—Don't tell me we've gone back to arranged marriages?" He tries to laugh. I think this is his idea of a joke. Or maybe he just wants it to be.

"Not exactly," I say.

I hear Alexei mutter something in Russian and then move to the opposite side of the room, as far away from me and my future husband as possible.

I am officially on my own.

"Your mother is of the opinion that it would be best for everyone if you and I were to marry," I choke out.

"Why?" There's a hard edge to the prince's voice, a deep mistrust in his eyes.

"It's a long story," I tell him.

"I have time," he says.

"But—"

"Oh, have mercy!" Lila snaps, then takes the prince by the shoulders and spins him around to face her. "Two hundred years ago, when the royal family was massacred, the baby lived. Grace is her descendant, and Grace's brother *should* be king, so Grace is going to marry you and have your babies so people will stop trying to kill her. Is that everything?" Lila eyes me, then edges away. "I think that's everything."

For a second, the room is silent, but then the door opens and Karina starts to sing. " *'Hush, little princess, don't you wait.'* "Karina reaches for me and refuses to let go. " *'The truth is locked behind the gates.'* "

I can feel the prince easing away as Karina comes closer. I don't know if he's afraid of me or the truth or this too-thin woman with the haunted eyes, but I can tell he hasn't just gone over the palace fences; he's gone through the looking glass and his world will never be the same again.

" *'Hush, little princess, pretty babe,'* "she sings again.

"Yes," I tell Karina. "That's nice." I try to soothe, but her eyes are growing wilder, her face paler. When her hands start to shake, Alexei lunges toward us.

"Come on," Alexei says, his voice soft. "Karina, come with me."

But his mother keeps looking in my eyes, and when she speaks again, the word is almost a whisper. "Caroline?"

"Caroline died," I tell her. "She's gone."

For a second, her eyes focus. Her gaze clears. It's like she heard me, understands. Knows. But then she sees the prince and spins on him, slaps him hard across the face and starts kicking and clawing. It takes both Alexei and Lila to pull her off while Noah shoves the prince behind him and tries to keep Karina away.

But no one can keep me back. Not ever again.

"What is it, Karina?" I ask, moving closer even as I should be pulling away. "What is going on in there?" I lean down, look into her eyes.

"They never knew." She sounds panicked but oddly lucid.

"Who, Karina? What didn't they know?"

It's like she's trying to find the words when the dreamy gaze descends again, falling across her face like a veil as she softly starts to sing. " 'The sunlight shines where the truth is laid.' "

"Karina, what are you talking about? Did my mother come to see you? What did you tell her?" *Is that why she's dead?* I want to scream but Alexei is shouting, pushing me toward the door.

"Stop! Leave her alone. Go home."

"But—"

"Just get out, Grace. You're upsetting her. Just go."

231

I could argue and I could fight, but even I know better than to stay where I'm not wanted.

Still, it's harder than I'd like to admit when I take my future husband's arm and give a gentle tug toward the door. We're almost to the stairs when I hear Megan call, "Grace, wait up a sec."

"What is it?" I hope I don't sound as frazzled as I feel.

Megan glances at the prince, who is waiting for me at the end of the hall, then drops her voice. "I've been doing some research into your mom's puzzle box. Turns out, there was this really famous Adrian carpenter-slash-inventor back in the 1800s. There are whole clubs that devote themselves to solving those boxes. There are desks, too. And chests and . . . lots of stuff."

"And you think he made my mom's box?"

"No." Megan's eyes glow. "I think *she* made it."

"It was a woman?"

Megan nods. "And when you search online, this is the only photo of her you can find."

The picture on Megan's phone really is quite daring. Black-and-white and no doubt taken in the late 1800s, the woman is wearing trousers and her gray hair is cropped short. She stands in a cluttered workroom, but behind her sits a gorgeous, ornate clock. It's easy to zoom in, look closer, and see the symbol I know so well carved into the base.

I cut my eyes up at Megan. "She was with the Society."

Megan nods her head. "I was thinking, if you want me to, I can work on your box while you do whatever you have to do now."

"What box?" When the prince speaks, it takes me a moment to even remember that he's with us.

"It's nothing," Megan says. She turns off her phone, slides it into her pocket.

I'm still looking at Megan, though, thinking about my mother and her secret lair—the work that killed her. And, suddenly the memories are too hot. I can't risk anyone else getting burned. "No. I need it," I say. "I want it. With me."

"Okay." Megan sounds surprised and disappointed but goes to get her backpack anyway. My mother's puzzle box is nestled safely inside, wrapped in an old sweatshirt. She hands it to me without another word.

But the prince is looking at me, as if wondering what kind of crazy person his mother is trying to fix him up with.

It is an excellent question.

"Come on, Your Highness," I tell him. "We need to get you home."

"What is this place?" the prince asks as we walk through the basement, and I have to give him credit. For a boy who just broke out of a palace and found out his family is trying to kill the girl they want him to marry, he seems to be taking it all in stride.

"Iran," I tell him. "Technically, this is the Iranian embassy. I know we shouldn't be here, but . . ." I don't bother to explain. I just wait for the usual cries of outrage and disbelief, but the future king of Adria just shrugs.

"Come on," I tell him as I head into the tunnel.

If it weren't for the sound of his footsteps, the occasional deep breath, I wouldn't know he's still behind me. I don't look back. Not now. Not ever. There are too many dragons in my past. Looking back only helps if they're no longer back there. But I know in my gut they are. Looking won't do anything but slow me down.

"Where are we now?" Thomas asks after a while.

"I don't know for sure," I tell him. "Probably somewhere under Egypt or maybe Australia."

"I mean, what are these?"

He catches up to me and makes me stop, gestures to the tunnels that stretch out before us and behind. Sometimes they branch and twist, but I know my way now, even without the little flashlight that lives inside my pocket.

"Tunnels," I say. I don't mean to sulk—really, I don't. But all the things I've seen and heard—what I know and will never in a million years understand—these facts are swirling inside of me. Too fast. It's going to make me sick.

"What kind of tunnels?" The prince sounds patient. He's not on the verge of a royal hissy fit. No, that honor is reserved for me.

"Old ones," I snap without really meaning to. It's not his fault. None of it. So I go on. "Really old. Like probably since-the-time-of-the-Romans old. For sure older than the wall."

"*The* wall?" the prince asks, sounding impressed.

"Yes."

He eyes the rough walls again with new appreciation. "Were they carved?"

"I don't know. I think so. But in some places they look natural. There are catacombs and stuff all over the city. Or under the city, I guess I should say. They even go out beneath the sea in places. But I think these were carved out. Sometimes you can see chisel marks. See?" I shine the light to a place on the wall where the line is too straight to be anything but man-made.

"I never knew there were tunnels," the prince says in disbelief. It's a tone I know. It's one that asks, *What else haven't they told me?* Then he meets my gaze and whispers, "Who?"

If the tunnel wasn't so narrow . . . if we weren't so close, I might not hear the question, but I do.

"I think the Romans. Maybe the Byzantines or the Mongols, but it doesn't really seem the Mongols' style, you know. So that's why I think it was—"

"Who wants to kill you?"

Oh.

I stop babbling, but the words don't come. I feel calmer than I should as I readjust my grip on my mother's puzzle box, then turn and start walking. I don't say a word as I lead Thomas through the tunnel, all the way to the ladder that I know will take us to a small alley behind the Israeli embassy.

When we're outside, the air feels cooler, and I'm suddenly chilled by the wind.

"Who wants you dead?" he asks again.

"We need to get you back to the palace before you're missed."

"Have there been attempts on your life, or is this just theoretical?"

He sounds so calm, so matter-of-fact. He's going to gather all the information and form a rational, informed opinion. He's not going to run off half-crazy and half-cocked.

If opposites do attract, then Prince Thomas might really be my soul mate.

But he's a soul mate I'm not going to answer.

"You shouldn't sneak out, you know," I say, then start the steep climb toward the palace. I don't stop and examine the irony of my giving someone else this advice. I don't stop and examine anything.

"You have to tell me," he says.

"It's not my place." I keep walking until I realize that the prince is no longer behind me.

He's standing, staring up the hill and then at the buildings that surround us. You can see the wall from here. And, beyond that, the inky-black waters of the sea. The moon is almost full as it climbs higher in the sky, and the gaslight burns atop the lampposts, lighting our way.

Thomas will be king of all of this someday—this and much, much more. But it looks very much as if he's seeing it all for the very first time.

"Are you in danger, Grace?" he asks me.

"At the moment? No."

"But you were. Is that why you moved into the palace?"

I don't answer. Which, I guess, is answer enough.

"Who tried to kill you?" He takes a step closer.

"Who do you think?" I practically shout. The words reverberate off the cobblestone streets and down the hill, echo out toward the sea. "My brother should be king. Who do you *think* wants us dead?"

I expect outrage or anger—for someone to strap me to a bed and pump me full of meds until I stop talking crazy. Nothing could surprise me more than when he looks down at the bundle in my hands and asks, "Where did you get that box?"

I'm so shocked that for a second I don't answer. "It's . . . It was my mother's."

"Where did she get it?"

"From her mother," I snap. If we're going to fight, I'd really like to get it over with.

"They told me about you," he says, but it's almost like a threat. "They said you had issues. I'm not supposed to believe you."

"That's a very solid game plan. But it doesn't mean I'm lying."

"No."

"Fine. Believe me. Don't believe me. I don't care. And, for the record, I don't want to marry you and have your babies either, but it's that or be hunted until I die, so . . ."

"That's a lie."

"Is it?" I look into his eyes and stalk closer. "You know the woman you just saw? The one who was singing that creepy, made-up song?"

"It's not made up," he snaps. I don't argue.

"Well, she was your mom's friend. Just like my mom was your mom's friend. And together they went looking for the lost

237

princess. That woman ended up in a mental institution for her trouble. My mom ended up dead."

The prince is backing away again, but he's no longer shaking. "They would have told me."

"Do you really believe that?" I don't mean to shout, and I don't mean to sound sarcastic. But some things can't be helped, I guess. "You didn't know that there were tunnels beneath the city. You look like you've never even *seen* the city after dark. Have you?"

He doesn't give me an answer, and I don't wait for one.

"You think you know your parents? Well, trust me, you don't. I don't care if they're royalty or military or schoolteachers or dentists or . . . I don't care and it doesn't matter. Because you never really know *anyone*. And that's the only thing I know for sure."

I don't realize it, but I've slowly turned as I've been speaking, and when I finish I'm looking up at the palace on the hill. Spotlights shine upon it, and from here I can see the tower Ms. Chancellor locked me in at the beginning of the summer. I can almost feel that old panic start to rise again, knowing that, in a way, I'm still trapped and I'll never be able to break free.

"So believe me or not, Your Highness, but that won't make it any less true."

I turn.

I stop.

I panic.

Because the future king of Adria is nowhere to be seen.

CHAPTER
TWENTY-THREE

I should run, I know. I should look. But the streets and alleys are like a maze here. Worse. They're like a maze where nothing runs straight and nothing runs even—where right now the prince could be running up toward the palace or down toward the sea. Or lower.

I look behind me. Thomas knows how to get into the tunnels now, so I bolt in that direction, expecting to see a flash, a peek. But the alley is empty and the opening to the tunnels is closed. I open the door and lean down, listen for the sound of running royal feet, but there is nothing but the *drip, drip, drip* of water. I know in my gut that I'm alone.

I stand and bolt back to the street, turning, looking. "Thomas!" I yell into the darkness, but Valancia is sleeping. I am alone. And the future king of Adria is gone.

•   •   •

I didn't lose the prince.

I didn't ask him to come with me. I didn't tell him to follow. I certainly didn't make him run off in the middle of the night down streets that I'm pretty sure he's never even seen before.

I absolutely did not lose the future king of Adria.

Or so I tell myself over and over throughout the night.

By the next morning I'm not entirely sure that anyone is going to believe me.

Maybe he made it back, I tell myself. He's a big boy—just a year younger than me. By the time I was his age I'd already lived a dozen lifetimes. But Thomas isn't like that. He's lived his whole life behind walls and gates and fences so high that the outside world never stood a shot of seeping in.

By his age, I was nestled deep inside a shell that was growing harder and harder every day. The world could still harm Thomas, I know, and that's what scares me.

I should tell someone, I think. But who? And what should I say exactly?

Funny story. So last night, I snuck out of the palace to go see the boy I like and my friends who are trying to prove that the royal family are murdering psychos, but then my pseudo-boyfriend's mom—who is an actual psycho—freaked out and I had to leave. Oh, and the prince fol- lowed me and heard all of this and then he freaked out and ran into the city and I didn't know where to find him, so I just gave up and came back. Now what's for breakfast?

240

No. I don't think that would help matters at all, so I don't say a word of it.

But I have to do something, I know, as I slide my mother's puzzle box beneath my bed, then dress and start downstairs.

I have to find my friends and divvy up the city.

Rosie and I can take the tunnels; Noah and Lila can scour the area around Embassy Row. It's possible Megan might be able to access some of the city's street-level surveillance cameras—maybe they caught a glimpse of the runaway prince.

It's not too late to find him, I tell myself.

It's going to be okay, I lie.

But as soon as I set foot on the first floor I know nothing is okay. The palace is alive, swarming with guards and uniformed members of the staff. It is a whirl of hushed words and hurried, frantic footsteps. For a second, I think I'm too late. That they know. Or, worse, that something has happened. This is what tragedy looks like, life has taught me. The palace is never supposed to be in disarray.

Everywhere I turn there are guards and workers and . . . florists.

I stop on the stairs and look down at the big room where I first met the royal family. Suddenly, I realize that this is a different kind of chaos.

"The party," I tell myself as I remember the king's coronation and the anniversary and the gala. I didn't think it was possible, but it's suddenly a whole lot harder to admit I might have lost their prince.

When the butler starts toward me, though, I know what I have to do.

"Good morning, miss," he says with a bow. "Is there anything you might require this morning?"

I stay silent a little too long, but the butler doesn't move. My tells are too obvious, too automatic. *I'll never lose them now*, I think as I realize my hands are shaking and my heart has started to pound.

"Miss?" he says.

"Prince Thomas . . ." I start. "I don't suppose you've seen him?"

"Why, yes, miss."

"Because I didn't ask him to—Wait. What?"

"His Highness is in the south corridor, miss. Is there anything else you might need?"

I'm too numb to speak. It's not until the butler turns and starts back up the stairs that I ask, "How do you get to the south corridor?"

I've found the prince, but as I rush through the crowded halls of the palace I realize I have no idea what I'm going to say when I reach him. Do I explain? Do I pander or condescend?

Some might tell him that he's crazy—that he didn't see what he saw or hear what he heard. But I could never do that to another human being, so I make up my mind to do the craziest thing of all: tell him the truth.

242

I don't know what to expect. Maybe the prince is rallying the troops, alerting the media, running away? Maybe he wants to get as far from the crazy new girl as possible. I certainly wouldn't blame him. I'd love to run away from me, too, most of the time.

This is a boy who has just learned that he has no actual claim to the throne he's been promised since birth, that his spouse has already been chosen for him, and that everyone he loves might want me dead.

Maybe he's decided to agree with them.

I may be running into anything, I realize, and still, as I turn the corner, I'm utterly surprised by what I see. Because not only is the prince standing in the corridor, looking out the massive windows, but he is not alone.

"Hello, Ms. Blakely," the king says. "We've been expecting you."

For a moment the whole thing is so surreal that I forget where I am—who I'm talking to. But then Thomas gives me a silent signal and I drop into the world's most awkward curtsy before the king.

Before the man whose family wants me dead.

As I slowly rise, it's all I can do to keep myself rooted—to make myself calm. The prince should be screaming for the palace guards, but it is just another morning as far as anyone could tell.

They don't look like king and heir, surveying their kingdom. They look like a grandson who has sought out his grandfather, needing a little advice.

My anxiety turns to full-on panic.

Then I see the object in the prince's hands, and my panic turns to rage.

"What is that?" I shout, but I already know what it is. I recognize the color and the shape and now, in hindsight, the brief recognition in the prince's eyes last night when Megan mentioned my mother's puzzle box and pulled it from her backpack.

"You got that out of my room? How dare you? That's mine! I've given up my life for you people. The least you can do is leave me a sliver of privacy."

"I didn't go into your room," Thomas says, defensive.

"That was my mother's—give it to me." I lunge for the box, but the prince steps back, out of reach.

I don't care that I sound like a petulant, spoiled child. I still snap, "Give it to me now!"

But when I lunge for the prince again, I find a seventy-year-old monarch standing in my way.

The king's voice is kind but strong. He doesn't sound like a killer when he tells me, "This box was not your mother's, Ms. Blakely."

For a second, I'm so stunned that I recoil. That's one of the curses of being me. I'm never really sure that I'm not lying.

"I'm sorry, Your Highness," I say. I need to be strong. "But you don't know what you're talking about."

"No, I'm the one who is sorry, Ms. Blakely. I should explain. This is not your mother's box, you see. I know because this box is *mine*."

The king turns and takes the box from his grandson. Carefully, he pushes and pulls the ornate carvings until, with a snap, the box pops open. He tips it on its side, and out slides a very old-fashioned key. He holds it up before me.

"Do you know what this is?" he asks.

"A key?" I say. I'm not trying to sound flippant. I'm just so tired and worn that I can't help it anymore.

The king smiles. "Not just any key, Ms. Blakely. This is a *key to the kingdom*. And I mean that quite literally. It fits these gates, you see."

But he's not pointing toward the front of the palace. He's pointing toward the tall iron gates that stand at the end of the south corridor. I realize that there is a sort of courtyard on the other side, and that is where the king leads us.

"Two hundred years ago the palace was smaller," he explains. "And, *these* were the gates that the guards threw open the night the royal family was killed and the coup began."

As the king speaks, I can't help but remember the ceremonial opening of the gates that kicked off the Festival of the Fortnight. The king must read my mind. "We just don't tell that to the tourists," he says with a wink. "It's not the gates that matter, after all. The whole thing is symbolic. Now."

He turns from me to run a hand along the ornate ironwork. "Not then, though. Two hundred years ago, these gates mattered very much. And this"—he holds the relic up to the light—"was their key."

I look at the old-fashioned key that still lies in the palm of the king's large hand. It doesn't look like it should hold any power at all. But once upon a time it changed the world.

"What most people don't understand," the king goes on, "what most people fail to realize is that no mob forms overnight. The royal family knew the people were angry. So the king ordered the gates closed and locked. And what no one ever says—what very few people even realize—is that the guards—the men who threw the gates open and let the mob run in—didn't have the key."

I look at the gates and the walls as if the truth were out there somewhere. But it isn't. I'm just not entirely certain it's in here, either.

"I don't understand," I tell him.

"This is the literal key to the kingdom, Ms. Blakely. And two hundred years ago there were only two in the world. One was held by the king and one was held by his brother. *This* is the king's key."

"Yeah," I tell him. "Of course. You're the king."

He nods. "I am. The king's key was given to me at my coronation. Just as it was given to my father before me and his father before him—all the way back to the War of the Fortnight. But this key did not belong to my great-great-great-grandfather. He *wasn't* the king, you see. He was the king's *brother*. And so a part of me has always wondered what became of his key. I told myself that it was lost to the war and to time, but now I highly suspect it lies locked inside *that* box."

He points behind me, and I turn to see the prince holding a second box.

"I lied," Thomas admits with a shrug. "I did go into your room."

But I'm no longer angry. There are no words for what I feel as the prince holds the box out to me, but for some reason I pass it to the king, who runs his hands along the smooth wood, almost reverently. Within a few seconds the puzzle Megan and I have been trying to master for days snaps open with a click. A second key comes tumbling out onto the king's palm.

"*So that's where that is.*" His voice is soft, and it takes a moment for him to meet my gaze. When he does, he's almost crying. "I don't know where your mother got that box, Ms. Blakely. But it has been missing for two hundred years. Ever since the night *this* key was used to open those gates and let in the mob that killed the royal family."

There are minutes—seconds— when the whole world can change and your life will forevermore be marked *before* and *after*. No one knows that more than I, and as I study the king of Adria, I know he's having one of them now. I just can't quite wrap my head around why.

"So a guard or someone stole the box," I say. "I'm sorry, Your Majesty, but I don't see . . ."

"You have a good heart, don't you, Grace?" the king asks me.

"That's probably up for debate," I say, and the king laughs. He doesn't know that I'm not joking.

"Have you learned to open the box?"

"No," I say, almost defensive.

"Very few ever do," the king says. "When you're raised in this house, then history is all around you. My ancestors hang on the

247

walls; my family tree is memorized in schools. My world should have no secrets, Ms. Blakely. No mysteries. And so since I was a boy, I have clung to one of the few unknowns that my family has left. A single question: What became of the second key?"

The king takes a breath and the prince eases closer.

"Oh, I told myself that the historians were right," the king says. "I assumed the box had been stolen—that it had been smashed or destroyed and the key removed. I was certain that explained it. But . . ."

"But if the box wasn't destroyed . . ." I fill in.

"Then it was *opened*, wasn't it?" he says. "By one of the two men in the kingdom who knew how."

The king draws a deep breath, as if telling this story means also tempting fate.

"Do you think Alexander the Second gave the guards this key, Ms. Blakely? Do you think *he* threw open the gates and let in the mob that would massacre his family?" The king shakes his head. For the first time, he looks old. "No. Of course he didn't. And so I have to think it was Alexander's *brother* who opened this box and turned over the key that stood between him and the throne."

"But that would mean . . ." I start, but I'm too afraid of the answer.

"It means my great-great-great-grandfather was a killer, Ms. Blakely. It means I am descended from a traitor, a usurper. It means I sit upon a stolen throne. But what I don't know is . . ."

The king hardens now. His gaze is so hot it almost burns. "Why are *you* here, Ms. Blakely?"

"Thomas," I say. I'm backing away and running on instinct. "I was looking for Thomas."

"No." The king shakes his head. "Why are you *here*?"

"I . . ."

Lies swirl inside my head, options spiral. I need Dominic or Ms. Chancellor—an embassy full of marines and every trick my big brother ever taught me to keep the bullies at bay. I need to run or fight, and I might do both if the king's gaze doesn't soften.

"Amelia lived, didn't she?" He's smiling now, and almost eerily calm. I look at Thomas, and I don't know what to say. The king doesn't seem like a villain in this moment—not the mastermind of my terrible fate. Is it possible he's as innocent as he seems? Is anyone? Ever?

"Amelia lived and her descendants live, and . . . and now I sit upon *your* throne, don't I, Ms. Blakely?" he asks, but he doesn't wait for an answer.

Instead, he does the strangest thing. He bows. To me.

"Get up! What are you doing?" I look up and down the hall, panic filling me. "You're the king of Adria."

"Am I?" he asks.

"Yes! I don't want to be a princess. My brother doesn't want to be king. We just want . . ."

Justice.

Revenge.

But I can't say any of that, so I just shake my head. "To tell you the truth, I don't know what I want anymore."

There's a window seat nearby, and the king eases me toward it. "Sit, Grace. Breathe."

I don't cry and I don't scream, but I don't run, either. I'm just so tired of running. Sometimes, Dr. Rainier says, your only job is to breathe, and so that is what I do. In and out. Until the king of Adria takes the seat beside me and says, "Now, Grace, I believe it's time you tell *me* a story."

So I do.

I tell him everything. About my mom and the Scarred Man and the fire. I tell him about the comatose PM and the night Jamie lay on the embassy's dining room table, his blood covering the floor.

I look up at the man I've been hating for weeks and say, "You didn't know any of this, did you?"

"No."

"You didn't try to kill me?"

"No. Though I would understand if you choose not to believe me."

I can't help myself. I look at Thomas, then back to his grandfather. "I believe you," I say, and the crazy thing is that it might even be true.

When the king stands, he pats my back. "Now why don't you go get some rest? You must be tired."

I stand, suddenly shaking. "But . . . what happens now?"

250

The king smiles and pats me on the back again. "Now you leave everything to me."

I bristle involuntarily and pull back. He already knows me too well and can read me too easily because he says, "Trust is hard, isn't it?"

"You have no idea."

"You can trust me," the king says. And as he does, Dominic appears over his shoulder.

"Yes, Grace Olivia," the Scarred Man tells me. "You can."

The king pushes me back toward my rooms. "Go, rest. I'll take care of everything. This fight isn't yours anymore."

He hands me my mother's box and his great-great-great-grandfather's key, and the prince and I start silently down the halls.

I can't read his tone when Thomas asks, "So does this mean you're not going to marry me anymore?"

"I don't know. Does it?"

He gives me a cocky smile, but neither of us says another word.

CHAPTER TWENTY-FOUR

Hope is a delicate thing.

A dangerous thing.

I had it once, back when I thought we were going to live in that little army town and I was going to graduate high school, maybe travel around Europe with my mom before I left for college. I thought I'd grow up, maybe meet a nice guy.

I thought I'd get a happy ending.

Those are the only endings anyone ever talks about, after all. What the world doesn't tell you—what you don't see in the movies and in books and on TV—is that not everybody gets one. And no one ever thinks they're going to be the very unlucky exception to the rule.

It's been over a day since the king took my burdens into his own hands, and now as I stand in the window of my room in the

palace, I can feel something inside of me. It bubbles and perco-
lates. It grows and swells. And it scares me more than any of
Dominic's warnings. There's a tiny voice in the back of my head
whispering that we are in the endgame of a two-hundred-year-
old chess match.

I might still get a happy ending, the little voice says, but I'd
give anything to quiet it, because I learned a long time ago that as
soon as I want something—as soon as I dare to believe—that's
when I get hurt.

"Well, isn't that a pretty sight?"

The maid is at my door, closing it behind her. The long blue
gown is draped across her outstretched arms. I want to tell her it's
too pretty, too perfect and stately and royal. I want to tell her to
take it back and leave me up here in my tower, where nothing can
possibly hurt me, much less my own foolish expectations.

But it's too late for that.

Because that's the thing about hope—you can never kill it
yourself.

"Are you excited for the party, Your Highness?"

"I'm not—" I start to correct her, then stop myself. She
doesn't want to hear me explain yet again that I'm not really a
princess, that I don't really belong here. So I save my breath.

"Yes," I say instead, terrified to realize that it's true. "I
think I am."

I expect the young woman to smile back, to be happy at this.
But it's like a cloud is passing across her face.

"I know you saw the king yesterday."

253

It sounds like an accusation, like I've done something wrong. I can just imagine the Society briefing their spies and setting their traps, wondering if it's time to maybe get rid of me once and for all.

"Yeah," I shoot back. "I did. And you can tell your . . . *sisters* . . . that I'll speak with whomever I please. I took their bargain. I'm here. And that's the last order I'm going to take."

The maid's smile is completely gone now. Her last words are a warning. "It would be a mistake to trust the wrong people."

She doesn't speak again as she helps me dress and does my hair. Carefully, she paints my face with makeup, covers my lips with something sticky and super pink.

I must look like a girl—I might even look like a princess, because an hour later there's a knock on the door, and I open it to find the prince standing in the hallway. He looks at me for a long time, staring, before he actually says, "Wow."

"*Wow* what?" I ask.

"You look nice." .

He sounds so surprised that I suppose I could be insulted, but I'm not. That's the thing about hope. It affects you in the most unexpected ways. I'm too optimistic to be hurt by insults. Even by compliments. Even by future kings.

Thomas rocks back on his heels and runs a hand through his hair. "I came to see if you wanted to go down together. My mom said I should ask."

"Okay," I say, trying to read Thomas's eyes. Is he afraid of his mother? Mad at her? Does he understand that someone wanted me dead, and apparently it isn't the king? If he knows his mother is a killer, I can't decide, and I don't want to be the one to tell him.

"I would have asked anyway, you know," Thomas says. "I'm not here because of her. But she did ask."

I can imagine Ann's train of thought. It would make for great optics, the sight of me walking in on the future king's arm. It would plant the seed, start the talk.

But that's not why Thomas is holding his arm out for me. It certainly isn't why I take it.

We're quiet as the prince leads me through the halls. When I try to start down the main corridor in the center of the palace, he tugs me in another direction.

He cocks an eyebrow. "Shortcut."

The hall is narrower here, less busy. "I was just thinking that I might make it all day without getting lost in this place."

He laughs. "I promise not to get us too lost."

"That's okay," I say. "I trust you."

I'm not just talking about the mazelike halls, and I know the prince can tell. I'm shocked to realize that it's even true. I do trust him. And I trust the king. I only wish I could trust the future.

"I met your mom once."

Thomas's words come out of the blue, and I can't help myself: They stop me.

"What?"

"I met her," he says again. "It was a few years ago. She came to see my mom. I remember it because . . . well . . . not many people come to see my mom."

I know what he means. The palace is huge and crowded. And lonely. My friends haven't been to see me once since I moved in. Not even Rosie has stormed the gates. They have their reasons— good ones, I'm sure. But it's easy to imagine that after a few years inside these walls I might not have many friends left outside of them. I tremble to think that, someday, I might end up just like Ann.

"Anyway, that afternoon I found your mom wandering around the corridors but laughing about it. She'd been wandering for almost an hour," Thomas tells me with a smile. "She'd gotten turned around, too."

It's one more thing my mother and I have in common, I guess. We both came here and lost our way. I don't let myself think about the rest of it: about how easily that can be a person's downfall.

"I showed her to the doors and waited while one of the embassy cars pulled up to get her. I kept thinking about that last night. About how now maybe you'll get to leave," Thomas tells me, but he sounds a little sad. Like maybe he'd give anything to leave, too, but knows he never will. "My grandfather will take care of it, Grace. You will be free of these responsibilities soon."

"Maybe," I say, and I can't help myself. I feel a little sorry for Adria's future king.

We must be getting closer to the party because faint traces of music come floating down the hall toward us. There's the low rumble that comes from a crowd of people in a massive room with excellent acoustics. And with every step my hands tingle more, my heart pounds.

I'm just about to tell Thomas that I have to go back—that there's been some kind of mistake—when, up ahead of us, a door opens.

It's too late to move when a woman bursts into the hall, bumping into me. I teeter a little, and without my grip on Thomas's arm, I might stumble.

I might fall.

But I don't. Instead, I find myself frozen, staring into the eyes of the woman before me.

"Excuse me, Madame Prime Minister," I say.

But the PM just glares at me. If looks could kill, I'm pretty sure I'd be dead by now.

"You kids have fun tonight!" a big voice booms, and I catch a glimpse of the king just past the prime minister's shoulder.

"Yes, Grandfather," Thomas says, then pulls me forward. I know there's no use in looking back. It's started now. And looking back won't do anything but make me turn to salt.

I blame my new designer shoes for the fact that my footsteps are unsteady.

I blame the fact that I can't breathe on the blue dress's tiny waist.

"It's okay, Grace." Thomas places his hand over mine and squeezes. "I told you my grandfather would see to it. And he has. Very soon you will be free of me."

I'm supposed to laugh. I suppose I really should smile. Telling the king sounded good in theory—it made sense at the time. But now that it's real and there's no going back, I can't shake the feeling that I'm about to make everything worse.

But Thomas doesn't understand my silence.

"It is okay, you know." He looks a little sheepish. "I wouldn't want to marry me, either."

We're nearing the end of the hall, and the music is louder. I can hear the dull hum of laughing, gossiping guests. We're so close to the party, but I have to stop.

"You're kidding, right?" I ask him.

"I know you have no reason to trust any member of my family, but I assure you my grandfather does not lie. If he said he will fix your situation, then it will be fixed."

"No. Not that." I shake my head. "You really don't know?"

"Don't know what?" He honestly looks confused.

"That basically every girl in the world is going to want to marry you."

He blushes a little. In his tux and white tie, he really is quite charming. He looks down. I half expect him to drag his toe across the carpet. "But not you."

Now *I* want to laugh. "I'm not princess material." I take his arm again, steer him toward the big open area at the end of the hall. The ballroom is down below. From up here, we are eye level

258

with the massive chandeliers and the arching ceiling inlayed with gold, painted by an old master.

"Okay. So who *do* you want to marry?" the prince asks as we reach the railing of the balcony and look down on the dance floor below.

But one boy isn't dancing.

He leans against the railing of the wide, sweeping staircase, looking up. I can't help but think back to that day at the beginning of summer when my biggest worry was impressing Ms. Chancellor and trying not to cause an international incident in the rose garden. I was his best friend's kid sister then, the bratty girl who was always climbing up trees and jumping off walls. So many things have changed, but one thing is constant: Alexei's still the boy who will try to catch me.

"Wait," Thomas says, following my gaze. "Don't answer that."

I'm pretty sure the prince and I are supposed to descend this gorgeous staircase together, arm in arm. Flashbulbs are supposed to go off. People are supposed to turn and stare. This is my big moment, my introduction. For the first time in my life, people are supposed to ask, *Who's that girl?*—and not out of horror.

I know the prince knows this. I also know he doesn't care, and that's why he pushes me toward the stairs.

"Go on."

I look back at him.

"He's not here for me," the prince says. Then he winks and walks away.

I can feel Alexei's gaze on me as I descend. I keep my hand on the railing and am careful not to hook my heel in my hem or anything else that might send me tumbling down the stairs and into his arms. Not that I'd mind the end result.

"What are you doing here?" I say when I reach him.

Alexei smirks. "I was invited." He pulls an invitation from the inside pocket of his tuxedo jacket. "A palace messenger delivered it personally this morning. I felt very important."

"You *are* important," I say. Then I can't help myself as I glance back at the boy who stands at the top of the stairs, grinning.

You're welcome, the prince mouths, then walks away.

"I—" Alexei and I both start at exactly the same time. Then we both stop.

I want to tell him about the prince and the king and the key. I want to say out loud that it might be over, that I've placed this problem in the hands of the most powerful man in the land—that it's no longer my burden to bear. I want to hug Alexei, kiss him, dissolve into him until all of the worry and dread that I've carried inside of me for weeks just fades away, rises up like the sound of the music.

But there's not time for that because a tiny blond blur is already streaming toward me.

"Grace!" Rosie says, plastering herself against me. "How are you?"

"I'm okay, Ro," I say, then look up at Alexei. Something about my face must show that something's changed, though, because the wider I smile, the more worried Alexei looks.

"Wait. What's wrong?" Rosie senses something and pulls back. "You look . . . happy. This worries me. Is anyone else worried about this?"

Megan and Noah have joined us now. They're holding hands, I notice. And Noah looks so handsome in his tux. Megan is in a red gown with small gold flowers embroidered at the hem. But as soon as Rosie says it, they both stop smiling.

"Yeah." Noah studies me. "What's wrong?"

"Why does something have to be wrong?"

"You're smiling," Megan says.

"I can smile!" I tell them. "It's allowed."

"Yeah. Sure," Noah says. "It's just . . . unusual."

I want to tell them that the status quo is changing, that this is who I'm going to be from here on out. But Rosie is scowling at me and shaking her head.

"Yeah. You look happy. Why are you happy?"

I'm not thinking. Really. It's not a *conscious* thought. But with the words I can't help myself—I glance in the prince's direction. He's in a group of people, but he's looking right at me.

I'm so excited to tell my friends about the box and the key and the king's promise to bring it all to an end, but Alexei follows my gaze. When Thomas gives me a wink, Alexei sees it, and bristles. He actually turns.

"Alexei, wait." I reach out and grab his arm. His tux is smooth and soft beneath my fingers.

"It was a mistake to come here. I should never have left Karina alone."

"How is she?" I ask before he can leave, before all my happy seeps away.

"Better." Alexei glances around the room, distracted. "She is better."

Noah and Megan share a look. Then Megan says, "She was lucid for a little while today. They must have had her super drugged up at the hospital. I really think that might be most of her problem. Maybe once all the drugs are out of her system . . ."

But Alexei isn't like Megan. Alexei is like me. He has long been immune to hope, so he just shakes his head. "I should not have left her alone."

"Wait." I grab his hand and pull him back, then look at all my friends in turn. "Something happened yesterday morning. I think . . . Well, I mean, if everything works out, then I think it might be over."

At first, my friends are stunned and silent. Confused. They're as afraid to hope as I am, and before any of them can start to wonder if this is just another aspect of my messed-up mind, the band begins to play the Adrian national anthem, and everyone in the ballroom turns. For a second, I think they're looking right at me, but then I realize, no, they're looking higher, to the balcony above.

A uniformed man with a booming voice stands at the top of the stairs. As soon as all eyes are upon him he steps to the edge and yells, *"His Royal Highness, the king!"*

Almost as one, every soul in the ballroom drops into a bow or a curtsy when the king appears on the balcony overhead. Princess Ann and Thomas's father are beside him.

A murmur is moving through the crowd, a wave of whispers that seem to say that nothing is as it seems. As I rise, I realize that someone has set a microphone stand on the top step. The king moves toward it, and the whispers get louder.

"What's going on?" Megan asks. "The program didn't say anything about the king giving a speech."

I can feel my friends' gazes burning into me, but I can't take my eyes off the man at the top of the stairs.

"Friends, family, distinguished guests," the king begins.

And there it is, deep inside of me, that tiny, fragile bubble that feels a lot like hope. I can feel it start to rise in spite of my best intentions.

"I am the luckiest of men to have worn the crown of Adria for fifty years. It has been my honor to be your king. But . . ."

The king falters. It's like he's going to cry—and maybe he is. At least that's what I feel like doing.

"But I come to you tonight and admit . . ." Again the king stumbles. Sweat covers his brow. And that bubble inside of me . . .

It bursts.

At the top of the stairs, the king of Adria reaches for the microphone stand, but he can't seem to grasp it. It tips and falls,

263

crashing down the stairs. On the dance floor, the king's subjects are quiet. A stunned disbelief fills the crowd as the man takes a hesitant step, but it's like his legs can't hold him—like he is an hourglass and a crack has appeared, sand rushing out, as the king stumbles.

He sways, then pitches awkwardly forward and crashes down the massive staircase.

It is a long, long way to fall.

Gasps and cries fill the ballroom, but the people of Adria are stunned. Frozen. I can see Thomas pushing through the people who stand like statues, trying to get closer to his grandfather, who has landed, limp and broken, on the polished parquet floor.

I'm not surprised when Dominic is the first to reach him. It seems like all of Adria is holding their breath as he reaches for the king, presses a hand gently against his neck even as he yells in Adrian for someone to bring a stretcher, for the crowd to make some room.

But then he goes silent. He hangs his head for a moment and pulls his hand away.

It seems to take forever for the Scarred Man to find the words.

"The king is dead."

Then he looks to the top of the stairs, where Thomas's father stands, Princess Ann beside him.

The king's eldest son—his heir—is deathly pale as Dominic finishes. "Long live the king."

"*Long live the king,*" a shocked crowd echoes, their gazes shifting. But I don't speak. I just stare at the woman who has hunted me and my brother for months, who wanted my mother dead.

Ann is the only person in the ballroom who doesn't seem the least surprised.

I don't know how she's done it, but I know what a killer looks like. I've been seeing one in the mirror for years, after all, and a part of me wants to rise up and point at the new king's wife, shout *murderer* for all to hear.

But the truth is the king was well—the king was safe—until I told him.

I knew the rules. I broke the rules. And the king paid with his life.

The king is dead, I think. *And it is all my fault.*

CHAPTER
TWENTY-FIVE

People don't run, don't scream. It's more like two hundred and fifty formally clad strangers are struck silent at the same time, and yet beneath it all there is an undercurrent of panic. Of disbelief.

This isn't happening, the good people of Adria are thinking. Things like this don't just happen—not in public, not out of the blue. But it's not a dream. The guards who are coming in and urging the crowd toward the doors prove that. It's as real as the paramedics who rush inside with their gurney and their bags, everyone knowing they're too late.

Thomas's cries echo through the ballroom—too loud and too familiar. That's what shocked disbelief sounds like.

Shocked disbelief and fear. And rage. And guilt.

It's a sound I know better than anyone.

I'm starting to pull away—to go to him—when something passes across my field of vision, and for some reason I turn and watch as the prime minister rushes away, her movements calm, her mood cool. And I realize that it wasn't just Ann's deal that I broke when I told the king my story.

Alexei's hand is on my arm. He's trying to drag me away, into the flow of the crowd. But when have I ever gone with the flow?

So I break free, pushing against the grain, away from the chaos, following the woman in white, who is going down a smaller, more inconspicuous hallway. I know it leads to a private entrance and exit. It's the one the royal family uses. I guess the prime minister, too.

"Did you do this?" My voice echoes in the long, narrow space, and the PM stops.

We're alone, I realize. I guess her guards are getting the cars, blocking the corridor. I don't know. Don't care. I'm too busy studying the woman who stands before me, slowly turning.

"Do what?" the PM says.

"Don't lie to me. Stop treating me like I'm an idiot—like I'm a child."

"You are a child!" The PM is practically yelling. It's as if this is the point that's been haunting her—taunting her—for ages. I should have been squashed months ago. That I'm still here, a thorn in her side, makes her want to rage.

And in that moment, her walls go down. I can see right through her.

267

"He told you tonight, didn't he?"

"What?" she snaps and draws back.

"He told you he was going to help me, didn't he? Of course he did. You're the prime minister. He'd have to let you know he was going to do something. But what is it you and your council like to say? *'Adria is a pivotal cog in the wheel of the world, and we cannot have it destabilized'*? You knew. And you had to stop him."

I don't like what I can't help thinking.

"Did you kill him?"

The PM tries to act indignant. "The king's heart was bad. Everybody knows this."

"He was going to stop it!" I shout because I want to—I want to scream. "He was going to fix it!"

"It has been fixed!" She holds her long skirts in her hands and leans toward me. It's like she's getting ready for a fight. "There is one solution that doesn't end with anarchy—with chaos and an economic ripple that could turn into a tsunami sweeping across the globe. And *that* is the solution that we have. That is the solution we agreed to."

I back up, eye her. *"Did you kill him?"*

My voice is too calm, too even. It makes the PM realize how far down the rabbit hole of rage she's already chased me.

She straightens and drops her hem. "The Society does not murder monarchs, Ms. Blakely."

I don't know why, but a part of me actually believes her as she goes on.

"I learned of this madness not ten minutes before the king fell. I would have tried to talk him out of it. I would have . . . If the infernal man hadn't been in such a hurry . . ."

"It's your fault," I tell her. "If you and your Society would have just helped. If you'd listened. It's your fault!"

"No." The PM shakes her head. "The king's death isn't our fault, Ms. Blakely.

She looks like a queen as she gathers up her skirts again and pivots. *"It's yours."*

I always knew I could break anything. Everything. And now I guess it's official.

One conversation with me can kill a king.

I know it's true. My words are poison, my mere presence a fire. A part of me wants to run as far and as fast as I can before I spread like an epidemic.

Another part of me wants to stand right here and let the palace burn.

When I make it back to the ballroom, the king's body is gone. The crowds are, too. But the ghost of the party still lingers in broken glasses and spilled food, overturned chairs and a dull, haunting ache that fills the ballroom like a pulse.

There's a painting overhead of King Alexander II and his queen and the little princes. They're my family, I have to think, as I look up at the painting with fresh eyes, trying to see some

kind of resemblance. But it's no use. Even their ghosts have probably moved on.

"She did it, didn't she?"

I jump at the words and spin, and that's when I see Thomas
sitting on the floor behind me, directly in front of the painting of
our mutual ancestors that hangs on the opposite side of the
ballroom.

"My mother is a monster," he says flatly. "You told me. And
that says everything, doesn't it? You come in here—a total
stranger—and you tell me that my mom has been trying to kill
you. My own mother! And I believe you. What does that say about
her? What does that say about *me*?"

"Thomas—"

"I think I've always known it. Is that crazy? I think that sounds
crazy. But just because something's crazy doesn't mean it isn't
true, you know?"

He looks up at me and I nod. I do know. Far too well.

"I'm going to—" He tries to stand. "I have to tell someone.
My father. The authorities. Someone. I have to tell someone it's
her fault."

"No." I put my hand out and stop him. "It's my fault."

"No." The prince shakes his head.

"Your grandfather would be alive today—right now—if I
hadn't told him. If I hadn't kept picking at it and picking at it and
making everything worse."

I make everything worse.

"Grace, no," the prince says, but I just hear my mother screaming.

"Grace, no!"

I shake my head. I start to rock. Someone dims the lights in the ballroom until only the gaslight in the sconces remains. There's gaslight all through the palace, covering the grounds. It is the color of fire, and I close my eyes and try to block out the glare.

"Grace, no!"

"You're shaking." The prince's arm is around me. He's pulling me tight. I should be comforting *him*. He's the one who's lost a loved one. He's the one who's been betrayed.

But I can't stop shaking, saying, "It's my fault. It's my fault. It's my fault," over and over again like a prayer.

He rubs my back, slow and steady. "Why do I get the feeling you think everything is your fault?"

He's not teasing.

"Because it is. Because I——" I start, but he cuts me off.

"You're not that important," Thomas says, stopping the loop that's been playing inside my head for years. "It's not an insult. It's just the truth. If you think you're to blame for everything, then you'd have to be responsible for everything. And you aren't. And even if you marry me and pop out a dozen royal babies, you won't be, will you?"

Somehow, in this crazy place and time, it seems like an extremely valid point.

271

"No," I admit.

"Good. Because if it's your fault, then it's my fault, too. I'm the one who told him about the box." The prince looks away, his gaze set on that far-off painting, that far-off time. "And now I'm the reason they're going to put him in one."

"Will you go to the funeral?"

"*We* will go to the funeral," he tells me. "My mother is going to like *the optics*. You comforting me in my time of grief, stepping in, being there for the family. She'll have us married by the time I'm twenty."

I should hate the sound of that, the truth of it. But I don't feel anything anymore. Now it just seems like the end.

"Maybe it's for the best. Maybe we should just accept it."

"Somehow you don't strike me as a person who accepts things."

Silence draws out. In the distance, I hear a vacuum cleaner. They're going to want to clean the room and polish the floors. But I just keep looking at that painting.

"They didn't get a funeral," I say.

"What?"

"King Alexander and the queen and the little princes— someone came and cut them down, took the bodies away. They were never seen again."

Does the prince know about the Society? About the secrets and the lies on which this very country was founded? I don't know. And, honestly, I don't really care.

He just looks up at the painting and says, "I know. It's practically the Holy Grail of Adria. People keep trying to find them.

People petition my grand—I mean, people used to petition my grandfather all the time to get access to royal lands or records or . . . whatever. People are always looking for dead bodies."

It's like he remembers in a rush. The truth comes back, and he sinks lower. I sit beside him, and he falls into my arms.

"It's not your fault," I say, because it's what people always say to me, even though it's never true and it never helps. I say it again and again. "It's not your fault."

A glass breaks.

The prince and I pull apart as if we've been caught, and when I look up I see Alexei. He must have stepped on one of the fallen glasses, but nothing is as sharp as his gaze before he turns and walks away.

"Alexei!" I yell. I start to stand, to run after him, but then I remember the boy whose life I'm basically destroying.

"Go," Thomas tells me. "Go to him."

So I do.

CHAPTER TWENTY-SIX

It's hard chasing after Alexei. Sometimes it feels like his legs are twice as long as mine, so I pick up the full skirt of my fancy dress and run as fast as my delicate shoes will let me.

Out the doors and through the gates, he doesn't look back. And I keep running. My heels try to catch between the cobblestones, but I don't care. I can't stop running.

I do not dare stop running.

Some might think I look like Cinderella, fleeing from the ball, but I can't shake the memory of another night and another party. I know in my gut that, once again, something bad is about to catch up with me.

So I run faster.

"Alexei!" I yell, but he doesn't slow down. His long legs stride over the cobblestones, and I have to hold my dress higher. The stones are damp and the hill is steep, but I'm not afraid of falling.

"Alexei, stop!" I yell when I finally reach him. I grab his hand and pull him to a stop, and he spins on me.

"Go back to your prince, Gracie."

"He's not my prince!" I snap. "I never wanted him to be *my prince*."

Alexei gives a huff. "I thought this was your birthright. I thought you were *born to be a princess*."

I slip closer, grab the lapels of his tuxedo with both hands. "I lied. I do that."

"Yeah. You do."

For a second we just stand together. No doubt all of Adria—all of the world—is huddled around their TVs and computers right now, listening to the news from the palace. The king is dead. The succession is happening. The nation will be in mourning. *I* should be in mourning. The hope I had two hours ago is dead, gone. And it will never be alive again. Now there is only moonlight and gaslight and the look in Alexei's blue eyes.

"So the prince seems . . . nice," he tells me.

"He is nice," I say.

"You don't sound happy about it," he says.

I look up at him. "Nice guys are overrated."

And then Alexei's arms are around me, and he's pulling me close, holding me tight. But my hands are still between us—there is still so much between us—and I push against his chest, holding myself apart.

"I have to marry him," I blurt out. I can't look in his eyes, so I stay focused on his perfect white tie. I want to straighten it even though it isn't crooked. I want a legitimate excuse to touch him. I want to find a reason to make this last.

But there isn't one.

"I thought that I could stop it. The king knew. That's what I was trying to tell you guys. He was going to stop it. So they killed him. No. I'm not sure the Society knew in time, but Ann did. Ann knew. So *she* killed him. She'll kill anyone. She will. She'd kill you."

Suddenly, I force myself to look at him. I need to see those blue eyes just one more time as fear grips me.

"She would kill you," I say, and I know that it's true.

But the look that Alexei gives me isn't one that I'm expecting. "She's welcome to try." He smiles and pulls me closer. My hands slide to his shoulders. I'm pressed tight against his chest.

"I have to marry him," I repeat before Alexei and I can get any closer. In a lot of ways. "This was a warning as much as anything. If they can kill the king . . . I have to marry him."

Alexei pulls me tighter. "You're not married yet."

And then his lips are on mine and my fingers are in his hair and everything fades away, the streets and the darkness and the prince who is a few blocks and an entire world away.

Nothing matters except this and here and now. Nothing matters except us.

But there never can be an *us*, I know now. Not ever again.

276

And so instead of sinking into Alexei, I make myself pull away. Someday soon I know I'll regret it, regret not making the most of these brief moments while they lasted. But what's going to haunt me more in the future—memories or regrets? I honestly do not know.

"Gracie . . ." Alexei starts. He pushes a piece of hair out of my face.

"There's something I have to tell you."

"No. No more talking," he says, then kisses me again, so hard that I almost forget my fears and my guilt and the dread that has been simmering inside of me for ages.

But, eventually, the kiss ends and I ask, "Is your mom really lucid?" for reasons I don't know.

"Gracie, don't."

"Don't what?" I ask.

"Don't get your hopes up."

And that makes me break away. It's like I'm being held by a stranger.

"Do you honestly think I'm capable of that? Well, I'm not." My voice is dry and joyless. "Don't worry. I will never get my hopes up ever again."

"Shh, Grace." Alexei tries to hold me again, but this is a completely different kind of embrace. He knows I'm on the verge of running—not toward but away.

"She killed the king," I say, because it's the only fact that matters. "She killed the king."

277

"I know," Alexei says and smooths my hair. Then his arms are gone and his hand takes mine. "Come on."

He doesn't take me to Iran. Not to Russia or the US or any of the embassies on the row. Instead, Alexei leads me to a narrow, winding street just like a hundred others in Valancia. In fact, I probably couldn't find it again if I tried, but I'm not thinking about the future. And I'm not thinking about the past. I'm just trying to memorize every second of this moment because I know it may very well be our last.

When Alexei walks up the steps to a narrow town house, somehow I'm surprised when he reaches into his pocket for a key and unlocks the door.

When he smiles at me, I raise my eyebrows.

"Dominic," he explains, because of course Dominic has a safe house. He probably has a dozen.

The apartment is old but neat. Clean and tidy but without frills. A lovely woman comes rushing toward the sound of the opening door, saying, "You're back! I'm so glad. I was . . ." Karina trails off at the sight of me. Her entire countenance changes when she says, "I know you."

Carefully, I glance at Alexei, who nudges me closer to his mother. "Yeah. I—"

"Caroline," she says, and my spirits fall. But then she brightens. "You look just like Caroline, so that means you must be . . . Grace?"

I must have been holding my breath because I can feel myself exhale.

"Yes," I say, relief rushing over me. "Yes, I'm Grace."

And then I see—really *see*—Alexei's mother for the first time. Her hair is short and clean and curls into a natural wave just like her son's. Her eyes are brighter, less tired. But, most of all, she seems present in a way she never has before.

I don't know what they were giving her at that facility, but I can imagine. I know better than anyone that the medicine can be far worse than the disease. I know how it feels to be here but not here, in the now but locked in the past.

She isn't shaking. Her eyes don't dart around the room as if there might be an attack at any moment. But there's still an edge to her—the never-ceasing pulse of someone who knows just how bad things can turn and just how quickly.

I know because I carry it myself.

" '*Hush, little princess . . .*' " Karina starts to sing, and panic rises within me. I can't let her slip away—not now. Not after she has come so far.

"No. Stay with me, Karina," I say, reaching for her. "Stay here."

"Your mother wanted me to sing that for her, the last time I saw her."

I look at Alexei. It's like we've both felt a piece of the puzzle start to fall into place.

"When did you see her?" Alexei asks. "When did you see Caroline?"

Karina brightens at the name. "Caroline? Oh, I'd love to see Caroline. Is she here?"

And my heart falls again. Alexei's hand rests at the small of my back as if to comfort me and remind me that there are no miracles.

"No," I say, and Karina's face falls. "She's not here."

"That's too bad," Karina says. "I haven't seen her in . . . well, I think it must have been months."

"Yes." I force a smile. "I think it's been a while."

"We're very dear friends, your mother and I. Did you know?"

I swallow and force out the word. "Yes."

"We were thick as thieves when we were girls. Me. Your mother." Karina turns. Her entire body stiffens, and when she speaks again it's like the words are laced with acid. "And *her*."

I know who she means, but still I have to ask, "Ann?"

Karina spins on me. "Don't say her name!"

She's rocking now, a back and forth so subtle it might be missed by someone who doesn't know, someone who hasn't been there. But I see it, and I know it's like a ticking clock. Karina is going somewhere deep inside her mind and we might be running out of time.

"What happened, Karina?" I ask softly.

She walks to the window. Light from the street falls through the parted curtain and slants across her face. But she's not looking outside, I know. Alexei's mother is looking *back*.

"Do you know about the little princess?"

She doesn't turn as I say, "I know Amelia lived."

"Oh, yes," Karina says, brightening slightly. "She lived and she grew up. Did you know that? And she had *a baby* and then her baby had babies. They were in the Society—they had to be. So we—my friends and I—we wanted to find them."

The longer Karina speaks the younger she seems. It's easy to imagine her as a little girl, gathering with her two best friends, deciding to search for treasure.

"And then . . ." Karina steps closer, out of the light. "We found them. Oh, how I wish we hadn't."

Alexei's hand is warm on my back. "How did you find them?" he asks.

"There were whispers," Karina says, her voice low.

"What kind of whispers?" I ask.

"The families who took the babies home kept records, you know. They made notes and plans for the day when Amelia would need to claim her throne. But it never happened. Maybe because peace came and no one dared to disturb it. But I think . . ." She steps a little closer. Her face actually glows. "I think Amelia was *happy*. No momma wants to change that. So the records were hidden or lost, but we found them. At first we thought that her descendant was . . . *her*. But we were wrong, weren't we? It isn't *her*."

She practically spits the final word.

A part of me wants to spit, too.

"No," I say. "It isn't her."

"It's Caroline. *She* is the heir. She told me when she came to see me." Karina smiles. She giggles like a little girl.

"What did she tell you?" I ask, but Karina is turning back to the window, singing softly.

" 'Hush, little princess . . .' "

"Karina!" I snap, because I need to keep her here; I don't dare let her slip away.

"She wanted to know about the song," Karina says.

"What about it?"

"She didn't know all the verses. Most people don't. But my grandmother knew about Amelia. She believed Amelia should have been put on the throne—many in the Society did, you know? Many do to this very day. And so Grandmother used to tell me stories about the princess and sing the song. She made me learn it when I was just a little girl. I so wanted Alexei to be a girl so I could teach him. Isn't it a pity?"

It's like she doesn't know her son is in the room. And maybe she doesn't.

She brightens again, looking at me. "Has Caroline taught you the song?"

"Why don't you remind me?" I say. "Please, could you sing it now?"

She does and I listen very carefully.

Hush, little princess, dead and gone.
No one's gonna know you're coming home.
Hush, little princess, wait and see.
No one's gonna know that you are me.
Hush, little princess, it's too late.

The truth is locked behind the gates.
Hush, little princess, pretty babe.
The sunlight shines where the truth is laid!

"That's it?" I ask when Karina's finished. "That's all she wanted? To learn the song?"

"She said she had to go to Adria. She needed proof," Karina says. "Nothing was ever going to happen without proof."

I don't dare look at Alexei. I don't dare to let myself believe. But the fact remains that my mother was looking for something. She came here. She found it. And if I could find it, too . . .

Maybe I could get someone else killed, I realize, and I feel sick.

Alexei doesn't see it, though. He just asks, "What kind of proof?"

"The bodies, of course!" Karina sounds like she's just been invited to a birthday party. "She said she'd found the bodies . . . or she *thought* she knew where the bodies would be. She was going to have to come back to Adria to be certain."

And now I find myself hurtling back in time—to Paris and the bridge and the desperate look in Ann's eyes.

"The tomb," I say, turning to Alexei. "In Paris, Ann asked about a tomb."

"What tomb?" Alexei asks.

"The king and queen and little princes. Their bodies were lost in the war. If Mom needed proof she was Amelia's heir—"

"Then your mom needed DNA," Alexei fills in.

"So if she really found the proof—"

283

"Then she found the tomb. And for whatever reason, she went to the palace and told Ann about it."

Alexei's voice is as hard as my heart. "And Ann tried to have her killed."

Karina starts to shake. Her voice is too high. "I told her not to go. I warned her. I said that *she* wasn't our friend anymore. I said that *she* had changed. And *she* was the one who sent me to that place. *She* did it. *She*—"

"It's okay, Karina," Alexei says, reaching for his mother. "It's okay."

"Caroline said she'd get me out. Caroline said that she was going to come to Adria and get her proof and then she was going to get me out!"

Alexei's mother is shaking. Tears fall from her eyes. Her voice breaks. "Did she send you to get me out?"

"Yes," I say. "She did."

And in a way it's even true.

We've held Karina for too long and I can see her slipping, descending into whatever peaceful place she's built inside her mind. When she starts to sing again, " *'Hush, little princess . . .'* " I know it's not for me.

She walks to a chair and curls up like a kitten, singing herself to sleep.

Alexei covers her with a blanket and then takes my hand, leads me outside.

We're halfway to the palace before he speaks again, leaning low to look into my eyes.

"Don't."

"What?"

"Don't go back there." It's like he's been fighting with himself for ages, trying to keep from fighting with me, too, but it has to be done and we both know it.

"I have to," I say.

"You're Grace Olivia Blakely. You don't have to do anything you don't want to do."

"This isn't optional," I tell him, but I'm really arguing with myself.

"Yes." Alexei shakes me slightly—like he's trying to shake some sense into me. "It is. Go to the US embassy. Come with me to Russia. Come with me to *Moscow*. We'll get on a plane. We'll borrow Noah's mother's van and drive all night. I don't care. Just get lost, Grace. Run away. Disappear and I'll go with you."

"I can't."

When Alexei presses his palm into my cheek, I can feel it like a brand.

"She killed the king, Gracie," he says, voice low. I don't bother to mention that there's blood on my hands, too.

I look into his eyes. "She won't kill me."

"How do you know?" he challenges, and I pull away.

"Because I'm playing her game. And she's winning."

CHAPTER
TWENTY-SEVEN

I'm not surprised that I don't sleep. When I close my eyes, I see the king fall. I hear the crowd gasp. I can feel Ann's gaze upon me, and I know she saw it coming. She's seen everything coming for ages, and it's far too late for me to catch up.

So I throw off my covers and ease into the dark, still halls. Walking, pacing. It feels like I'm stuck inside the castle from "Sleeping Beauty," dormant but alive and waiting for the right moment to wake up.

I shouldn't be surprised when I find myself in the big sitting room where Ann invited me to tea right before the Night of a Thousand Amelias—right before Jamie almost died.

These are the windows where the bodies of the royal family hung two hundred years ago. The Society would have cut them down from here. They would have taken them through this room, out into the palace, and then . . . where?

Where did my mother find them? There are hundreds of miles of catacombs beneath the city—maybe thousands. The Society has a secret underground headquarters and their own private island. There are caves in the hills and lakes and a sea so big and so blue that it feels like this is the end of the world.

The Society wanted to keep the bodies safe, and they did it, I have to think. They just did it a little too well.

"Karina Volkov is crazy."

I'm not surprised to hear Ann's voice. I'm not even afraid to turn and see her by the doors. I didn't lie to Alexei. She has me right where she wants me. I'm not a threat to her, and she knows it, so for the moment I really don't have anything to fear.

"Don't look so shocked, Grace," Ann says, sidling closer. "There's nothing that goes on within the palace that I don't know. And, besides, I told you this was my favorite room. Did you really think I wouldn't know you had stopped by?"

"I'm just leaving." I start toward the doors, but Ann blocks my way.

"Stay." It's an order. The smile that follows is false. "Tell me, how is my old friend?"

"I don't know what you're talking about," I try, just because that's what's expected. I'm supposed to lie and Ann's supposed to sneer and neither of us is supposed to give a single inch.

"Did you really think I wouldn't know that you ran out of the palace earlier in a rather dramatic fashion? Did you think I wouldn't know who you were following? I don't want you to see her, Grace. She's too dangerous and you're too important."

"I'm leaving," I tell her. I'm almost to the door when Ann speaks again.

"The authorities know she's here, Grace. And I'm beginning to think it's time for Karina Volkov to go back where she came from."

"Why?" I snap. "Hasn't she suffered enough?"

"You've seen her. You've spoken with her. Does she seem stable to you?"

"There was never anything wrong with her. You did that. Being in that place did that. Spending ten years in a place like that would make anyone crazy!"

The calm smile that Ann gives me is enough to make me scream. "And you would know, wouldn't you, Grace?" She cocks an eyebrow but doesn't really wait for an answer. "Besides, what I've done I've done for Adria. I've done for peace."

"Yeah. When I hear *peace* I always think *hunt my friends down like rabid dogs.*"

Ann's anger is rising. It's like she's tired of having to explain this to me time and time again. "The Society agrees with me, you know. Adria needs peace and stability. Our plan—our bargain—assures that. Amelia's kingdom was taken from her. Righting that wrong has been my life's work. It was your mother's work! Having the heir marry the prince was her idea. But you still fight it."

"And the king . . ."

"The king's death is a tragedy." Ann sounds sincere. "My husband and son and I will mourn him fiercely."

"But he had to die," I fill in.

Ann just shrugs.

I want to slap her. I want to claw her eyes out. I want to hang her from that window and let the whole world see how ugly she really is.

But I can't do any of that. Because even without Ann, the Society would still want me here, and the Society is too powerful to fight. Like it or not, I'm the solution to a two-hundred-year-old problem, and no amount of rage on my part is going to change that any time soon.

"Good night, Grace," Ann tells me, heading for the door. "Do get some sleep. Tomorrow will be a trying day. We will need to prepare to bury our king, after all."

It's not an observation. It's a threat. And I stay, shaking, long after she's gone.

I should find my room, my bed. I should do *something* to make this right, but I just look out the big windows, wishing I could go back in time.

To save the king.

And my mother.

And the people who cut those bodies down and dragged them who-knows-where.

But that's not true, I realize. My mother knew where the bodies were buried, and she came here—into the belly of the beast—and told the one person she thought she could trust. Someone she thought would help.

My mom trusted Princess Ann, I remember. It makes me want to cry, the realization that bad decisions must run in my family.

My breath fogs against the thick glass windows, blocking out the city and the walls. They could be anywhere out there, beyond those gates, and . . .

Karina's voice comes back to me. I can almost hear my mother sing.

" 'The truth is locked behind the gates . . .' "

And I know.

My mother didn't come to the palace to tell Ann about the bodies.

My mother came to the palace to find them.

CHAPTER
TWENTY-EIGHT

When morning comes, the king's still dead, but it takes Thomas a moment to remember. I can actually see the grief pass over him, watch as reality seeps in. And I know the moment he realizes that it wasn't all a dream.

"Get up," I tell him, and he bolts a little, afraid. In spite of everything, I manage to smile. This must be what Noah felt like on my first night here when he dragged me from the safety of the embassy to Lila's party on the cliffs. That was a lifetime ago, I think as I plop down on the edge of Thomas's bed. I've changed out of my pretty blue ball gown, and I no doubt look like what I am—a worried, guilt-ridden girl who might never sleep again.

"What are you doing here?" Thomas rubs his eyes. "What time is it?"

"Get dressed." I throw him a T-shirt. "It's two hundred years ago, and I need your help."

Thomas doesn't call me crazy. He doesn't even tell me that we're wasting our time. But that doesn't mean he understands.

"Tell me again," he says when we reach the sitting room where Ann served me tea last summer and explained that these were the windows where, two hundred years ago, everything started.

"My mom found the lost tomb," I tell him. "Which was bad because tomb means *bodies*. And bodies mean *DNA*. And DNA means *proof*. And so that's why your mom wanted her dead," I say so matter-of-factly that I have to stop and make myself remember who I'm talking to. "Sorry."

"It's okay," the prince tells me. "I always knew, you know? Not that she'd done . . . this. But that she could. I think a part of me always knew."

"I never knew," I tell him.

"About what?"

"About any of it," I have to admit. "I thought my mom was an antiques dealer, a collector who had been raised in Adria. I had no idea that this"—I gesture at the ornate room before us—"was even possible. People don't live like this."

The prince eyes me. "I live like this."

And it's true. This is the only life he has ever known—will ever know. For the first time, I realize I'm not the only one whose destiny is completely out of my hands, and a part of me kind of feels sorry for the prince. But that's not the reason why we're here.

"I always thought my mom came here to tell your mom she found the bodies, but last night I realized . . . what if my mom actually came here to *find* them?"

"Grace—"

"If my mom came here to find the bodies, then *we* can find the bodies."

"Grace, they're gone. They were smuggled out of the palace centuries ago. Everybody knows that."

"Do they?" I have to ask. "I mean, think about it. Some people snuck into the palace and cut the bodies down, yes. That we know. But looters were everywhere that night. The whole city was filled with mobs. War was raging."

"Yeah. And the bodies got lost in the chaos."

"Have you ever tried to carry someone who's unconscious? Well, I have—"

"Why am I not surprised?"

"Alexei's heavier than he looks," I add quickly. "And carrying him was hard. I could barely drag him twenty feet. Think about it. Why drag four dead bodies across the city when you have a whole palace to hide them in? Especially if you know that you can always come back once the dust settles and give them a proper burial?"

I know my theory makes sense, but the prince doesn't quite believe me, I can tell. He's looking at me like I'm confused or naïve. But not crazy. Never crazy. And I kind of love him for it.

He's still shaking his head, though. He's still trying to make me see.

"You don't get it, Grace. The palace is huge, yes, but every inch of it has been remodeled and modernized and refurbished in the last two centuries. I mean, *two hundred years* have gone by. If the bodies were here, don't you think someone would have found them before now?"

Sometimes I really hate common sense. That's why I go to such great lengths to avoid it.

There's a desk in the room with an old-fashioned pen set and really fancy paper. I rush toward it and draw the Society's symbol the best I can, then hold it up for Thomas to see.

"Look at this," I say.

"Okay."

"Have you seen it anywhere in the palace?"

"No. Why?"

"I think it might mark the hiding place or be some kind of clue. Think hard. Maybe it's carved into some wood or etched into stone or . . . something."

"Grace, the palace is huge. There's no way—"

"The truth is locked behind the gates!" I practically scream.

There's a look that people get when they don't want to give a crazy person bad news. We need our delusions, or so it seems. The prince just met me, and already he knows how fragile I am, how breakable. And he doesn't want to be responsible for my final, fatal crack.

"Grace—"

"You said you saw my mother here. You said you saw her wandering around the palace. When was that?"

"I don't know." Thomas runs a hand through his messy hair. "Years ago."

"Was it three—almost four—years ago? Think."

Thomas looks down at his feet, as if trying to remember. After a moment, he nods, certain. "Yes. We talked about how I'd just gotten my braces, so yeah. That would be right."

It's like I've been holding my breath for years. For centuries. But I can finally exhale when I say, "That was when she found them."

I can tell by the look in Thomas's eyes he doesn't quite believe me. That's okay, I think. I probably shouldn't believe me, either.

"Think about it, Thomas. That day, when she was wandering around, she wasn't lost. She was looking. And she found them."

"Grace, that's—"

"Where was she?"

"I don't remember. It was a long time ago, and—"

"Thomas, think!"

I don't mean to shout.

I don't mean to rant and rave. Thomas is a good guy. He's on my side. He didn't choose to be a part of this, but neither did I. When he nods and leads me down the hall, I have to tell myself that we're not looking for bodies.

We're looking for a way out.

All around us, Adria is in mourning. Heads of state are paying their respects. Palace officials are running to and fro, getting ready for the official funeral. Thomas's grandfather is dead and his father is now king, but the prince is here with me.

I have to wonder if maybe we aren't both crazy.

But as soon as Thomas leads us down the south corridor I know in my gut we're almost there.

"The gates," I say as the old palace gates come into sight up ahead. I can't keep from singing.

"'Hush, little princess, it's too late. The truth is locked behind the . . . gates.'"

They're open now, and nothing stands between the south corridor and the atrium-like room that probably used to be a courtyard. The floor is cobblestone. In the center of the room there is a fountain.

More hallways and corridors and staircases diverge from this space and I turn around, suddenly lost.

"This used to be the outside, right?" I ask, but I think Thomas knows I'm really talking to myself. "So did they mean *behind*, like coming out of the castle, or *behind*, like you're coming in?"

Thomas shakes his head. "I don't know. I didn't know it meant anything until now."

Together we move toward the high iron gates that used to stand between the palace and the world but now stand open for all to see.

Thomas and I each take a gate and try to pull them closed, to move them in any way, but they don't budge.

"They're stuck," Thomas says. "They probably haven't moved in two hundred years, remember."

I push harder. I pull with all my might. But then I stop and look closer at the gate before me, the old scrollwork and handles and the way the gate has swung back to perfectly block a tiny alcove in the wall. The bolt is extended, keeping the gate in place.

"They're not stuck," I tell him. "They're locked."

I opened the puzzle box this morning and pulled out the key that the king had been searching for almost his entire life. It hangs around my neck now, tucked beneath my T-shirt. When I bend down to examine the gate more closely, I can feel the cold metal against my skin, swinging on its chain and rubbing against me. Suddenly, I have to wonder.

"Could it be this easy?"

I pull the key from my shirt and hold it to the keyhole and give Thomas a look that says *wish me luck*.

Then I insert the key into the lock.

And turn.

And the gate swings.

The alcove beyond is shallow and damp. It was probably something of a guardhouse once upon a time, just room enough to keep a few provisions.

There's a brazier where they probably kept a fire in winter, some hooks on the wall.

There's a long, narrow window in the wall, and the sun is shining bright outside. Dust dances in a beam of light that slices through the dim room and then down a tiny, narrow staircase that doesn't belong in this century or even the last.

" *'The sunlight shines where the truth is laid,'* " I sing in disbelief. Thomas looks at me.

"Grace, is that . . . ?" Thomas starts. I can't blame him for not being able to finish.

"Maybe."

I inch toward the old stone stairs. The mortar is crumbling and the space is dreary and damp. This room belongs in a castle in the old, medieval sense of the word. The stone around me looks like the same kind that they used to build the wall a thousand years ago. This part of the palace is old. Ancient.

And the future king of Adria is beside me.

"What do we do now? We can't just go down there. Can we?" Thomas asks—and he's got a point. Now is not the time to rush. It's not the time to panic. Old Grace would have rushed in where angels feared to tread, but the last person to come here may have been my dead mother and that makes even me cautious.

I tell myself that the bodies have been hidden for two hundred years. Twenty minutes more won't matter.

So I turn to Thomas. "Now we go find Dominic."

"Who?"

The question stuns me. For a second, I stand, gaping, and I have to remind myself that this boy doesn't know me. He's not going to call me crazy.

Not even when I say, "The Scarred Man." The words are quiet, almost reverent. "I have to find the Scarred Man," I say, and I know now, more than ever, that it's true.

Because this time I know that he's on my side.

"He loved my mother," I explain. "He'll know what to do. We can trust him."

298

"Okay." Thomas nods. "We'll split up and find this Dominic and then we'll meet back here."

"Sounds good," I tell him.

We start back down the south corridor then split up when we reach the main hall.

As soon as Thomas is out of sight—as soon as he's safe—I reach for my flashlight and turn back. Maybe because I'm being stupid. Maybe because the last person who went down this proverbial rabbit hole ended up dead.

But, more than likely, it's just because there are some paths you're destined to walk alone.

CHAPTER TWENTY-NINE

It smells like the tunnels. Like centuries of dust and damp and mildew and . . . secrets.

The stone steps are steep and dusty but not dark. I walk in that beam of light, past torches that still hang from the walls as if waiting for the guards to change shifts—for an emergency to send them down these stairs. Maybe for supplies. Maybe reinforcements. I just know that with every step, I get further from my own time and closer to my mother. Closer to Amelia. Closer to the truth.

When at last I reach a cold stone floor, I stop and get my bearings. Cobwebs cling to my hair and to my clothes. I'm walking through a century's worth of dust, and it feels at least ten degrees colder here than it did in the rest of the palace. The ceiling is made from stone and ancient wood, and I can't hear the servants who are rushing from room to room upstairs, getting ready for the onslaught of dignitaries and world leaders who will come to mourn the king. Somewhere, Thomas's father is dealing with the fact that the job's now his. And Ann . . .

Ann is probably thinking that she's won.

And she's probably right.

But I keep walking anyway.

My flashlight's small, and its beam is thin as it sweeps across a room that's full of crates and boxes. There's no telling what it used to be, but now it's filled with old pieces of furniture and marble busts.

There are heavy barrels along one wall, cases of what look like wine on the other. But this isn't the palace's wine cellar, I can tell. No one has been here in ages. It's like a time capsule, like a display at a museum.

There's a rack nearby with swords and belts, like the men who wore them have just changed shifts and will be back in a few hours, ready to start another day. There's a heavy table in the center of the room, surrounded by chairs that are so solid and so heavy that I wonder if I could even move them.

A pair of old ceramic cups sit on the table, like their owners might come back at any time and finish their drinks.

I don't know what I expected to find. Surely there wouldn't be a sarcophagus or a marker. There was never going to be an X to mark the spot.

I feel silly for a second. Defeated. But then I see the beam of light that falls from the room's lone window. It's high on the wall, probably just above the ground, and it's barely enough to fight the darkness that surrounds me, shining like a spotlight upon a stage.

Except . . . not a stage.

The table.

I walk to the huge wooden artifact in the center of the room. This isn't one of the grand antiques that fill the palace, but I have no doubt it's just as old. Heavy and rough, this was built for hard use by hard people.

Scuff marks and burn marks mar the surface. A thick layer of dust covers the whole thing, and I run my hands across the scrapes and scars of careless use and then, in the center . . . something else.

I lean over the massive relic and brush with all my might, blowing away the dirt and dust that have settled into the symbol I've seen all over this city. Never has it made my heart pound like this.

The Society was here, they might as well have carved. And now I know I'm close.

I could scream or fight, but I force myself to back away and look at the room anew. Crates, shelves, barrels, and weapons. But no big boxes. The stones along the wall look undisturbed. And I have to think.

They would have been hidden quickly, probably in the dead of night. Maybe the Society members who came for the royal family intended to return once the coup was over. This is hardly fit to be a royal grave. And it's not, I realize. It's a royal mystery.

I step toward the table again, but this time I almost trip when my toe catches on the edge of an old, faded rug. It must have been heavy at one time. No doubt placed down here to fight the chill, but that's not why I feel a shiver in my bones when I look at it.

Now the chairs that seemed so heavy a moment ago fly across the room like feathers as I toss them aside. The old table creaks and groans and crashes to the floor when I grab one side and hurl with all my might, toppling the furniture and pushing it aside.

Now there's only the old rug that has lain beneath the Society's symbol for ages, just waiting for someone to look.

I hold my breath and take a corner. The rug starts to disintegrate beneath my hands, but I keep pulling and pulling until I can see the stone floor give way to wooden planks. It used to be a door, I can tell, and I think about the tunnels that crisscross the city. Many caved in ages ago, filled with rocks and dirt and debris. There's not a doubt in my mind this used to be one of them.

Now the trapdoor is nailed shut, and the wood is still solid.

I know I should wait for Dominic. We need tools and more light—workers and archaeologists. This is history that I'm unearthing, and even though I know that I should wait, I can't. This secret is like the telltale heart, ticking beneath the floor of this room, and I have to make it stop.

Iron sconces are set throughout the room. On the ceiling, you can actually see the soot and scars from hundreds of years of fires that burned through the night. But the torches are cold now, and when I reach for one, I have to use all my strength to jerk it free—but it comes off, dirty and dusty in my hands.

Heavy.

The iron is solid, and I swing as hard as I can, sending it crashing into the wooden planks that fill that section of the floor. I swing again and again and again, until wood splinters and dust scatters.

I'm breathing too hard, coughing and gagging, but I can't stop until the old door breaks and I'm able to reach down and pull it open, watch as the narrow beam of light from the window shines onto four ancient bundles that lie, resting in the shallow space below.

A part of me wants to ease forward and pull back the ancient cloth, look down at the remains just to be sure. Another part of me wants to turn and run from this dark place, go just as fast and as far as I can.

But all I can manage to do is sing.

" 'Hush, little princess, wait and see. No one's gonna know that you are me.' "

And then I hear it, a shuffling behind me. I start to turn, expecting to see Thomas and Dominic, but instead a pain shoots through me, jarring me forward.

I double over and I sway, but I see nothing but stars.

When I wake up, I can't be sure that I'm not dreaming.

At first, I think I'm back in the little cabin on the island. That the thumps and thuds I keep hearing are the sounds of Alexei and my brother fighting and training in the cool ocean air.

But the floor beneath me is too cold and too hard. In spite of the mind-numbing pain that is reverberating through my head, I desperately want to sneeze. But as I try to push myself upright it's all I can do not to vomit, not to sway and sink back to the floor again. I've known pain like this only once in my life, and that was when I was twelve and jumped off the wall.

There's not a doubt in my mind that, this time, my foolishness really should kill me.

But worse than the pain and the nausea and the confusion is the fact that I'm almost certain I smell smoke.

"Oh, good. You're awake."

Ann sounds so calm and so at ease as she walks around the room. There's a gun in her hand, though, and she's lit all of the old-fashioned torches. Storm clouds must have covered the sun, because flickering fire is the only light and the room smells like smoke and death.

"You found them, Grace." She stops and looks down into the shallow grave where my ancestors lay, waiting. "I've lived here for eighteen years, and I never found them. Can you believe it? I feel like a fool. I feel like . . . it is a shame, really."

"What's a shame?" I ask, because I don't know what else to do.

"It's a shame that now they have to disappear again. Forever."

I push myself upright, ignoring the white-hot pain that still shoots inside my head.

"Funny, I didn't even know this room was here," the princess says as she walks around the room's perimeter. "But I guess no one did, did they? After a century or two I suppose it's easy for things to get forgotten. Even a room that seems to be used mainly for the storage of lamp fuel."

That's the smell, I realize. Something more powerful and pungent than gasoline, and a new terror shoots through me. One of the big barrels has tipped over. A hole has been punched in the side and liquid is seeping out, running across the floor and then pooling in the shallow grave.

"What are you doing?"

"Isn't it obvious? I'm going to burn the bodies," Ann says, and then she laughs. "And I'm afraid you'll have to die as well."

Maybe it's that she looks like Karina.

Maybe it's that she sounds like me.

But it's more clear than ever that Ann's not well. That this isn't about bloodlines and legacies and history anymore. It might have started that way, but now it is about power and some misguided belief that two hundred years later we can make it right.

She is a woman obsessed, and I wonder about the weight of carrying this kind of secret—this responsibility. As a child, Ann decided to right a two-hundred-year-old wrong, and for most of her adult life she thought she'd succeeded. She'd thought her son was the answer. And then she learned that she was wrong. That— if anything—her son was at risk.

I know how the human mind can be—how it's both wonderfully strong and terribly frail, and how, if necessary, a person can rewrite history, even if only for themselves.

306

Ann has done that. She's given her life to this cause and now . . .

She's ready to give mine.

"You've won," I say. "You're the princess and I'm here. I took your deal. In a few years, Amelia's heirs will sit on the throne."

"No!" Ann shouts. "If you had taken my deal, you wouldn't be here, trying to find your mother's precious proof! And now . . . well, Amelia's heirs *will* sit on the throne someday. But not yours."

"I don't think Jamie'd be good at bearing children," I say, even though it's not funny. "He doesn't have the hips for it."

"Oh, Gracie. Did you think you're the only female descendant? I'll find the next one in line. And then . . . You did this to yourself, Grace. *I* wanted it to work! But no. You had to dig and dig. You're just like your mother. Neither one of you could ever leave well enough alone."

"It's not going to be easy to find another girl desperate enough to go along with your scheme, you know. Or do you already have someone in mind?"

I don't really care about the answer. I just have to keep her talking.

Dominic will be here soon.

Dominic will find me.

Dominic will save me because he couldn't save my mother and the Scarred Man isn't the type to fail twice.

But then sparks fly from the torch in her hand, igniting a

trickle of lamp fuel that trails across the floor. Flames flare to life and smoke fills the room, and I'm no longer in a palace. I'm on a deserted street.

I'm listening to my mother yell, *"Grace, no!"*

The fire pops and cracks as the old, dry wood of the shelves catches and flares to life. And a part of me knows that this is what I want, isn't it? For the proof to disappear? For there to never be anything that ties any member of my family to this place ever again?

It would save Jamie.

It would save his children and grandchildren and . . .

But the palace is hundreds of years old, ancient and weathered, and it has natural gas running through almost every room.

Maybe the fire wouldn't spread and grow and consume all it touches.

But maybe not.

The fire hasn't reached the bodies, and so far it's still contained. It's not too late. Yet.

"Ann, stop!" I shout. "Listen."

"I am through listening to you, Grace Blakely."

"Lighting a fire here is suicide."

Behind me, I can hear shelves spark and crack. Cases of wine crash and shatter on the stone floor, and the smell of the lamp oil fills my lungs. It's seeped into the cloth around the bodies and the wood of the old trap door. It's covering my hands and pooling at my feet.

"The heir has to return," Ann says. She sounds like Karina. Like me.

Then there are noises on the stairs—footsteps and running and—

I know the moment when Ann hears him. She jerks her head toward the stairs, and for the second time in my life, I see the Scarred Man through the smoke. He's strong and fast, and I'm not the only one determined to change how the story ends this time.

But he doesn't know that Ann's down here. He probably can't see her or the gun, and this my chance, so I leap up and rush toward her.

Ann's hand is outstretched. There's a scream—a cry full of terror, and I realize too late it's coming from me.

"No!" I yell, and throw myself across the room, but it's too late, and Ann's firing. Bullets slam into Dominic's chest, and he drops to the ground.

His gun crashes, then slides across the floor, and the truth hits me: It's far too late for anyone to save me.

The lamps are sparking, and I know the moment the second pool of oil on the floor catches. There's a great *whoosh* as the fire grows and spreads.

The smoke is rising, filling the room, and I know I could turn and run for the stairs. I could make it to fresh air and freedom.

I could save myself. But some things aren't worth saving.

I've spent months chasing freedom, and now it lies before me, just a few feet away, cold and dormant on the floor.

What I *want* is to be free of this place and this world and this curse that will haunt me for the rest of my life.

What I *need* is revenge.

Before me stands the woman who ordered my mother's death, who chased my brother and bargained with my future.

I reach for the gun.

I see the Scarred Man through the smoke, rising from the ashes. And I hear my name.

"Grace, no!"

It's my mother's voice, and I know what this is: my chance to do it differently.

To go back and let it burn.

Ann is walking to the grave. There's a torch in her hand, and even through the smoke I know it's almost over. She just has to drop that torch into the pool of oil that surrounds the bodies, and the DNA will be gone. The proof. The lifelong mission that doomed my mother.

But my mother's not dead because of those bodies. She's dead because of the woman who stands over them, and so I close my eyes for a moment. I try to block out the smell of smoke and the color of fire and the voice that keeps shouting, "Grace, stop! Grace, no!"

I squeeze my eyes closed and I hear the shot. I smell the smoke, and I know that I can't end it. That it's too late and I'm too lost. I've done it. I know. I'm in a room with a two-hundred-year-old secret, letting history repeat itself.

I look down, but my hand shakes. Empty. And nothing makes any sense.

"Grace?"

The voice is not my mom's this time, and I turn to look at Thomas. The gun is tumbling from his hand as his mother crumbles, blood-soaked, to the floor.

CHAPTER THIRTY

I spend the night in the embassy. In my mother's bed and my mother's room, but my mother's ghost isn't here when I wake up.

No.

That honor goes to Noah.

"It's about time!" he tells me.

"Is she up?" Rosie says from the corner. "Good."

Soon I'm surrounded by my friends, but it's Lila who has my full attention.

She isn't smiling. She's no doubt heard all about the fire and the rumors of the shooting. My mere presence in this bed is enough to tell my friends that it's over, but it's not. And Lila and I are the only ones who know it.

Her brother looks at her. "What's wrong with you?"

She hands me a sweater. "Get dressed. It's time."

When we reach the headquarters of the Society, it doesn't look like it did the day Ms. Chancellor first brought us down here. Chairs have been assembled and the big tables have been pushed to the sides. Once again, the women all sit in a circle. Some of them I recognize from Paris. Some I've seen at the palace or meeting with Ms. Chancellor. No one makes introductions, and the truth is no one has to. They all know who I am: Grace Olivia Blakely, the not-so-lost princess of Adria.

When Lila and I step onto the little balcony that overlooks the big room, every head turns.

"It's good of you to join us, Ms. Blakely," the Englishwoman from Paris tells me.

"I'm happy to be here. Alive," I say.

"Grace." It's Ms. Chancellor who eases toward me. "How do you feel?"

"How's Dominic?" I ask because it's all that really matters.

"He'll be fine. And Thomas. He's . . ." I know what Ms. Chancellor can't say. It might be years before anyone knows how Thomas is.

"If we might have your attention, Ms. Blakely . . ." Prime Minister Petrovic signals that the women are growing restless. "We have asked you here today to discuss recent developments."

"You mean how I found an ancient, hidden tomb and got attacked by a lunatic princess while this noble Society didn't do a darn thing to help me?"

"We had a bargain, young lady," the British woman tells me.

"Yes. Well, I'm pretty sure all bargains are voided once one of the parties tries to set the other party on fire. Isn't that correct, Ms. Chancellor?"

"Yes, that does seem like legal precedent to me."

But the women of the Society aren't as happy I'm alive as I am.

"I know you wanted me to marry Thomas. I know you wanted me to have little royal babies so that no one ever found out Amelia survived. And I get it. I do. This"——I gesture to the ancient headquarters around us——"is secret. *We* are secret. Two hundred years ago Amelia needed to be kept a secret to keep her safe. But now . . .

" *'Hush little princess, it's too late. The truth is locked behind the gates. Hush, little princess, pretty babe. Sunlight shines where the truth is laid.'* "

When I stop singing, Ms. Chancellor studies me, her eyes shining with unshed tears.

"Our ancestors wrote that song. Our mothers and grandmothers have been singing that song to us for generations because they *wanted* the bodies to be found. Amelia was never meant to be a secret forever."

I watch the words sweep over the room, but no one nods. No one speaks until the PM leans closer.

"As tragic as yesterday's events were, the fact remains that we face a crisis," the PM says. "The very thing we have longed to prevent is inevitable. The king, queen, and two princes have now been recovered . . . without Amelia. Now there is DNA, and . . .

314

I do not know how much longer we can keep it a secret. We are all at risk."

"You're right," I say. For once, I agree with her. "As long as there's a secret, there's a risk. So it cannot remain a secret."

"Ms. Blakely, we cannot take a chance with Adria's future!" says a woman with a French accent who I last saw in Paris.

"I'm not saying we have to risk Adria's future. I'm asking you to have faith in mine."

The women seem to consider this. It takes a moment for the PM to speak again.

"The king left you a legacy, Ms. Blakely. You are mentioned specifically in his will."

"I don't want my legacy. I don't want anything from him. Whatever it is, you can give it to Thomas."

"Oh, I assure you, Grace," the prime minister says, "you want this."

CHAPTER
THIRTY-ONE

There are five coffins at the front of the church. Two kings. A queen. And two little princes, both under the age of ten.

It's caused quite a stir, of course. The finding of the bodies, literally unearthing a secret.

There are those who think Thomas's grandfather should have had his own service—one final moment in the spotlight all alone. But I know better. He spent his whole life looking for the people who now lay in the coffins on either side of him.

It's too much to hope that people won't notice who isn't here. The official story is that Princess Ann, prostrate with grief, has been taken ill and is unable to be by the sides of her husband and son. The unofficial stories vary. None of them come close to the truth.

When the prime minister finishes her remarks, she looks at me, as if wondering if I'm really going to go through with this.

She smiles at me, and I'm so shocked it takes me a moment to realize that she's giving me one last chance to chicken out. I probably should. This is probably a harebrained scheme. A foolish mistake. So of course I stand when she introduces me, and then I make my way slowly to the front of the cathedral.

There are hundreds of people looking at me, not counting the millions watching on TV. My palms sweat and my blood burns, but I keep my gaze on the coffin of the king. I have to say what he'd have said if only he'd had a little more time.

"I'm not much for public speaking," I choke out, then add, almost to myself, "for public anything, really. I'm here today because, evidently, the day he died, the king made some changes to his will. He asked me to do this in the event of his death, so I'm not up here for me, you see. I'm up here for"—my voice quakes—"for the people who can't be up here themselves."

I try not to look at the television cameras or Thomas and his father. I don't want to notice how there are representatives from every royal family in Europe and the Middle East—presidents and prime ministers from many others.

I don't want the world to see me, know me—to have verified once and for all that I am exactly as crazy as advertised.

"The day before the king died, he and I had a conversation. He was a really nice man. A good man. And when he found out I was in trouble, he wanted to help me, and . . ." I choke back a sob and try to find the words. "I suppose everyone knows now that the king isn't alone here today. You've all no doubt heard the news that we recently found the lost tomb of King Alexander the

Second and his wife and sons. What you might not remember is that he had a daughter, too. And the daughter's remains aren't here because . . . well . . . the daughter lived."

A shocked murmur goes through the crowd, but I can't stop now. If I stop, I may never start again, so I keep talking.

"For generations, some people have believed that there would always be a threat to Adria so long as Amelia lived. As long as her descendants lived. But the king never believed that. No. He knew there would always be a threat so long as Amelia's descendants remained a *secret*. And so I stand before you today . . ."

I take a deep breath.

"My name is Grace Olivia Blakely, and I am a lost princess of Adria." The murmurs grow louder just as, at the back of the cathedral, doors open. "And I'm not the only one."

My heart is in my throat when I see the boy who is now walking down the center aisle toward me. His back is straight and his steps are strong—only a faint trace of a limp remains. And I want to cry because my brother is alive and well and here and so handsome he is like the sun and it almost hurts to look at him.

But, most of all, my brother is not alone.

A parade of men and women follow. Some are teens like us. Some are small children. Most are grown men and women in the prime of life. I've never met them, but I know them. And I know exactly why they're here and what they want.

Freedom.

We don't want the throne. We don't want fame or fortune or the responsibilities that come with a kingdom.

"There are sixty-three of us," I say into the microphone. "Sixty-three living, breathing descendants of the king and queen who we lay to rest today." Megan inches up beside me and slips me a stack of papers. They're cool and almost heavy in my hands as I hold them up for the world to see.

"And I give you sixty-three signed documents, stating that we have, every one of us, chosen to abdicate the throne."

A kind of gasp goes through the crowd—a ripple through the world. Then I find Thomas and his father where they sit on the front row. "Your father was a good man, Your Highness. A great king. And you and Prince Thomas deserve his legacy. The rest of us?" I can't help myself. I laugh. "We want to earn our own."

For a moment, I forget about the cameras and the crowd, and I think about the secrets that have brought us here.

Then I look at Thomas. I remember the one that's set us free.

CHAPTER THIRTY-TWO

Winter doesn't feel like it used to. After the fires of my life, I should never feel cold again. But I do. Jamie would warn that it's because I'm too thin. Noah would tease and say it's because I have a cold heart. But Alexei doesn't say anything. He just puts his arm around me and pulls me close as we wait for the door.

Ms. Chancellor is there when it opens. I'm reminded of my first day back on Embassy Row, of the teasing, cautious look in her brown eyes as she studied me, like she couldn't quite decide whether or not I was as crazy as advertised. I was more. And I was less. And so it shouldn't be any surprise that I would end up here eventually.

"It's time," Ms. Chancellor says, her voice no louder than a whisper and yet it seems to echo when she leads us inside the cold, sterile room.

The walls are gray and cinder block. The light's a harsh fluorescent glare. There is wire on the windows and stains on the ceiling, and just this room alone would be enough to make my palms sweat, my pulse race. Part of me wants to close my eyes and rock and pulse with the tension that is always thrumming inside of me.

But another part of me never wants to close my eyes again.

So I ease forward slowly. I choke out the word "Hello."

The woman on the bed is in a hospital-issued gown that gaps in the back. The sheets are stiff; I know without even touching them. They've been bleached so much and for so long that they'll be raw against her skin. She'll itch but she won't be able to scratch. The leather restraints that bind her wrists are too tight—the shearling lining is no doubt stiff and tough and rancid after years of other people's sweat and blood and anguish.

For a second, I just stand here, slightly out of reach, rubbing my own wrists, fighting the force inside me that is always there, like an undertow, threatening to pull me back in time.

But the voice from the bed keeps me here.

"Let me loose," the woman snaps. She sounds imperial despite the burns that have scarred her skin, the wild look in her eyes, and the rough, jagged edges of her hastily chopped hair.

I ease into the chair near the bed, try to soften my tone. "You should be careful, you know. You don't want to hurt yourself."

She jerks in her restraints. "I don't belong here!" she is shouting as Ms. Chancellor steps closer. There's a doctor at her side. The hospital is taking us very seriously, I know. This is a high-profile case.

"She appears to be overwrought," Ms. Chancellor says to the doctor. "She may need something."

The doctor nods and reaches into the pocket of his lab coat. "I agree."

I don't know what's in the vial. I don't care. They all feel the same on the inside. They're supposed to feel like peace, like bliss. But to me they always felt like your heart was covered with frostbite. They made me so numb I actually burned.

I watch her face fill with terror as the doctor injects the drugs.

"What is that? No! No! Let me loose. Free me this instant. I'm the princess of Adria and I demand to be freed!"

Since the funeral, people all over the globe have been claiming a place as one of Amelia's descendants. Lost princesses are a dime a dozen, and no one takes her seriously. The doctor never even bats an eye.

Ms. Chancellor's mouth ticks up and she tries to smooth the woman's hair. "Rest now, Karina. You're in good hands."

"My name is Ann!" the woman shouts. "I'm Princess Ann of Adria, and I command you to free me now!"

The doctor studies her, as if he's starting to see the resemblance despite the burns that mar her face, but the scars are too much and we are all so sure. "She is clearly very troubled," the man observes. But I must say, she and the princess do resemble one another. You say they were friends once?"

"Yes," Alexei says. "As girls. Then they became estranged. My mother was always . . . spirited . . ."

Then the doctor leans down. "Your son has brought you to us and we're going to take good care of you, Karina."

Her eyes are wild. "Do you know who I am? My name is Ann! I'm Princess Ann and . . ."

The moment the drugs enter her system, the woman on the bed's outrage starts to fade, replaced by an eerie, surreal kind of calm.

"Do you know who I am?" she asks again, and this time it's really a question.

"Rest, Karina," Ms. Chancellor says. Then she adds, too low for the doctor to hear, "You will never be able to hurt yourself or anyone else ever again."

Her eyes are heavy. It's like the drugs and the lies and the misery are trying to drag her under. Soon, she might even give up the fight and go, so Alexei leans down and looks into eyes that are nothing like his own.

"Good-bye, Karina. I think you're exactly where you belong."

The woman tries to fight again, to scream, but no sound comes and everyone shuffles quietly toward the door.

Everyone, that is, except me.

For a moment I'm alone inside a memory. A nightmare. I take a deep breath and remind myself that I'm a long way from being the girl on the bed.

"I didn't do anything!" she yells to no one in particular. She struggles against her restraints, which is a mistake, I know. But she'll learn for herself soon enough. "I didn't do anything!" she yells again.

I ease close and lean down. My voice is a whisper.

"It's okay, Ann," I tell her. "It's not your fault. *It was an accident.*"

Then I turn and walk away.

CHAPTER
THIRTY-THREE

When I was twelve years old, I broke my leg jumping off the wall between Canada and Germany. I had something to prove then, some competition with myself that I didn't even know I wasn't winning.

Now years have passed and I'm back up here, high atop a wall that my ancestors convinced their husbands to build. It has kept Adria safe for a thousand years, standing guard against whatever enemies might float in on the tide.

I built my walls higher. Thicker. Stronger. But as I sit here watching the sun dip on the far side of the Mediterranean, I can feel them start to crack.

For the first time in a long time, I'd be content to let them crumble altogether.

When I hear a noise, I turn.

And for the first time in a long time, I am not afraid.

"I thought I'd find you here," Alexei says, but he doesn't even have to say that, really. He just gives me a look, and I know he knows what I'm thinking, what I'm feeling. He puts an arm around my shoulders, and I know he feels it, too.

"Here you are!" Rosie's voice carries on the wind. Then she turns and shouts back to Germany. "She's up here!"

And soon Rosie and Noah and Megan are climbing onto the wall and taking a place beside me. A moment later, Lila's here, too, with Jamie following behind. He's not as strong as he was, not as fast. But when my brother smiles and throws back his head and laughs at something Lila is saying, he's more golden than the sun, and that feels right. Perfect. We sit with our legs thrown over the high balustrades that were made to shelter archers and lookouts and guards.

But we are the lookouts now, and our battle is over.

Only Megan dares to break the silence. "Hey, Grace, how's Thomas?"

"I don't know," I admit. "His mom's gone and his dad is king." Thomas saved my life, but he changed his world, and I know better than anyone how far and how fast those ghosts can chase you. "I don't think anyone knows how Thomas is and probably won't for a really long time."

"Uh . . . about that." Rosie actually stumbles. I never thought I'd hear timidity in her voice, but she sounds almost afraid as she admits, "He and I . . . talk. Sometimes."

Now it's Noah's turn to laugh as he turns to Rosie and raises an eyebrow.

"What?" She shrugs. "People like me. I am very likeable. And he's kind of freaked out because . . . well, because of everything. And also because his dad wants him to be more in touch with the people from now on, so he's going to start at the international school tomorrow."

"Just like Gracie," Alexei says, taking hold of my hand.

I hope the world never knows exactly how much Thomas and I have in common. I hope Thomas never knows, either. Maybe his ghosts will stay locked up in the middle of nowhere. I wish for him only the very best kinds of crazy.

Ms. Chancellor is inside, returning phone calls and briefing my grandpa, who is back to work part-time. I have a school uniform laid out on my bed. A stack of brand-new notebooks and pens. This is my new normal, and I know I'm supposed to eat something, start getting ready for bed. But I've spent so much of my life looking back that I can't waste this chance to look forward for just a little while longer.

The sun is at the horizon now, and the sky streaks with reds and golds. The whole world seems to be wearing a halo, and for a second I let myself savor it.

I let myself believe.

Alexei's arm is warm around my shoulders and a cool breeze blows in off the sea. Between us, we speak seven different languages, but not a one of us says a word.

We sit in silence as the sun sets, marking the end of the day.

Marking the beginning of everything else.

ALLY CARTER is the *New York Times* bestselling author of *All Fall Down* and *See How They Run*, the first two books in the Embassy Row series, as well as the Gallagher Girls and Heist Society series. Her books have been published all over the world, in over twenty languages. You can visit her online at www.allycarter.com.